JANE AUSTEN THE NOVELIST

Jane Austen the Novelist

Essays Past and Present

Juliet McMaster

First published in Great Britain 1996 by
MACMILLAN PRESS LTD
Houndmills, Basingstoke, Hampshire RG21 6XS
and London
Companies and representatives
throughout the world

A catalogue record for this book is available
from the British Library.

ISBN 0–333–59926–8

First published in the United States of America 1996 by
ST. MARTIN'S PRESS, INC.,
Scholarly and Reference Division,
175 Fifth Avenue,
New York, N.Y. 10010

ISBN 0–312–12753–7

Library of Congress Cataloging-in-Publication Data
McMaster, Juliet.
Jane Austen the novelist : essays past and present / Juliet
McMaster.
p.   cm.
Includes bibliographical references and index.
ISBN 0–312–12753–7
1. Austen, Jane, 1775–1817—Criticism and interpretation.
2. Women and literature—England—History—19th century.   I. Title.
PR4037.M35   1996
823'.7—dc20   95–14700
                                                             CIP

10   9   8   7   6   5   4   3
05   04   03   02   01   00   99   98   97

Printed and bound in Great Britain by
Antony Rowe Ltd, Chippenham, Wiltshire

To Valentine and Hugh,
kind sister and brother-in-law,
with lasting affection,
and thanks for your years of toleration and support
of my Jane Austen doings

Contents

List of Illustrations

Texts and Abbreviations

References to Jane Austen's works are to R. W. Chapman's editions:

The Novels of Jane Austen, ed. R. W. Chapman, 5 vols, 3rd edition (London: Oxford University Press, 1932–4), 5th impression.

Minor Works, ed. R. W. Chapman (London: Oxford University Press, 1954), reprinted with revisions 1963.

Jane Austen's Letters to her Sister Cassandra and Others, ed. R. W. Chapman, 2nd edition (London: Oxford University Press, 1952).

E	*Emma*
Letters	*Jane Austen's Letters to her Sister Cassandra and Others*
MP	*Mansfield Park*
MW	*Minor Works*
NA	*Northanger Abbey*
P	*Persuasion*
PP	*Pride and Prejudice*
SS	*Sense and Sensibility*

Preface

To begin with an anecdote: On the day I draft this preface, Jane Austen has claimed attention in no less than four book projects – all of which are either in process, like the one I am writing at this very minute, or projected for the future. And if a single critic is involved in four at a time, how many books on her must there be out there, growing week by week?

Here's how the day has gone. With my colleague and co-editor, Bruce Stovel, I have been contacting contributors about last-minute changes to the volume of essays we call *Jane Austen's Business*, a collection resulting from the large-scale conference of the Jane Austen Society of North America which he and I convened in the autumn of 1993 at Lake Louise, in the Canadian Rockies. The contributors include such people as Margaret Drabble and Elaine Showalter, and the conference, in spite or because of its remote setting, drew six hundred delegates. That's one book project.

Also on this day arrived readers' reports on a projected *Cambridge Companion to Jane Austen*, very positive. (How could a reader *not* be positive about such a Companion?). That volume Ed Copeland of California and I are co-editing, and we have the go-ahead on it from Cambridge University Press.

Also on this day came a phone call from a colleague in Texas, sounding me out as a co-editor of a volume of essays that may result from the *next* Society conference, to be held in New Orleans on the theme of revolution in Jane Austen's writings. A prominent Austen scholar in England is interested in such a volume for a British press he is connected with.

And then of course there's the present volume, of my own essays past and present, with an opening essay on "Jane Austen as a Cultural Phenomenon," which engages these very issues of how many people are reading Jane Austen, and how many books there are on her. Why do I feel as though I am riding a wave? – indeed thundering in to shore with the surf breaking all around me.

It may be a phenomenon peculiar to the circles I move in that Jane Austen is receiving unprecedented attention; but if so, those circles are certainly getting bigger and bigger. Jane Austen is news. Jane Austen is business. In academe her status has never been higher, and has had an extra impulse with feminist approaches. And the popular following is even greater than in the heyday of the Janeites, early in the century. I'd rather join the stampede (a fairly decorous one, let me admit) than disapprove of it. The essays that follow have been written as part of an academic career; but I hope they speak also to those who read Jane Austen simply for recreation. They are about what we all care for: the development of her art; her characters and their language; her sense of community; and love.

Jane Austen's habit of mind is to move easily from the particular example to the general proposition, and back again, with a due enrichment of both. In writing and rearranging the essays that follow, I have tried to do something similar, alternating the long-distance look with close-up examination. Some of these essays are overviews of an overarching theme, some individual studies. The first essay, on Jane Austen's growing place in our culture, is the one written most recently, and I draw on my long association with the Jane Austen Societies on both sides of the Atlantic, as well as on my experience in teaching and criticism, to examine the extraordinary popular following that she still attracts, as well as her high status among academics. Why all the fuss about Jane Austen? – ask the ones who are not making the fuss. That is a large and general question, and part of the answer is a documentation of the fuss.

The essay on "Hospitality" as a recurring concern in Austen's works was written for a particular occasion, as is still apparent. It engages large issues of the social ties that bind the characters of the novels together (or divide them), and define her society. The same can be said of the final group of essays on love in her novels. Here I challenge Charlotte Brontë's contention that Austen as a novelist lacks passion. Not so, I claim. Three of these essays first appeared in a little book called *Jane Austen on Love*; the last, on the "Women in Love," is new to this volume, and will be detected as being of more recent date in showing the influence of feminist criticism, which has so changed and enlarged our way of reading the novels. Within these general essays, however, I still tend to move in to close examination of individual texts – my principle being that if you're dealing with a stylist of Jane Austen's calibre it's a waste not to quote her amply.

In between come several close-up studies. I rejoice in Jane Austen's juvenilia, and have probably paid more sustained attention to "Love and Freindship" and "The Beautifull Cassandra" than anyone else in print. The tantalising fragment *The Watsons*, too, coming as it does between Jane Austen's two creative periods of the 1790s and the 1810s, invites more attention than it has received, and I'm not one to turn down an invitation. I have no such excuse for writing about *Pride and Prejudice* and *Emma*, as they have been, and continue to be, very thoroughly worked over. But I claim a right to have my say too.

These essays have been written over two decades, and I don't pretend to a unity of approach. In preparing them for this volume, I have sometimes added a new reference (where it seems indispensable) from the large body of criticism which has emerged since they were written. But it would be anachronistic to attempt a full-scale updating. These essays haven't a single thesis; rather they are the separate products of years of reading Austen's novels with attention and admiration, and teaching them with joy. Though I have written in the meanwhile on several other authors – Burney, Thackeray, Trollope, Dickens, the Brontës, George Eliot – Jane Austen is the one I return to with most delight in "the achieve of, the mastery of the thing!"

Since I have ventured to be personal and confidential in these essays, I should explain that it seems to me that Jane Austen is a writer who does almost magically engage her readers' whole personalities. As generations of her readers have found, she breaks down the barriers between the orders of reality, and makes us like or dislike her characters as if we actually knew them. One finds it difficult to maintain a proper professional distance in talking of her novels. I confess this in advance, lest the less-than-critically-distanced material in, say, the chapters on "The Beautifull Cassandra" and "Hospitality" should seem unseemly.

It has been my good fortune to have addressed the members of the Jane Austen Society of England (once) and the Jane Austen Society of North America (many times). By the time this book emerges, I shall have tried my luck with the Jane Austen Society of Australia too. These are such audiences as almost to spoil one for any other. If there is a tone of levity in some of the following essays, many of which were first delivered to these Societies, blame the audiences, not me. They were the ones who encouraged me.

Acknowledgements

I am grateful to the University of Alberta for its generous and ongoing support of my research, including grants to enable me to go places to give these papers. For helping me to develop and define these ideas, and for kindly listening to them, I thank my students, both undergraduate and graduate, as well as the Jane Austen Societies, and many individuals within them. Among the many students, colleagues and friends whose help and advice I would particularly like to acknowledge are Joan Austen-Leigh, Garnet Bass, Diana Birchall, Astrid Blodgett, Pat Clements, Ed Copeland, Martin Friedrich, Isobel Grundy, Susan Hillabold, Heidi Janz, Gary Kelly, Michael Londry, Peter Mitham, Shirley Neuman, Ilona Ryder, Elaine Showalter, Christina Sommerfeldt, Bruce Stovel, Eileen Sutherland, Karys Van de Pitte, and Mary Beth Wolicky; also the late Jack Grey, who was so generous in his encouragement to so many of us who work on Jane Austen. My husband, Rowland, has as always stimulated my ideas as well as listened to them; and he has even put up with being turned into a bit of a Janeite himself.

Many of these essays have been published before, and I am grateful to the editors and presses listed below for permission to publish them here. "Teaching 'Love and Freindship'" was first published in *Jane Austen's Beginnings: The Juvenilia and Lady Susan*, edited by J. David Grey (Ann Arbor: UMI Research Press, 1989), 135–51. "*Pride and Prejudice*: 'Acting by Design'" was first published in *The Novel from Sterne to James: Essays on the Relation of Literature to Life*, by Juliet and Rowland McMaster (London: Macmillan, 1987), 19–36. "Jane Austen on the Symptoms of Love" was an address to the Jane Austen Society at Chawton in 1977, and printed in the Society's annual report for that year. "Surface and Subsurface in Jane Austen's Novels" appeared first in *Ariel*, 5:2 (April 1974), 5–24. "Love and Pedagogy" was invited for *Jane Austen Today*, edited by Joel Weinsheimer (Athens, Georgia: University of Georgia Press, 1975), 64–91. The last three, as I have explained, were also published in my *Jane Austen on Love* (Victoria: English Literary Studies Monograph series, 1978). Published in *Persuasions*, the annual journal of the Jane Austen Society of North America, were "'The Beautifull Cassandra' Illustrated," (10, 1988, 99–103); "'God Gave Us Our Relations': The Watson Family," (8, 1986, 60–72); and "The Secret Languages of *Emma*," (13, 1991, 119–31).

Part I

1

Jane Austen as a Cultural Phenomenon

In an essay which he left tantalizingly unfinished at his death in 1975, Lionel Trilling was prompted to speculate on "Why We Read Jane Austen." He had been impressed by "a phenomenon of our contemporary high culture, the large and ever-growing admiration which Jane Austen's work is being given."[1] The essay vibrates with a certain personal intensity for me. In my student days I read Trilling with great admiration; and when I was fairly launched in my academic career, and was organizing a Jane Austen Bicentennial conference at my university, it was a great triumph that Lionel Trilling agreed to be a speaker. Then came the disappointment and the sadness that he couldn't come after all; that he had cancer. And before the bicentennial year was out he had died. His essay for the occasion, which he had nearly completed, was not available for the collection I edited from the conference;[2] but it came out as a lead article in the *Times Literary Supplement*.[3]

The essay can't be said to have answered the question, once and for all, of why we read Jane Austen, partly because it remains unfinished. Trilling begins with his experience of discovering that a full 150 eager students were bent on crowding into his course on Austen, though he had intended it to be only a seminar. (With engaging humility, he seems to discount the possibility that many of them were there not so much for Jane Austen as for Lionel Trilling.) Then, after touching on some speculations that the eager students perceived "Jane Austen's novels presented a mode of life which brought into question the life they themselves lived" (209), lingering over "the charming visual quality" of her world (211), and the fact that it is "charged with moral significance" (213), he enters into a discussion of the findings of the anthropologist Clifford Geertz about the conception of identity and the self in the Javan and Balinese cultures. It is not clear how he intended to loop this argument back to Jane Austen; nor can I (to adapt Milton)

Call up him that left half told
The story of Jane Austen bold.

In fact the story of Jane Austen as a phenomenon in our culture has
not waited for Trilling or anyone else to tell it, but has gone on unfolding. I can't complete Trilling's essay, nor would he have had the last
word if *he* had completed it. But I have had my own modest equiva-
lents of his crowded classes on Jane Austen, and I have participated
in the burgeoning Jane Austen Societies on both sides of the Atlantic;
so I have had my own chance, in the intervening years, to observe the
phenomenon.

I would differ from Trilling in his conception of her prominence as
a mainly academic matter, as belonging only to "high culture." Since
James voiced his exasperation with her status as "darling and pet,"
says Trilling, "she became ever less the property of people who,
through being nice people, were excluded from the redemptive strenuosities of the intellectual life" (206). The touch of academic snobbery
aside, the comment doesn't accord with the observable facts. Jane
Austen's popular following is as large and as loud as it has ever been,
and moreover they are now more organized and articulate than before.
Her standing in academe is also high and unquestioned. There may
be occasional scraps going on between the academic and the non-academic readers of Jane Austen as to whose property she is, with some
sneers of healthy contempt on both sides. But what I see more than
that is a happy discovery of common ground. At many a conference,
an audience of declared Janeites – who may be physicists, housewives,
real estate salespersons, or whatever – come to hear specialized academics speaking on aspects of the art, psychology, and social history of the novels, and they buy the books and debate the ideas. The
specialized academics learn that to address so informed and discriminating an audience – though a non-academic one – is a privilege
surpassing the more cerebral rigours of debating literary theory with
their peers. Jane Austen becomes a meeting ground for friendly
exchange between academics and general readers. The regrettable
thing is that such meeting grounds tend nowadays to be relatively
few and far between. For providing one, Jane Austen gathers the more
credit.

The epithet "Janeite," in its own context, can be as loaded a term
as "black" in the racial context. The focus on the first name is itself a
declaration. James's impatience with "their 'dear,' our dear, everybody's dear Jane"[4] was part of his reaction against the nineteenth-cen-

tury adulation of her, the cult whose cultivated absurdities were calculated to prompt a backlash. The use of the first name is of course a claim to intimacy: There have always been those who want to think of Jane Austen as their special private friend, their "own particular Jane."[5] The history of Austen nomenclature would itself make an interesting cultural study, for certain attitudes manifest themselves in each form of address. Those who disdained what they took to be the gushing tone and tendency to idolatry associated with the use of "Jane" no sooner separated themselves from "Janeites" than they gathered their own label of "Austenites."[6] There has also been an established tradition of calling her "Miss Austen," even long after her death made the polite form of address inappropriate. For instance, the same 1866 article of the *Englishwoman's Domestic Magazine* refers to *"Charlotte* Brontë," but *"Miss* Austen" (my italics), though in the same context and sentence.[7] And yet, as those cognizant of her society's mores are swift to point out, "Miss Austen" is incorrect, since Jane Austen was a younger sister, and so would have been referred to as "Miss Jane," with "Miss Austen" as the title for her elder sister. Sides are still being taken in recent decades. The feminists' tendency to speak of her as "Austen," *tout court*, was combated by the editor of *Persuasions*, the annual journal of the Jane Austen Society of North America: "Speaking of Jane, this editor has a very pronounced dislike of hearing our author referred to as 'Austen,' as if she were her father, her brother, or her nephew. This rather recent vogue – of calling women by their surnames without title – [is] indulged in by feminists and provincial newspapers. . . . In these pages, Jane Austen . . . will be referred to as Jane Austen, J.A., or Jane, for Miss Austen she was not."[8] "Jane" is permissible in this camp, but not "Austen." "Janeite" has been used as a term of abuse, to signify those whose admiration is undiscriminating and fanatic. But it is also proudly claimed as a label for those learned in Jane Austen discourse. There is a bumper-sticker extant that proclaims, "Janeite and proud of it."

James's reactionary phrase about "their 'dear,' our dear, everybody's dear Jane" is memorable not so much for the emphasis on the "dear" as for the repetition of the possessive adjective. She is theirs; she is ours; she is everybody's. Her admirers are not content to read her; they want to possess her. They want her to be their own particular Jane. And since she can't really be everybody's, each admirer has to create a camp, a little army of those who admire her in exactly the right way. There are those who claim she is perfect: George Henry Lewes was the champion of this view, with his echoing claim of 1852:

"First and foremost let Jane Austen be named, the greatest artist that has ever written, using the term to signify the most perfect mastery over the means to her end."[9] Elizabeth Barrett Browning's "curt" response to the proposition was to damn by faint agreement: the novels, she concedes, are "perfect as far as they go – that's certain. Only they don't go far, I think."[10] Lewes and the publisher's reader of *Jane Eyre*, W.S. Williams, again urged Austen's perfections on Charlotte Brontë, who responded with the famous and familiar comments about her lack of passion and lack of poetry. Here it is again interesting to find the men as the champions, the women as resisting what they take to be disproportionate praise.

It has more often been the other way round. The most outspoken antagonists – Mark Twain, D.H. Lawrence, H.W. Garrod – have been male, and they notably respond out of their maleness. Mark Twain, casting himself for the nonce as a Bowery barkeeper, reacts as virile male who (like Huck Finn) refuses to submit to petticoat government.[11] D.H. Lawrence denounced her as "old maid."[12] His champion F.R. Leavis is like James in bestowing praise with one hand and taking it away with the other. He places her at the head of his Great Tradition of the English novel, but never gets around to saying why she belongs there.[13]

The history of the squabbles among Janeites and anti-Janeites seems sometimes like the battle of the sexes disguised as a critical argument about Jane Austen's merits, or lack of them. When the battle got going, in the latter part of the nineteenth century, women were beginning to find a critical voice and to use it; and some of the reaction against Jane was surely a male reaction against the vocal female admirers. In his intriguing history of "Janeites and Anti-Janeites," Brian Southam tends to associate the gushing tone with the women, the measured discrimination with the men. Anne Thackeray (whom he calls "Miss Thackeray") provides "rhapsodic apostrophe and gushings of delight." The women's evident self-parody as the game got going is passed over, though E.M. Forster's "I am a Jane Austenite, and therefore slightly imbecile about Jane Austen" gets praise as comic. And it is Henry James who provides "the most astute analysis of the origins of Janeitism."[14]

The feminist readings, and reactions against them, are a notable feature of the current state of the Jane Austen scene. For better or worse, the record shows, readers and critics respond both to Jane Austen's works and to commentary on them out of their maleness or their femaleness.

James's famous comments, because of when they were made and who made them, have a certain status and authority: Trilling suggests (though he doesn't actually say) that they were the turning point at which Jane Austen was rescued from the garrulous and undiscriminating fans, and delivered to the discriminating intellectuals: she now belongs to those who partake in the "redemptive strenuosities of the intellectual life." Southam seems to agree. In playfully parodying those who peddle "everybody's dear Jane," James seems to establish a climate of proper rational estimation. There is no explicit claim that men have a monopoly on proper rational estimation. But to read his criticism in context is to discover some deeply embedded assumptions about gender and merit.

James's comments appear in his 1905 essay, "The Lesson of Balzac." Balzac, as James presents him, is a literary figure who qualifies, among a select band of authors, as one who can "fit with a certain fulness of presence and squareness of solidity into one of the conscious categories of our attention" (116).[15] Women novelists, it turns out, aren't so good at filling this space, either squarely or roundly. James asserts that the Novelist may be either "he or she (and I emphasize the liberality of my 'she')" (117). But in spite of this vaunted liberalism, he then proceeds to bring forward the women novelists – George Sand and the Brontës, besides Jane Austen – and to find them wanting. The metaphors become increasingly gender-specific. The work of "Madame George Sand," he says, "presents about as few pegs for analysis to hang upon as if it were a large, polished, gilded Easter egg, the pride of a sweet-shop if not the treasure of a museum" (117). Who would not rather be denounced than so praised? (The image of the pegs recalls Walter Shandy's bitterly misogynist comments about having a wife "with such a head-piece, that he cannot hang up a single inference within side of it, to save his soul from destruction."[16])

Then, still lingering with "the nameable sisterhood," James gets to Jane Austen. He makes a show of doing her and her "light felicity" justice; she is "one of those of the shelved and safe, for all time, of whom I should have liked to begin by talking." But clearly she does not fit with sufficient "fulness of presence" into "the conscious categories of our attention": in fact, "Jane Austen . . . leaves us hardly more curious of her process, or of the experience in her that fed it, than the brown thrush who tells his story from the garden bough" (117). It is strange that the master James, with all his sensitivity, has entirely missed the minutely calculated strokes of that fine brush Jane Austen wielded over her piece of ivory (*Letters*, 469). He reduces her art to the song of the brown thrush who simply warbles native wood-notes wild. It is stranger still that, being so little "curious of her process," he should wish to have begun his study with a discussion of her art. He rejoices that, after a long period of neglect, she has become "the prettiest possible example" of a rectified critical estimate; but on the other hand he notes that the tide of her popularity, augmented by the commercial interests of booksellers and illustrators, has risen beyond "the high-water mark . . . of her intrinsic merit and interest" (117). "So what's all the fuss about Jane Austen?" is the modern equivalent, a sentiment usually voiced by men.

He continues to respond out of his maleness to her femaleness. "We," her readers, he says, have "more or less – beginning with Macaulay, her first slightly ponderous amoroso – lost our hearts to her" (117). (James, as Beerbohm's caricatures show, was himself somewhat ponderous by this time.) Now she is upgraded from unconscious brown thrush to human needlewoman at her tapestry; but she is still, apparently, only minimally conscious:

> The key to Jane Austen's fortune with posterity has been in part the extraordinary grace of her facility, in fact of her unconsciousness: as if, at the most, for difficulty, for embarrassment, she sometimes, over her work-basket, her tapestry flowers, in the spare, cool drawing-room of other days, fell a-musing, lapsed too metaphorically, as one might say, into wool-gathering, and her dropped stitches, of these pardonable, of these precious moments, were afterwards picked up as little touches of human truth, little glimpses of steady vision, little master-strokes of imagination. (118)

This attractive genteel lady nodding over her needlework gets not much more credit for her creations than the brown thrush. He believes that her very "master strokes" are achieved by mistake. I am sufficiently an admirer of James to regret it when he writes fatuously. And I regret it even more when his fatuosities are cited as setting the critical record straight!

"The Janeites," Kipling's short story of 1926, humorously recasts James from Jane Austen's amoroso to her legitimate offspring. The story has a curious place in the Janeite debate, and not least for its reversal of the usual gender alignments. As one who has had occasion to note the current demographics of Jane Austen societies, in which women are a large majority, I welcome the strong masculine bias of the story; for it reinforces an image of a Jane Austen who is for both sexes as well as for all seasons.

The story is set after the First World War, among veterans who reassemble to remember. The principal character is a hulking working-class heavy gunner, Humberstall, who has been "'Blown up twice'" (148).[17] After the first time, when he might have gone back to civvy street with honour, he nevertheless insists on rejoining his unit, though with his brainpower notably diminished. (His credentials as macho male are impeccable.) Since he is not fit to work the guns any more, he is given a job in the mess, and so hears much of the conversation of his Major and Captain. In civilian life, one of them is a lawyer, the other a private investigator; and hence, as a natural consequence, both are misogynists. The one lady they admire, indeed idolize, is Jane (her last name is never mentioned). With elaborately implied analogies to masonic secrets and rituals, her writings become a code, and knowledge of them qualifies you for membership in a select and privileged society. (Today's Jane Austen societies know all about that, though they are less deliberately exclusive.) Phrases from the novels become passwords; the guns are named "Bloody Eliza," "The Reverend Collins," and "The Lady Catherine de Bugg." Humberstall, though his experience as a gunner has been blown clean out of his head, nevertheless wades into the six novels, and comes to respond to them deeply and mysteriously. Conversation in the mess graduates from narratives about the courthouse and the detective agency to learned theology on Jane. "Then they went at it about Jane – all three, regardless of rank," Humberstall recalls (153). The ultimate *mot*, blissfully delivered by an ex-schoolmaster when he is "bosko absoluto," is the claim that Jane, instead of dying without "lawful progeny," actually "*did* leave lawful issue in the shape o' one son; an' 'is name was 'Enery James" (153-4).

The whole unit of the Heavy Gunners, Humberstall excepted, is wiped out when the Somme front collapses in 1918. Humberstall, who has had all his clothes blown off him except his boots, totters to a hospital, where an allusion to Miss Bates wins him admission, beef-tea, and an extra blanket. The Jane passwords avail him in the female-dominated world of the hospital as in the male preserves of the heavy gunners and the veterans. How James would have hated all this!

I have lingered over the Kipling story partly because it is so different from the Jane Austen occasions I witness now, at the other end of the same century, when Jane Austen studies are dominated by women. When the term "Janeite" is used abusively now, its referent is usually expected to be enthusiastic, gushing, female, and self-consciously "cultured." It is rather pleasant to find Kipling characterizing the Janeites as aggressively male, and the study of her as bridging all barriers of rank, class, education, and even – ultimately – gender. Humberstall, though working-class, shell-shocked, punch-drunk, and "apt to miss 'is gears sometimes" (173), and though his understanding of the novels is hazy at best, nevertheless recalls the days of his immersion in Jane as the happiest of his life (166).

On civvy street Humberstall is a hairdresser; this is the one concession to female concerns that marks this outstanding Janeite. His professional connection with female vanity has not soured him, as the lawyer and private investigator have been soured. Although "The Janeites" depicts a dominantly male world, gender continues to be a major issue.

Kipling's "The Janeites," then, seems to be written in answer to Henry James, with the joke about his being the son of Jane forming a cheerful reproach to an insufficiently respectful son.

The gender battle continues, and the recent phase features a reaction to feminist readings of the novels. Deborah Kaplan's *Jane Austen Among Women*,[18] for instance, which proposes revisions to the biographical tradition, is a book which I am told visitors to Jane Austen's House in Chawton love to hate. I hear lately of a male group within the Jane Austen Society of North America who plan a counter-attack to rescue Jane from the feminists, where some think she is in durance vile. And (to bring this impressionistic survey up to the minute) even the present writer may have been detected in a gender bias of her own.

The hot news item of the 1990s about the fate of Chawton House, the gracious home that belonged to Jane's rich brother Edward Austen Knight, is fraught with regional, national and gender implications. After the likelihood that it would be turned into a luxury hotel, one would expect Janeites to unite in relief that the American Sandy Lerner is to buy it and convert it into a centre for the study of early women writers. But some (predictably perhaps) resent American ownership; some seem offended that Jane should have to share glory with anyone else; and others seem to fear a feminist take-over. The story keeps unfolding. Janeites – or (perhaps I should less provocatively say) the readers, admirers, and scholars of Jane Austen – continue wary of those in their ranks who do not read, admire, or study her in just the correct way, in just the right company. Jane Austen is territory over whom we do battle, because for one reason and another she touches us where we live.

The gender issue, then, is only one of those fault lines along which Jane Austen's readers divide. In today's culture, Jane Austen remains remarkable for her continued appeal in both the popular and the academic market. I have reason to be widely acquainted in both groups. To speak first to the popular. There are thriving Jane Austen societies on both sides of the Atlantic. The Jane Austen Society in England has nearly 5000 members. About four hundred of them meet annually in Chawton in the summer to hear an address by an expert, attend a brief business meeting and have strawberries and tea on the lawn. I have attended intermittently, and I notice that the event is burgeoning and attracting booksellers and other commercial entrepreneurs. On that day and during the rest of the year, there are some 27 000 visitors to Jane Austen's House in Chawton, and it now has a growing trade in books, gifts and memorabilia.

The Jane Austen Society of North America, which had its first meeting in 1979, is more elaborate still, with nearly 3000 members. Because its membership is far-flung over the continent, when they do meet they do so for two or three days, and the programme grows in complexity and inventiveness. Its 1993 meeting (of which I was one of the organizers), held in the spectacular mountain setting of Lake Louise in the Canadian Rockies, attracted some 600 delegates to hear the 30-odd speakers, and to engage in other celebrations. There is always a Jane Austen Bookshop. Ancillary attractions on hand for the event were an illustrated novelette sequel to *Persuasion*, a "dance at Uppercross," with some hundreds of delegates in Regency dress, and a full production of a musical version of *Persuasion* called *An Accident at Lyme*. Clearly such an event gathers around it a considerable cluster of Austen-related businesses and other enterprises.

Subject matter for both British and American events includes presentations biographical, historical and critical, and plenty of matter in between, such as crossword puzzles, quizzes, sequels, adaptations, tapes, costumes and quilts. The Jane Austen Society in England produces an annual report in pamphlet form; the Jane Austen Society of North America produces an annual journal, *Persuasions*, and a bi-annual newsletter, *JASNA News*. In addition to the main body of JASNA, there are regional "chapters" of the society all over North America, each with its own cluster of eager members, and most producing their own more or less elaborate newsletters.

Enthusiasm is a keynote. ("I like the name 'Which is the Heroine?' very well," Jane Austen wrote to her niece Anna about her novel in progress, ". . . – but 'Enthusiasm' was something so very superior that every common title must appear to disadvantage" [*Letters*, 393]). It's nice to know Jane Austen approved of enthusiasm, even if only in a title. The Society is a band, a numerous one, who might well chant "Janeite and proud of it." They – or, let me say, *we* (for I am proud of it too) – dress up like Mrs. Allen in *Northanger Abbey*, learn the dances that Elizabeth danced with Darcy, take lessons in loo and speculation, and bandy quotations from the novels. Not all of this is sharply critical, but it does all proceed from a large knowledge of Jane Austen's writings, and a keen desire to extend that knowledge. As a sample of the tone of enthusiasm, here is a quotation from the account of the Lake Louise conference in *Persuasions*:

> Nora Stovel called us all to order with great delicacy and aplomb so we could hear Margaret Drabble read a short story which she had created *just for us*. It was a kind of sequel to *Persuasion* and we were entranced with the adventures of "Bill Elliot" and his contemporaries.[19]

The fastidious critic might call that gushing, and require a "sharpening of the critical edge." The voice is certainly female, and enthusiastic. But not necessarily therefore undiscriminating. Discrimination preceded the enthusiasm, and was the reason for it. Certainly I defy any male or anti-Janeite, with or without critical edge, to find these enthusiastic JASNA members lacking in either knowledge of Austen's texts or astute and discerning things to say about them.

The academic camp, for all their sharpness of critical edge, tends to be less vividly engaging. But Jane Austen is territory keenly competed over in academe too. In the five years up to 1993, I count in the *PMLA* Bibliography nearly 40 books and dissertations devoted in whole or in part to Jane Austen, and some 200 articles. Together those amount to thousands of pages of print – many more than she published herself in her whole career. Some of the critics who produce all this are among the most distinguished in academe. Jane Austen provides grist to the mill of most of the past and current movements in criticism, and one may find interpretations Marxist, Freudian, biographical, new historical, structural, deconstructionist, and, of course, feminist.

A kind of production that is apt to be more patronized by the enthusiasts than the academics is the plethora of adaptations, sequels and spinoffs of Austen's works. In 1993 alone there were two sequels to *Pride and Prejudice* published, *Presumption*, by "Julia Barrett," and

Emma Tennant's *Pemberley*;[20] and I know of another one waiting in the wings. Also launched at the 1993 conference was Joan Austen-Leigh's *Mrs Goddard, Mistress of a School*,[21] an epistolary novel that recounts the events of *Emma* through the eyes of a minor character. I myself have perpetrated an illustrated children's book from one of Jane Austen's juvenilia (of which more hereafter). A student of mine, in satiric mode, has proposed a canny canine novel to be called *Pug* ("a sort of cross between *Finnegans Wake* and *Lassie*")[22] in which we see the action of *Mansfield Park* as observed by Lady Bertram's lapdog. The parodists are lurking again.

And it is not only the presses that groan with fresh books and pamphlets and journals and newsletters about Jane Austen. There are the stage, screen and television adaptations, which then become marketable as audio- and videotapes; the jigsaw puzzles, cards and mockups; a growing trade in made-to-measure Regency outfits; Jane Austen sweatshirts, watches and tote bags; and nighties embroidered with the legend, "Not tonight, dear – I'm reading Jane Austen."

It is tempting to keep the list going; but I must restrain myself. This much is still enough to make the point that Jane Austen is not only a novelist but (by now) an industry. For some she is more: she is a way of life.

The two major groups within the industry, the enthusiasts and the academics, are by no means mutually exclusive categories. The majority of those who address the two Societies at their meetings are academics; the enthusiasts listen and eagerly participate, and the academics find they have plenty to learn. Then many of the academics are enthusiasts too. (I count myself as one of these hybrids.) But there is inevitably some strife between the two camps, as between the Janeites and the critics, the women and the men, the old guard and the young Turks. "I *am* a bit concerned . . . that we are becoming too academic," wrote J. David Grey, one of the founders of JASNA, to his co-founder, Joan Austen-Leigh, in 1980, just after the Society had got going.[23] The Janeites are a courteous crew – none more so – but I saw one slam the door on a talk describing a post-structuralist approach to *Emma*. A compliment I haven't quite come to rejoice in runs, "I loved your paper, Juliet – it's not like those *academic* ones" (with disgusted emphasis). The hostilities – as far as they go – are regrettable. And one can't dismiss them with a breezy "Who cares?" as one might with a more laid-back author, such as Mark Twain, for example. For those who read and know Jane Austen *do* care, and care immensely. Her novels are a training in fine discriminations.

But they are not a training in super-fastidiousness, or for the hyper-refined. Robert Ferrars, who devotes his most intense mental operations to selecting a tooth-pick case (*SS*, 220), is not a sympathetic character. And for the most part it is possible for the academics and the enthusiasts to look beyond their differences to the immense amount they share.

Lionel Trilling, like James, is fastidious about the Jane Austen industry, and would like to keep her for the intellectuals, and only a refined few among them. "The making of Jane Austen into a figure has of recent years been accelerated. . . . I find it difficult to say why I am not on comfortable terms with the figurative process generally and as it touches Jane Austen in particular" (207). He objects not only to the popular adulation, but to the academic proliferation; he admits (with a recognizably Jamesian cadence) that he does not want to augment "the abundant, the superabundant, the ever more urgent intellectual activity that was being directed toward a body of work whose value I would be the first to assert" (207). There is the problem in a nutshell. We all want to write about Jane Austen, but we each of us want to be the only one doing it. We want everyone to admire Jane Austen, but we each suspect the others do it the wrong way. We want her to be our own particular Jane, and to share her with a multitude too.

I come back, then, to Trilling's question: why do we read Jane Austen? Granted that there are as many answers to that as there are readers to articulate them; yet still some salient and recurring reasons suggest themselves as common to men and women, amateur and academic, aficionado and recent convert.

Jane Austen's oeuvre – the six slender novels, the minor works, the letters – is slim, and you can come to know it very well indeed. Moreover, with her finely turned phrases and her elegant economy, she is eminently quotable. There is a great cultural advantage to being well known, as the example of Shakespeare shows. Once the critical mass is achieved, the snowball effect begins, and those who don't possess the knowledge already feel the pressure to acquire it, and to pressure others to acquire it. Such instruments of popular culture as the old *Punch* and *The New Yorker* can add Jane Austen references to the Shakespeare, fairy tale and nursery-rhyme references that their readership can be expected to respond to. "Very nice, Miss Austen," says a Regency publisher in a *Punch* cartoon, to a bonneted lady across the desk, "– but all this effing and blinding will have to go." If you miss the point of a *Punch* joke, you'd better read your Austen and get with it: That's the message.

We come to know the characters very well indeed, too. It's not just that the oeuvre is slim and easy to reread; but the characters become commentators on each other ("But Harriet Smith, I have not half done about Harriet Smith," says Mr. Knightley, insistently [*E*, 38]), and lure us into the discourse; so that even the most distanced and disciplined reader succumbs with pleasure to the temptation to think and talk about these verbal creations as though they were real people, jostling against the other personages in our world, and sometimes displacing them, because in being more fully knowable they seem more fully real.

And then Austen provides, with grace and clarity, both familiarity and difference. Her six plots about a young woman's initiation, growth to maturity, and choice of the right husband have a familiar and predictable outline, a recognizable rhythm of allegro and andante that is as pleasurable as the expected movements of a known concerto. And yet among the similarities and achieved expectations there is always also the difference – the change in tempo, the unexpected minor key, the surprise. We have no sooner noticed the similar predicaments of Fanny and Anne than we must discriminate their differences, and explore the modulations. The samenesses and differences, and the fine modulations in between, are eminently discussable.

Her ironic mode and her economy of understatement make her novels a rich field for critical exegesis. Her fiction is layered, poised, balanced; it maintains a fine equilibrium between text and subtext, between assertion and qualification. The tacit politics silently cry out for vigorous and vocal articulation; the unobtrusive art solicits sophisticated attention and adumbration. What she doesn't claim for herself we professors feel the need to claim for her.

Her world, similarly, is at once like our own, and distanced from it; safer, and more dangerous. People turn to Jane Austen in times of chaos. Her novels, like Trollope's, were read in the trenches, as an assurance of stability and serenity somewhere, sometime. In the wake of the 1994 earthquake in Los Angeles, residents I know picked up their Jane Austen books first from the rubble on the floor. But before we patronize her for her remoteness from our hectic modern life and for the serenity and safety of her vicarages and country gardens, we need to remember too the real threats and pains in a world where a vulnerable old spinster like Miss Bates needs protection from "those who might hate her" (*E*, 21); where Edward Ferrars' life and happiness can be ruined when a Lucy Steele gets her hooks into him; where a Henry Crawford can idly work at making a "small hole" in Fanny

Price's heart; or where marriage to a Mr. Collins is preferable to all other available alternatives. One can see that as funny, or as horrible. Jane Austen's world is morally ordered and fully significant, in ways that make us wistfully envious, as we muddle along with our messy lives in our permissive culture. For her, *everything* matters. It's not surprising that we should all want a piece of that action.

Notes

1. Lionel Trilling, *The Last Decade: Essays and Reviews, 1965–75*, ed. Diana Trilling (New York and London: Harcourt Brace Jovanovich, 1979), p. 204. For subsequent quotations from this essay I supply page numbers in the text.
2. *Jane Austen's Achievement: Papers Delivered at the Jane Austen Bicentennial Conference at the University of Alberta*, ed. Juliet McMaster (London: Macmillan, 1976). Ian Jack kindly came at short notice to deliver a paper in Lionel Trilling's place. Other papers were by Lloyd Brown, Barbara Hardy, A. Walton Litz, Norman Page, B.C. Southam, and George Whalley.
3. *Times Literary Supplement*, 5 March, 1976, 1–2.
4. Henry James, "The Lesson of Balzac" (1905), in *Literary Criticism: French Writers, Other European Writers, the Prefaces to the New York Edition*, selected by Leon Edel and Mark Wilson (New York: The Library of America, 1984), p. 118.
5. *Our Own Particular Jane* is the title of a play by Joan Austen-Leigh which consists of scenes from the novels and responses to them. Compare Katherine Mansfield: "The truth is that every true admirer of the novels cherishes the happy thought that he alone – reading between the lines – has become the secret friend of the author." *Novels and Novelists*, ed. J. Middleton Murry (London 1930; Boston: Beacon, 1959), p. 302.
6. For a fuller account of the battles between different camps, see Brian Southam's "Janeites and Anti-Janeites," in *The Jane Austen Companion*, ed. J. David Grey, A. Walton Litz and Brian Southam (New York: Macmillan, 1986), 237–43.
7. See "The Victorian 'Society' View," in *Jane Austen: The Critical Heritage*, ed. B.C. Southam (London: Routledge & Kegan Paul, 1968), p. 201.
8. Joan Austen-Leigh, "Editorial," *Persuasions* (annual journal of the Jane Austen Society of North America), 4 (1982), p. 2.
9. "The Lady Novelists," *Westminster Review* 58 (July 1852), 134. Reprinted in *Jane Austen: The Critical Heritage*, p. 140.
10. Letter to Ruskin of 5 November 1855; quoted by B.C. Southam, *Jane Austen: The Critical Heritage*, 25.
11. See Southam, p. 240.
12. In "Apropos of Lady Chatterley's Lover," 1930.
13. F.R. Leavis, *The Great Tradition* (London: Chatto & Windus, 1948), p. 1.

14. Southam, p. 248. My intention is not to accuse Mr Southam of sexism, but to show the inevitable gender biases even in measured criticism.
15. This and the following quotations from the James essay (cited above) are from pages 116 to 118.
16. Laurence Sterne, *Tristram Shandy* (1760–67), II, xix.
17. Rudyard Kipling, "The Janeites" (1926), in *Debits and Credits* (London: Macmillan, 1949), 147-76. I supply page references in the text.
18. Deborah Kaplan, *Jane Austen Among Women* (Baltimore and London: Johns Hopkins University Press), 1992.
19. "JASNA Meets at Lake Louise," "by a Janeite," *Persuasions*, 15 (1993), p. 19.
20. *Presumption: An Entertainment*, by Julia Barrett (actually Julia Brown Kessler and Gabrielle Donnelly) (New York: M. Evans, 1993); *Pemberley, or Pride and Prejudice Continued*, by Emma Tennant (London: Hodder & Stoughton, 1993).
21. *Mrs Goddard, Mistress of a School*, by Joan Austen-Leigh (Victoria: Room of One's Own Press, 1993).
22. Michael Londry, "Pug," for English 455, University of Alberta, 1993.
23. Quoted by Joan Austen-Leigh, "The Founding of JASNA," *Persuasions*, 15 (1993), p. 12. The current President of JASNA, however, Garnett Bass, in her report in the same volume, celebrates "the easy footing on which academic and amateur enthusiasts mingle and exchange ideas" in the Society (p. 15).

2

Teaching "Love and Freindship"[1]

Do the juvenilia belong in the classroom at all? is a fair question, given the scarcity of time in most courses for covering great works of literature. If you have a chance to teach *Pride and Prejudice* or *Mansfield Park*, dare you jettison it for a selection of items from *Volumes the First, Second,* and *Third*? Put this way, the question possibly requires the answer "No." I am too confirmed an admirer of the six great novels to miss any opportunity of teaching them when it arises. I have taught *Pride and Prejudice* at the High School level and to university freshmen, and *Emma* to freshmen and in survey courses on the English novel. And from time to time – O frabjous day! – I have the chance to teach all six novels in a specialized undergraduate class, or in a graduate course. In these last cases, I make time for some of the juvenilia, and particularly for "Love and Freindship," as a way into the novels. Graduate students, who have some knowledge of the sentimental tradition that it parodies, are bowled over by it. And even in teaching Jane Austen at the lower and less specialized levels, I usually get in "Love and Freindship," if only in the form of some selected readings, as a way into the Jane Austen novel at hand.

But though by these means I have managed to teach "Love and Freindship" several times, I confess it has always been as an adjunct to teaching the major novels. So far, that is. But my experience has brought me to the conclusion that in the right context it can stand alone as a teaching text. A course in romanticism, for instance, could include it as a succinct critical text, since it is a marvellously pointed and intellectually acute reaction to romanticism, and a codification of its conventions. With its brevity and concentration, its control of diction and mastery of burlesque, it would be a joyful addition to courses in composition and rhetoric at both basic and advanced levels. In recent years Sandra Gilbert and Susan Gubar have chosen "Love and Freindship" as the representative work by Jane Austen in *The Norton Anthology of Literature by Women*, and so it is not only newly available

18

as an accessible text, but also likely to receive new prominence in courses in women's literature.[2]

One great advantage that this work has, and shares with the other juvenilia, as a text for teaching to young people is that it is written by one of themselves. In teaching at high school and freshman levels in particular, where the English instructor is apt to be faced by a number of students more or less resistant to literature, it is a shrewd move in the game to beat the generation gap by infiltrating the opposition forces with an author who shows so many signs of sharing *your* concerns, while being on *their* side of the gap. This kid with the marvellous control of language and assured command of an extensive vocabulary, this writer with an intense and exuberant involvement in other literature, is a mere teenager, a 14-year old. Perhaps, suspects the resistant student who may yet become a convert, there is something in literature after all.

The approach one takes in teaching "Love and Freindship" will of course vary according to the context in which it is taught. If it is a part of a course on romanticism or the history of the novel, then the emphasis will naturally fall on the war of ideas and the burlesque of the novel of sensibility. If it is a text in a course in composition and rhetoric, clearly the language and narrative technique will be to the fore. And when I am teaching it as an adjunct to the teaching of Jane Austen's other works, then it is useful to focus on the intimations of things to come, the themes and technical concerns that are to be developed in the great novels. By way of giving some coverage to all these possibilities, I will divide this essay into three parts, roughly on past, present, and future: one on the burlesque element as a reaction to literature that has gone before, one on "Love and Freindship" as a text standing on its own, and one on this little work as looking forward, a pointer to the novels yet to come.

LOOKING BACK: THE BURLESQUE

For the informed graduate student who comes to it via wide reading in the eighteenth-century novel and the novel of sensibility, "Love and Freindship" has a particular and unrivalled delight – almost such as it must have had for its first readers, Jane Austen's sister and brothers, who were steeped in the unselected and uncanonical fiction of the day. To come to young Jane Austen's reaction via *The Man of Feeling* or *The Fool of Quality*, or even *Clarissa* or *Evelina*, is to feel a bracing breeze of wit after a cloistered absorption in emotion.

But fortunately the wit is accessible to the less specialized student too, for you don't have to wade through *Laura and Augustus*[3] and the other novels that are being parodied to get the point. Their conventions and narrative procedures are brilliantly and unfairly generalized, selected and lampooned for us. As A. Walton Litz points out, "The Juvenilia are remarkably self-sufficient, and most of the burlesque passages are self-explanatory."[4]

Even the unsophisticated student may learn from the text itself – from Sir Edward's speech, carefully planted early in the work – that it bounces off other texts. Sir Edward is reacting to the romantic effusions of his son: "Where, Edward in the name of wonder (said he) did you pick up this unmeaning Gibberish? You have been studying Novels I suspect" (81). For the reader uninitiated in the fiction Jane Austen was burlesquing, it can become a stimulating exercise to deduce the characteristics of the novels young Edward has been studying.

How would an intelligent but not necessarily widely read student respond to the following question on "Love and Freindship"? It reads, let us say, "Making clear the evidence on which you base your conclusions, deduce the major characteristics of the kinds of novel Sir Edward suspects his son of reading." First, the student would need to look carefully at what young Edward has just been saying. I quote here from his mini-autobiography, delivered on the first night of his acquaintance with Laura and her parents, which includes the dialogue with his father:

> "My Father . . . is a mean and mercenary wretch – it is only to such particular freinds as this Dear Party that I would thus betray his failings. Your Virtues my amiable Polydore (addressing himself to my father) yours Dear Claudia and yours my Charming Laura call on me to repose in you, my Confidence." We bowed. "My Father, seduced by the false glare of Fortune and the Deluding Pomp of Title, insisted on my giving my hand to Lady Dorothea. No never exclaimed I. Lady Dorothea is lovely and Engaging; I prefer no woman to her; but know Sir, that I scorn to marry her in compliance with your Wishes. No! Never shall it be said that I obliged my Father."
> We all admired the noble Manliness of his reply. (80–81)

The tirade received with such admiration by its later audience is designated "unmeaning Gibberish" by Sir Edward. This already points to two symmetrically opposed sets of values among the characters of the work; and with some close reading or some helpful guidance the student may align these values with Sense and Sensibility, in their extreme forms. Young Edward's values (as deducible from this passage alone) include a vaunted scorn for material considerations, an opposition on principle to fathers, a determination to be independent of parental guidance even at the cost of his own comfort and convenience, an extraordinary readiness to form instant intimacies beyond his family, and a strong propensity to talk about himself: we are already well on the way to the values of Sensibility (at least of Sensibility as here exaggerated and satirized), which are to be more elaborately adumbrated in the rest of "Love and Freindship"; and these are the values, clearly, that are enshrined in the novels that his father suspects Edward of reading. Since the same values are also articulated at large by the heroine, Laura, the student may expand from Edward's mini-narrative to his wife's larger one, and may move also from thematic concerns to technical ones. Laura, as heroine of sensibility, gives us a version of the novel of sensibility, with its routine gestures of sighing and swooning, prodigious coincidences, birth-mystery plot, embedded life-histories of different characters, and improbable layout in epistolary form. All this and much, much more (as the brochures say) the intelligent but unread student can deduce for herself from an attentive reading of the text, because of the vivid exaggeration of Jane Austen's parody.

The more fully initiated graduate student, meanwhile, may receive more recondite pleasure from the same passage, the pleasure of recognition. "Love and Freindship" is one more document in the ongoing eighteenth-century debates on true and false sensibility, marriages of interest and romance, the disinterestedness of true friendship, and the proper extent and limits of parental authority. Richardson's Clarissa Harlowe, for instance, had already delivered such a lecture as Sir Edward would have approved to her friend Anna, who was inclined to despise her sensible and eligible suitor because, like young Edward's Lady Dorothea, he was unexciting: "[You] have nothing to do [Clarissa tells her friend] but to fall in with a choice your mamma has made for you, to which you have not, nor can have, a just objection: except the frowardness of our sex . . . makes it one that the choice was your mamma's. . . . Perverse nature, we know, loves not to be prescribed to; although youth is not so well qualified . . . to choose for itself" (Letter 73).[5] Clarissa puts it mildly; her uncle Anthony's phrase, "a most horrid romantic perverseness" (Letter 32.4), might be closer to describing young Edward's reaction to Lady Dorothea. For the well-read seeker after sources, of course, "Love and Freindship" provides a veritable Happy Hunting Ground. Where shall we find the original for the wonderful recognition scene, in which poor Lord St. Clair is reunited with four grandchildren (all by separate mothers, and unaware of each other) in as many minutes? (91–92). In Fielding's *Joseph Andrews* ("I have discovered my son, I have him again in my arms!")?[6] In Smollett's *Humphry Clinker* ("You see, gentlemen, how the sins of my youth rise up in judgement against me")?[7] In Sheridan's *The Critic*, as Walton Litz suggests?[8] Or (my candidate) in Fanny Burney's *Evelina*, where Sir John Belmont, introduced to the girl who claims to be his daughter, responds with a dry irony worthy of Mr. Bennet, "It is not three days since, that I had the pleasure of discovering a son; how many more sons and daughters may be brought to me, I am yet to learn, but I am, already, perfectly satisfied with the size of my family"?[9] Fourteen-year old Jane, familiar with these and many more, generalizes and caps them all with Lord St. Clair's bevy of supernumerary grandchildren. Well may he enquire nervously, "But tell me (. . . looking fearfully towards the Door) tell me, have I any other Grandchildren in the House" – and, after dealing out banknotes all round, beat a hasty and permanent retreat (92).

An undue emphasis on "Love and Freindship" as burlesque of other novels has the danger of giving the impression, particularly to the unsophisticated student, that Jane Austen despised the fiction of her day. Henry Tilney can help here. Although he is the hero in a novel largely devoted to parody of the Gothic novel, and is an able parodist himself of Mrs. Radcliffe, he declares, "The person . . . who has not pleasure in a good novel, must be intolerably stupid. I have read all Mrs. Radcliffe's works, and most of them with great pleasure" (*NA*, 106). This intimate relation of admiration with mockery needs to be understood as informing "Love and Freindship" too. Reading novels and critically reacting to them were clearly the great delights of young Jane Austen's life. And her delight needs to emerge as well as her mocking judgement when we teach her youthful burlesque.

Suppose that "Love and Freindship," instead of being written by a 14-year-old girl for the small circle of her family, had been written by Byron – as it well might have been, in the same wicked mood in which he wrote "English Bards and Scotch Reviewers": it would surely have been published in its own day, and read, and laughed over, and quoted, and become part of the canon. B.C. Southam, who is careful to acknowledge the occasional and fugitive nature of Jane Austen's juvenilia, nevertheless calls it "the most amusing and incisive of all eighteenth-century attacks upon sentimental fiction."[10] For the acute perception of the flaws of a certain mode, and the limber articulation of them, are not only remarkable for a 14-year-old girl, they are remarkable for *anybody*. This document of the history of ideas is the product of a first-class mind as well as of an agile creative imagination. The tenets of the cult of sentimentality, many of which were common to the romantic movement, are marvellously grasped, dramatized and reduced to absurdity. In fact Jane Austen uses the logical strategy of *reductio ad absurdum* with brilliant consistency. Each treasured position of the sentimentalist is identified, exaggerated and pursued to the point where it becomes a reversal of itself. Laura, Edward, Sophia and Augustus, the adherents to the cult, are like a comic version of Milton's Satan, who can produce a fine intellectual argument in support of his insanely perverse proposition, "Evil, be thou my Good."

Romantic individualism, chiefly manifested here in the rejection of social sanctions as epitomized in parental advice, becomes ultimately self-annihilating; as we have seen, Edward can't consider marrying Lady Dorothea, even though he likes her, because his father advises it. In the same way other treasured watchwords of the sentimental cult are consistently turned upside down. Sensibility itself, the capacity to feel tenderly for others, becomes callousness: at the outset Laura admits that though her sensibility was at one time "too tremblingly alive to every affliction of my Freinds," she now feels for nobody's afflictions but her own (78). Sophia enacts this hyper-refinement of the emotions: "Alas, what would I not give to learn the fate of my Augustus! to know if he is still in Newgate, or if he is yet hung. But never shall I be able so far to conquer my tender sensibility as to enquire after him" (97). Romantic reverence for the beauties of external nature becomes one more way of turning in upon the self:

"What a beautifull Sky! (said I) How charmingly is the azure varied by those delicate streaks of white!"

"Oh! my Laura (replied she hastily withdrawing her Eyes from a momentary glance at the sky) do not so distress me by calling my Attention to an object which so cruelly reminds me of my Augustus's blue sattin Waistcoat striped with white!" (98)

"The world is too much with us," wrote Wordsworth, giving memorable voice to the romantic's rejection of a hyper-civilized society and of things worldly; "late and soon, / Getting and spending, we lay waste our powers." Laura and her fellow romantics believe that they live according to the spirit of this rejection. Edward scorns his father, the representative of social authority, as "a mean and mercenary wretch," and expects to live the life of the lilies of the field, who toil not, neither do they spin. But as our students quickly notice, this innocent assumption that the world owes them a living leads directly to various acts of theft and embezzlement, and numbers of banknotes are "gracefully purloined" (88) with some skill by these untaught children of nature. Decades later, Dickens was to render this sinister reversal of a vaunted indifference to material things in the figure of Harold Skimpole, a character based on another romantic, Leigh Hunt. Skimpole confesses proudly "to two of the oldest infirmities in the world: one was, that he had no idea of time; the other, that he had no idea of money." He claims, "I covet nothing. . . . Possession is nothing to me." But he proceeds cheerfully on the assumption that others must support him, and like his forebears, Laura and her associates, he elevates his freeloading into a moral principle. "I almost feel as if *you* ought to be grateful to *me*," he tells his benefactor, "for giving you the opportunity of enjoying the luxury of generosity."[11] Jane Austen's Sophia can similarly turn the moral tables on her benefactor when, being caught in the act of "majestically removing" his banknotes to her own purse, she angrily calls their owner the "culprit" (96).

This pattern of turning romantic principles into their own reversal is most fully and inventively developed in the presentation of freedom of choice: Laura and company believe that they are free spirits, children of nature, living a life of spontaneous response, rejecting the hardened conventions of their parents' society, and expressing themselves habitually by the "spontaneous overflow of powerful feelings" that is Wordsworth's definition of poetry. That is their construction of themselves. As Jane Austen exposes them, however, we see them as the veritable slaves of their own convention of freedom. Their responses are rigidly codified, their language is a prescribed jargon, their attitudes are *de rigueur*; their very swoonings are performed with a paramilitary precision, "Alternately on a Sofa" (86). Far from being free individual spirits living lives untrammelled by the stultifying conventions of society, they conduct their lives by a code so rigid and exacting that it extends to the name (it must be classical like "Laura" and "Augustus," not homegrown like "Bridget"), stature (it must be above the middle height), and the colour of the hair (it must be auburn).

All this comes most comically to the fore in the episode at Macdonald-Hall, where Laura and Sophia, who have hitherto been exiles from society, become authority figures themselves. The 15-year-old Janetta

Macdonald proves malleable, and her new role models, with considerable zest, set about her conversion from Sense to Sensibility. She is engaged to Graham, but Laura and Sophia take things into their own hands. "They said he was Sensible, well-informed, and Agreable; we did not pretend to Judge of such trifles, but as we were convinced he had no soul, that he had never read the Sorrows of Werter, & that his Hair bore not the least resemblance to Auburn, we were certain that Janetta could feel no affection for him, or at least that she ought to feel none" (93). Laura and Sophia, with their own rigid notions of propriety, prove to be even more arbitrary and tyrannical than conventionally tyrannical parents; and they symmetrically reverse the requirements of such parents as Clarissa Harlowe's by detaching Janetta from the prudent suitor and marrying her to an opportunistic fortune hunter.

To identify, exaggerate, and reduce to their own absurd opposites these tenets of the dying cult of sentimentality, from which the new cult of romanticism, phoenix-like, was about to rise, and to do all this in the dramatic form of a brief narrative, is surely to have achieved something considerable in the history of those movements, as well as to have produced a marvellously funny pastiche. "Love and Freindship" as burlesque, as a reaction to previous and contemporary texts, deserves a place in courses on the eighteenth century and romanticism.

THE TEXT ITSELF

Although "Love and Freindship" inevitably makes its first impact as a burlesque of earlier fiction and assumptions, it also deserves attention for its own intrinsic value, and for its internal ironies. Students in a course on composition would have plenty to learn from the control of language and the narrative structure of this brief but eventful story.

The series of letters that constitutes "Love and Freindship" sets it up as a narrative of instruction. Isabel asks Laura, the friend of her youth, to recount "the Misfortunes and Adventures of your Life" for the moral benefit of her daughter, Marianne (76). Laura quickly assumes that she is to appear in her own story as the *positive* moral example: "may the fortitude with which I have suffered the many Afflictions of my past Life, prove to her a useful Lesson," she prays (77). But the attentive student who matches the beginning with the ending will notice that Isabel is far from admiring the youthful Laura's conduct. When they meet in the stagecoach which coincidentally contains all the surviving personages of the story, Laura delivers an oral version of her life story, but Isabel tends to be disapproving. "Faultless as my Conduct had certainly been during the whole course of my late Misfortunes & Adventures, she pretended to find fault with my Behaviour," notes Laura indignantly (104). Isabel, it appears, has gone through some moral evolution in the course of the narrative: having been once the bosom "Freind" of Laura and the chosen companion of her youth, she learns from her friend's experience and her recounting of it that Sense is morally preferable to Sensibility. Hence her scheme in eliciting Laura's written narrative is to provide her daughter Marianne with a *negative* example, not the positive one that Laura fondly assumes. Marianne as reader is to learn to *avoid* Laura's sentimental excesses, and is so to be converted from Sensibility to Sense, as her mother was before her. Although Jane Austen doesn't labour the point – in fact she merely tosses it in – there are intricacies and ironic possibilities in this narrative set-up that are worthy of a more elaborate tale.

Laura herself is immune from any moral benefit to be derived from her experience: the only moral she can draw from it is the one she relays from the dying Sophia, about the imprudence of wilful fainting fits (102). She remains satisfied that since "I had always behaved in a manner which reflected Honour on my Feelings & Refinement," she must be irreproachable, and so have nothing to learn (104).

The many interpolated narratives within Laura's narrative suggest that the young Jane was meditating (though certainly not solemnly) on narratology. What is narrative *for*? All the characters, whether on the side of Sense or Sensibility, clearly lap it up. On that memorable coach ride between Edinburgh and Stirling, the characters deliver autobiographies at an astonishing rate. First, at Sir Edward's entreaty, Laura tells the story of his son's death; next, Laura "related to them every other misfortune which had befallen me since we parted"; next, Isabel gives Laura "an accurate detail of every thing that had befallen her since our separation"; finally, Augusta supplies "the same information respecting herself, Sir Edward & Lady Dorothea" (104–5). Laura's curiosity for such personal narratives is insatiable. After this marathon of telling and listening, while the others are regaling themselves with "Green tea & buttered toast," Laura seeks out her cousins, and "we feasted ourselves in a more refined & Sentimental Manner by a confidential Conversation" (106) – consisting, of course, in further "entertaining Narration" (108). Apparently Laura actually lives off people's lives and adventures. To keep her supplied with this verbal grist to her mill can be exhausting, and poor Edward may be said to have died from the effort:

> "Oh! tell me Edward (said I [when his phaeton has overturned]) tell me I beseech you before you die, what has befallen you since that unhappy Day in which . . . we were separated –"
> "I will" (said he) and instantly fetching a deep sigh, expired –.
> (100)

What, besides a substitute for toast and tea, do Laura and the others get out of each other's stories? It seems that the morally approved characters, Sir Edward and his ilk, get moral enlargement and some matter for thought: the raw data can be sifted, interpreted, judged; it conduces to more than itself. But for the Sensibility crew, a life history is mere food for curiosity. Laura *telling* a story proposes to "gratify the curiosity of [Isabel's] Daughter" (77); Laura *hearing* a story desires Isabel only "to satisfy my Curiosity" (104). For such people a story begins and ends with itself, or rather with *the* self, and no mental or moral growth is involved in the transmitting of it. The teller gratifies the self, and slakes the listener's curiosity (or the "degrading thirst after outrageous stimulation" that Wordsworth was to complain about in the preface to *Lyrical Ballads*.) Jane Austen was to pursue the distinction between kinds of discourse in her later novels. Henry Tilney can rise to conversation, stimulating the mind beyond the individual and the particular toward exchange at a shared and general level; John Thorpe is capable only of talk. "All the rest of his conversation, or rather talk," the narrator discriminates in *Northanger Abbey*, "began and ended with himself and his own concerns" (*NA*, 66). Thus Sir Edward wants Laura to tell him of Edward, a third party. But Laura makes Edward's death only an episode among her own adventures, for she can proceed no further than the I–thou narrative.

The two species, with their opposed sets of assumptions about appropriate behaviour and appropriate discourse, have their own distinct languages. And identifying these languages, or the kinds of *patois* common to a group, or particular to an individual, can be a useful exercise in a course in composition and rhetoric. The conversation between Edward and his sister Augusta, representatives respectively of Sensibility and Sense, is a good starting point. Augusta has just suggested that Edward may need to apply to his father for the support of his new wife, Laura:

> "Never, never Augusta will I so demean myself. (said Edward).
> Support! What Support will Laura want which she can receive from him?"
> "Only those very insignificant ones of Victuals and Drink." (answered she).
> "Victuals and Drink! (replied my Husband in a most nobly contemptuous Manner) and dost thou then imagine that there is no other support for an exalted Mind (such as is my Laura's) than the mean and indelicate employment of Eating and Drinking?"
> "None that I know of, so efficacious." (returned Augusta). (83)

The whole conversation is longer, but even from this extract one can tell that the two interlocutors speak in two different registers; and if one's students in rhetoric can become sensitive to tonal register, much is gained. Edward adopts the grand style for the expression of his elevated emotions of scorn and indignation. Augusta calls him "you," but he calls her "thou," and his archaism is intended to capture the dignity of chivalric romance. His characteristic syntax is exclamatory ("Support!" "Victuals and Drink!") and histrionic. Augusta on the other hand is down-to-earth and colloquial, to match her practical concern with creature comforts. She speaks economically in sentence fragments, supplying only the noun phrases that answer his rhetorical questions (he means them to be rhetorical). And she, like her father, can handle irony ("None that I know of, so efficacious"), whereas it is characteristic of the adherents of sensibility that they are as incapable of using irony as of understanding it. Their speeches may of course be ironic for the *reader*, however. Here, for instance, Edward's outrage at the notion that Laura will need support from his father can be matched against the circumstances of the ending, when the widowed Laura retires on an allowance of £400 a year, supplied by Sir Edward (108).

An exercise in practical criticism of such a passage can alert students to different verbal styles. And because Jane Austen is here being deliberately crude and hyperbolic, even the unawakened freshman can get the point. The marvellous nuances and finely discriminated tones in the quite recognizable speech patterns of John Thorpe, Mrs. Jennings, Mary Bennet, Mr. Woodhouse, and the rest are yet to come. But meanwhile we still have broad burlesques by way of developing the student's ear, such as Laura's speech when mad. It is a take-off of Ophelia, even to being for much of its length in iambic pentameter. For instance:

> Give me a violin – . I'll play to him
> & sooth him in his melancholy Hours –
> Beware ye gentle Nymphs of Cupid's Thunderbolts [a hexameter this time],
> [A]void the piercing Shafts of Jupiter. (100)

The attribution of Jupiter's thunderbolts to Cupid, and of Cupid's piercing shafts to Jupiter, is a touch of madness cheerfully thrown in.

A full study of Jane Austen's language is not possible here, but I touch on what seem to me useful starting points, by way of suggesting how much is there to follow up. One kind of sensitivity that is particularly surprising in so young a writer is her fine ear for what is hackneyed and outworn. Laura and Sophia talk in catchwords, in ready-made clichés: "She was all Sensibility and Feeling. We flew into each others arms and after having exchanged vows of mutual Freindship for the rest of our Lives, instantly unfolded to each other the most inward Secrets of our Hearts" (85). So much is compacted into one sentence – the physical action, the content of the vows, the invoking of lifetimes, the unfolded secrets – that the sentence structure itself conveys the emptiness of the claims. The two heroines could as well be conducting their meeting by semaphore, like Girl Guides, waving successively the Sensibility flag, the Eternal Vow flag, and the Inmost Secret flag. And one of the sharp weapons in Jane Austen's verbal armoury comes into wicked play: the adverb. The fact that those inmost secrets are unfolded "instantly" utterly devalues them. Likewise we get the comedy of the ladies' fainting "alternately" on the sofa, a preview of the more subtly controlled irony, to be encountered hereafter, of Charlotte Lucas's deliberate setting out to meet Mr. Collins "accidentally" in the lane (*PP*, 121).

Jane Austen's major novels are famous for their restraint, for their delicacy, for their miniaturist's craftsmanship, etcetera. Not so the juvenilia. The juvenilia are wild and rowdy, full of extravagant exaggeration, exuberant jokes, nonsense, slapstick, and anarchic humour. "Love and Freindship" is the kind of work that provokes belly laughs. And like other funny books – *Pickwick Papers* for instance[12] – it has a plot that is subordinated to the jokes. It's not easy to remember the sequence of the action of such works. Laura and her lovers and friends rocket about between London, Wales and Scotland in a manner that is as difficult for the readers as for the characters themselves to keep track of. But of course this very chaos is intentional. "It would be almost impossible to summarize the action of 'Love and Freindship'," Litz points out, "since one of Jane Austen's aims was to satirize the intricate and unnatural plots of contemporary fiction."[13] She has, for instance, a birth mystery plot of an intricacy to dazzle and dismay. But one of the pleasures for the close reader of this wild text is that in the midst of the anarchy it has its own order and consistency. For years I have admired the revelation scene (in which Lord St. Clair discovers his four separate grandchildren) for its mere craziness: "Acknowledge thee!" exclaims the Venerable Stranger to Laura, "Yes dear resemblance to my Laurina & my Laurina's Daughter, sweet image of my Claudia and my Claudia's Mother, I do acknowledge thee as the Daughter of the one & the Grandaughter of the other" (91). Surely no one can follow such stuff! But lately, when I had set the passage as an exercise in practical criticism, I tried constructing a family tree, and found to my delight that it all works. Moreover, in working out Lord St. Clair's and other families, I found that a chart demonstrates a balanced familial symmetry among the figures of Sensibility and Sense. In supplying this chart, I claim to be the first genealogist who has taken Lord St. Clair's tree seriously.

I have indicated the characters of Sense in roman capitals, and the characters of Sensibility in italics. This makes it clear that while the heroine has a pedigree of unblemished Sensibility, the hero's family members are symmetrically divided. Sensibility needs the opposition of Sense to define itself. Sir Edward and Philippa, brother and sister, represent Sense and Sensibility respectively; the same is true of the next generation, Augusta and Edward. Sophia (Sensibility) is likewise opposed to her cousin Macdonald (Sense). And there is a similar symmetry among the morally mobile younger generation. Young Janetta Macdonald, who begins by espousing Sense, is converted by Laura and Sophia to Sensibility, and the sequence of her two suitors, Graham and M'Kenzie, confirms this. Young Marianne, for whom the letters are written, is presumably mobile in the other direction (if her mother's plan works), being converted by the moral action of this narrative from Sensibility to Sense.

The wild implausibility of the birth mystery plot and its revelation, and the other unlikely relationships, turn out to be not random and chaotic, but neatly patterned, to reinforce the major thematic oppositions of the tale.

Laura's and Sophia's Family

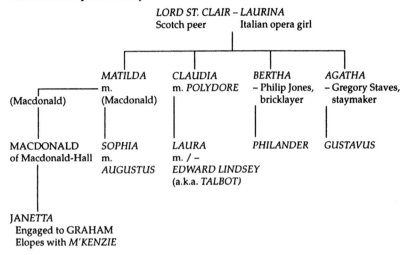

LORD ST. CLAIR – LAURINA
Scotch peer   Italian opera girl

MATILDA   CLAUDIA   BERTHA   AGATHA
m.   m. POLYDORE   – Philip Jones,   – Gregory Staves,
(Macdonald)   (Macdonald)   bricklayer   staymaker

MACDONALD   SOPHIA   LAURA   PHILANDER   GUSTAVUS
of Macdonald-Hall   m.   m. / –
    AUGUSTUS   EDWARD LINDSEY
        (a.k.a. TALBOT)

JANETTA
Engaged to GRAHAM
Elopes with M'KENZIE

Edward's Family

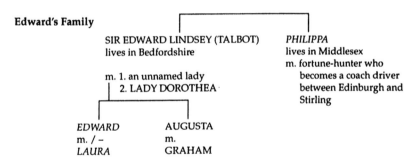

SIR EDWARD LINDSEY (TALBOT)   PHILIPPA
lives in Bedfordshire   lives in Middlesex
    m. fortune-hunter who
m. 1. an unnamed lady   becomes a coach driver
    2. LADY DOROTHEA   between Edinburgh and
        Stirling

EDWARD   AUGUSTA
m. / –   m.
LAURA   GRAHAM

Marianne's Family

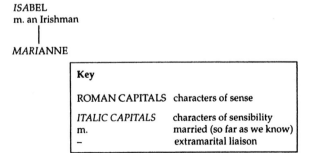

ISABEL
m. an Irishman

MARIANNE

Key	
ROMAN CAPITALS	characters of sense
ITALIC CAPITALS	characters of sensibility
m.	married (so far as we know)
–	extramarital liaison

Genealogies in "Love and Freindship"

And in the same way as the theme provides structure and pattern for the family tree, so the moral oppositions provide shape for the story. Browning is said to have claimed that if Jesus Christ had not existed, we would have had to invent him: the myth is so aesthetically à propos for the state in which humanity finds itself. Similarly, I sometimes think that if morality hadn't existed, Jane Austen would have found a way to invent it. For those sharp antitheses (between sense and sensibility, or between the self-centred and the outward-looking, or between wisdom and folly), those clean oppositions in "Love and Freindship" and the major works too, are there not just for didactic purposes, but because they supply form, a tense and a delightful aesthetic structure.

LOOKING FORWARD: INTIMATIONS OF THE MAJOR NOVELS

To discover Sense and Sensibility as located in siblings is to lead to the relation of "Love and Freindship" to the major novels.

Laura's chosen friend, Sophia, from fainting in the grass as the evening dew is falling, contracts "a violent pain in her delicate limbs, accompanied with a disagreeable Head-ake" (101), and presently dies, delivering the memorable advice about avoiding fainting-fits that is the overt moral of "Love and Freindship": I like to recall that the recipient of this advice is called Marianne, for it is Marianne Dashwood in *Sense and Sensibility* who contracts a violent cold ("with a pain in her limbs") after twilight walks in dew-wet grass, which proves almost fatal. And the two Mariannes are both educated from Sensibility towards Sense. This is only one of dozens of connections between "Love and Freindship" and the major novels. And if one is teaching it as an adjunct to the teaching of Jane Austen's major works, clearly the ongoing theme of Sense and Sensibility makes the most obvious starting point. "Love and Freindship" leads most clearly and directly to *Sense and Sensibility*. But the contrast between Sense and Sensibility, varied as the rival claims of reason and emotion, remains a central structuring idea in all the novels. "Beware of fainting fits . . . Though at the time they may be refreshing and Agreable yet beleive me they will in the end, if too often repeated & at improper seasons, prove destructive to your Constitution . . . My fate will teach you this . . . One fatal swoon has cost me my Life" (102). The oppositions of sense and sensibility, and reason and emotion, and the debate on the proper balance between them, continue to vibrate through all the novels, up to and including *Persuasion*. Anne Elliot, we know, completes the pattern. "She had been forced into prudence in her youth, she learned romance as she grew older" (*P*, 30). From "Love and Freindship" to *Persuasion* we can see Jane Austen go through much the same evolution.

An alternative clue, planted in "Love and Freindship"and running as a strongly uniting thread through the other novels, starts with Sir Edward's pregnant conclusion, when faced with his son's romantic outburst, "You have been studying Novels I suspect" (81). This leads not only backward into the novels Jane Austen was burlesquing, but forward into the novels she was to write herself. That is, we can go beyond the activities of parody and burlesque to the more interesting and dominant idea of literature as model for life. Jane Austen's characters, like Don Quixote, are intently engaged in a quest to make experience conform to literary precedent. Again, students of the whole canon can trace this idea as developed with increasing subtlety through Catherine's Gothic fantasy in *Northanger Abbey*, and Marianne's sense of entrapment in hackneyed language and hackneyed responses at the very moment that she is practising them, to the elaborate fictions that Emma imposes on life. Many of Emma's most serious errors arise from the assumption that fictional conventions are transferable to life. Her preconception that Harriet Smith, of unknown parentage, is a fit wife for a gentleman is ultimately traceable to the same conventions that Jane Austen parodied in the Lord St. Clair episode in "Love and Freindship": because there's a birth mystery about Harriet, Emma concludes she must be of noble parentage. The theme is dear to the hearts of Jane Austen and other well-read novelists (Cervantes, Fielding, Sterne, Thackeray, George Eliot, and James come especially to mind), because it is born of a consuming love of books. These are writers who *live* their literature, and are wryly conscious of the propensity. And they are sophisticated, too, being fully aware, long before Oscar Wilde told the rest of the world, that "Life imitates Art far more than Art imitates Life." Jane Austen's fictions, from her juvenilia on, demonstrate a constant and amused concern with the complex and sometimes hilarious interaction of life and literature.

"Love and Freindship" is as visible a step toward the mature novels in matters of technique as of theme. Jane Austen's giant step from the eighteenth century to the nineteenth involved for her a weaning from the epistle. *Sir Charles Grandison* and *Evelina* were undoubtedly habit-forming: "Love and Freindship" ("a novel in a series of letters"), "Lesley Castle" ("An unfinished Novel in Letters"), "A Collection of

Letters," and *Lady Susan* lead to "First Impressions"[14] and "Elinor and Marianne," the lost first epistolary versions of mature novels. And in those novels themselves the letter continues to be of crucial importance. What "Love and Freindship" shows in this evolution is Jane Austen's power of self-examination. It is easy to slip into a convention; but a finely conscious artist in the making already has a weather eye on the potential absurdities in a medium. In the opening she brilliantly conflates two separate conventions in order to burlesque both. She combines the convention of the perfect heroine, necessarily described in the third person by an omniscient narrator, with the first-person narrator of the epistolary novel, with hilarious effect: "Lovely as I was," writes Laura modestly, as though she were someone else, "the Graces of my Person were the least of my Perfections. Of every accomplishment accustomary to my sex, I was Mistress . . ." and so on (77–8). In other ways the letters draw attention to their own absurdity; for they are not written "to the moment," according to the Richardson formula, while the mind is in the midst of present distresses; they are recollected in tranquility, long after the event, and sent away in arbitrarily chopped-off chunks. Here is the self-critical creative mind at work. Full self-awareness belongs rather to sense than to sensibility, after all.

"That [M'Kenzie] certainly adores you (replied Sophia) there can be no doubt" (94). Sophia is here in the process of detaching teachable young Janetta from her old suitor and attaching her to a new one, as Emma is later to do with Harriet Smith. The passage is pregnant with other concerns that are to be lasting in the Jane Austen canon: not only the propensity to arrange reality according to a preconceived pattern, as Emma the imaginist does, but also the indoctrination and manipulation of one human being by another. The impress of a formed consciousness upon a relatively unformed one is the stuff that some of the best novels, but especially Jane Austen's, are made of. The pedagogic enterprise is a dangerous and fascinating one, and it may turn out well, like Henry Tilney's with Catherine, or disastrously, like Sophia's with Janetta or Emma's with Harriet.

But to return to our own students, and our pedagogic enterprises on their behalf (and our own). There is only so much we can tell them: the rest they must discover for themselves. And "Love and Freindship" is a text that will do much towards teaching itself. Although it is the product of subtle perceptions, and shows a subtle artist in the making, it is itself gloriously obvious. And unlike the self-centred romantics it parodies, it leads attention beyond itself, by its reach for other literature, by its healthy mockery of the unending circle of self, and by its exuberant play of mind.

Notes

1. This paper was first published in *Jane Austen's Beginnings*, ed. J. David Grey (Ann Arbor: UMI Research Press, 1989), 135–51.
2. Sandra M. Gilbert and Susan Gubar, eds, *The Norton Anthology of Literature by Women: The Tradition in English*, New York and London: W. W. Norton, 1985, pp. 209–32. Professors Gilbert and Gubar's close and revealing study of "Love and Freindship" in *The Madwoman in the Attic*, New Haven and London: Yale University Press, 1979, pp. 113–19, is an excellent feminist reading.
3. Marvin Mudrick has plausibly argued that Elizabeth Nugent Bromley's *Laura and Augustus: An Authentic Story: In a Series of Letters*, three volumes, London, 1784, is the most likely candidate as the single butt of "Love and Freindship." *Jane Austen: Irony as Defense and Discovery*, Berkeley and Los Angeles: University of California Press, 1968, pp. 5–12.
4. A. Walton Litz, *Jane Austen: A Study of Her Artistic Development*, London: Chatto & Windus, 1965, p. 18.
5. Samuel Richardson, *Clarissa* (1747–8), ed. Angus Ross, Harmondsworth: Penguin, 1985, p. 291.
6. Book IV, chapter 15.
7. Volume III, letter of 4 October.
8. Litz, p. 21.
9. Letter 78.
10. Brian Southam, *Jane Austen's Literary Manuscripts*, Oxford: Clarendon Press, 1964, p. 3.
11. *Bleak House*, chapter 6.
12. G.K. Chesterton, in his preface to the first printing of "Love and Freindship," also makes this connection: Jane Austen's inspiration, he says, "was the inspiration of Gargantua; . . . it was the gigantic inspiration of laughter." *"Love and Freindship" and Other Early Works by Jane Austen*, New York: Frederick A. Stokes, 1922, p. xv.
13. Litz, p. 19.
14. We can infer that "First Impressions" was epistolary from the fact that Jane Austen's father cited *Evelina* as the model when he wrote to the publisher Cadell in 1797. See A. Walton Litz, "Chronology of Composition," in *The Jane Austen Companion*, ed. J. David Grey, A. Walton Litz and Brian Southam (New York: Macmillan, 1986), p. 47.

3

"The Beautifull Cassandra" Illustrated

My idea for an illustrated version of "The Beautifull Cassandra," one of Jane Austen's early stories in *Volume the First*, was born at the 1987 conference in New York on the juvenilia. I had read the little story before, but it hadn't really registered with me until I reread it for the conference. And then I was struck all of a heap by its charm and its cheek.

"Cassandra was the Daughter & the only Daughter of a celebrated Millener in Bond Street," the story begins (*MW*, 44).[1] Her mother is the family bread-winner, and her father, who claims to be "of noble Birth," is a mere layabout, a childhood version of Sir Walter Elliot. Cassandra's day of adventures begins when she falls in love with one of the bonnets her mother has made, and elopes with it. Her adventures include the conspicuous consumption of six ices at a pastry-cook's, and a trip to Hampstead and back in a hackney coach: her progress there is rather like that of the grand old Duke of York with his troops in the nursery rhyme: "He marched them up to the top of the hill, / And he marched them down again." When the coachman demands his pay and she can find no money in her pockets, Cassandra resourcefully plonks her bonnet on his head and runs away. When she gets home to her welcoming mother, she "smiled & whispered to herself, 'This is a day well spent.'"

Jane Austen describes "The Beautifull Cassandra," rather grandly, as "a Novel in Twelve Chapters." But in fact it is a brief contained tale, only about 350 words without the chapter headings. It appears in *Volume the First*, and occupies five pages in the manuscript (which is now in the Bodleian Library in Oxford), and only about three pages in Chapman's edition. It has so far received hardly any attention,[2] and it is seldom mentioned in biographies or critical studies. But the young Jane Austen herself evidently had a developed sense of its place in her oeuvre: In "Catharine," another work dedicated to her sister, she jokingly referred to it as having "obtained a place in every library in the Kingdom, and run through threescore Editions" (*MW*, 192).

"The Beautifull Cassandra" is different from the other juvenilia: it is less sophisticated, in that it depends less on effects of burlesque and the in-jokes of the literati. It has a simple story-line, a journey from home to the big world and back. In fact (I thought when I first pondered it seriously) it's like *Peter Rabbit*, and many another story for children. My inspiration was to present it as a story for children, in the manner of Beatrix Potter. And so I envisage the characters as small animals, dressed in clothes of the period. My beautiful Cassandra is a mouse, and her adventures include encounters with a lizard, a guinea-pig, a squirrel and a cat. The hackney coachman is a frog, and his horse a tortoise. This may be taking an unwarrantable liberty with Jane Austen's text. But I don't think children would think so.

The illustrations reproduced here are only the line drawings of pictures that are in sufficiently gaudy colour.

Professors of English aren't expected to go to market with illustrations for children's picture books, even when the story is by Jane

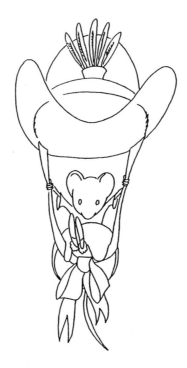

"Cassandra was the Daughter and the only Daughter
of a celebrated Millener in Bond Street"

Austen. When I approached the children's books arm of my usual publisher, Macmillan, they liked my idea and wanted my editorial matter, but said they'd commission their own illustrator. But I persisted with my pictures, and after many vicissitudes my *Beautifull Cassandra* at last emerged as a children's picture book, in full colour, with my pictures, and my afterword addressed to children.[3] Children like it. After all, it was written by one of themselves.

When you illustrate a story you have to think hard about it. I think I can now claim to be the world's expert on "The Beautifull Cassandra"! I have deeply pondered its relation to Jane Austen's life and other work. Consider the dating of it, for instance. Brian Southam, the major authority on Jane Austen's literary manuscripts, assigns the story to any time between 1787 and 1790.[4] But he overlooks what I take to be a suggestive piece of internal evidence, the fact that the heroine has just "attained her 16th year." Now I wouldn't want to claim that Jane's sister Cassandra, to whom the story is dedicated, is the same Cassandra who is the heroine of the story, the milliner's daughter. But all the same, the joke between the two sisters partly depends on the outrageous doings of the beautiful Cassandra as the possible doings of the actual Cassandra. As a working hypothesis, then, let's say that both Cassandras were in their sixteenth year when the story was written. Cassandra was born on 9 January 1773, nearly three years before Jane's birth on 16 December 1775. So at the time of writing Jane would have been in her thirteenth year: that is, twelve. This would make the year of composition 1788.

What else was Jane doing in 1788? Well, that summer she went to Kent with Cassandra and her parents to visit her great-uncle, Francis Austen of the Red House in Sevenoaks. Philadelphia Walter met them there, and wrote that Jane was "not at all pretty and very prim unlike a girl of twelve."[5] On the way home to Hampshire the Austen family stopped in London, and had dinner with Eliza de Feuillide and her mother, in Orchard Street. Now Orchard Street is just round a couple of corners from Bond Street, where the beautiful Cassandra's mother has her milliner's shop. Isn't it likely that the two sisters went window-shopping in the street famous for elegant clothing? (I can't help remembering that the old mare driven by the Watson sisters stops at the milliner's quite automatically! – [*MW*, 322].) On such an occasion sister Cassandra could well have declared herself in love with an irresistible bonnet, so providing the seed of the tale that Jane was to dedicate to her sister. It's still only a hypothesis, but I think it's a probable one. If Jane was for once to renounce her principle of writing about those three or four families in a country village, it's likely to have been after a stimulating visit to the metropolis.

I rejoice in the story for various reasons, but one of them is for its cheerfully liberated heroine. The young Jane is evidently reacting against the conventions that confine women. The genteel female, we know, was supposed to have a delicate appetite; but Cassandra "devoured six ices" in quick succession. Ladies were expected always to have their heads covered (one scholar speculates that Dr Johnson himself may never have seen a woman without either a bonnet or a cap; and he was a married man); but Cassandra, after she has cleverly used her bonnet to pay her coach bill, still confidently walks through the streets. Women aren't supposed to travel alone, and we know from Jane Austen's letters that she constantly had to make arrangements to travel under other people's escort. Fanny Burney's Cecilia, for instance, has to call for the protection of an utterly incompetent man, Mr. Simkins, "for her dread of being alone . . . in an hackney-coach, was invincible."[6] But Cassandra goes alone on an impulsive pleasure trip to Hampstead and back. Women were economically dependent on men, and even when they were paying the shot themselves would customarily hand over their purse to some man to do the paying for them. At the climax of *Cecilia* (which young Jane knew well) the heroine actually goes mad during the difficult business of paying off an importunate hackney coachman. But Cassandra manages her "peremptory" hackney coachman with great aplomb.

This isn't a moral story. It's a story of pure self-assertion and self-gratification, as are many stories about boys. To use a modern analogy: Maurice Sendak's famous trilogy, *Where the Wild Things Are, In the Night Kitchen*, and *Outside Over There*, has as protagonists two boys, Max and Mickey, and a girl, Ida. The boys are allowed to be authoritative and self-assertive: "Let the wild rumpus start!" says Max to the Wild Things; and it does. "Cock-a-Doodle Doo!" proclaims Mickey, with unabashed frontal nudity. But Sendak's girl, Ida, has a moral lesson to learn. While she is self-indulgently playing her horn, the goblins steal her baby sister and leave an ice-baby changeling in her place. Ida, haunted by guilt, has to go on a quest to recover the baby and placate her authoritative father.

Cassandra is more like Max and Mickey than Ida. She goes off on a self-indulgent binge, and copes resourcefully with her world and its economy, and is never made to be sorry or learn lessons. Her day has been "a day well spent," and highly satisfactory.

"The Beautifull Cassandra," like the other juvenilia, contains intimations of the great novels to come. Catherine Morland, who travels alone in an emergency, proves herself not to be a mere "shatter-brained creature" (*NA*, 234). Elizabeth Bennet is a descendant of Cassandra in being energetic and self-assertive, and we often see her running, or "jumping over stiles and springing over puddles with impatient activity" (*PP*, 32).

I think of Cassandra as the Mouse That Walks By Itself. She doesn't need anybody else. She only curtseys to the eligible Viscount, who might have turned out to be the hero of one of the novels. She passes by the trembling Maria and the inquisitive widow, and gets on with

"She placed it on her gentle Head & walked from her Mother's shop to make her Fortune"

her own affairs. So much for Love and Freindship. She has a brief romance with a bonnet, but she's ready to part with that too without regrets. Her love for the bonnet turns out to be only a matter of First Impressions.

The bonnet, besides Cassandra herself, is the most important character in the tale. And I have followed up Jane's and Cassandra's relations with bonnets through the *Letters*. She writes to Cassandra of one particular bonnet "on which you know my hopes of happiness depend." Sometimes she imagines a bonnet as alive, with its own personality. "I took the liberty a few days ago of asking your black bonnet to lend me its cawl, which it very readily did, & by which I have been enabled to give a considerable improvement of dignity to my cap" (*Letters*, 37). She may not have been a milliner, like the beautiful Cassandra's mother in the story, but she seems to have been a real pro at putting together the decorations for her headgear. "Instead of the black military feather [I] shall put in the Cocquelicot one, as being smarter; – & besides Cocquelicot is to be all the fashion this winter" (37-8). That was the passage that decided me to make one of the feathers in my Cassandra's bonnet cocquelicot (or scarlet, the colour of a poppy).

One day Jane went shopping for her sister to buy decorations for another bonnet. Flowers and fruit were in fashion, but she found the fruit was more expensive, so she had to consult Cassandra anew: "I cannot decide on the fruit till I hear from you again," she wrote. "Besides, I cannot help thinking that it is more natural to have flowers grow out of the head than fruit. What do you think on that subject?" (67). That was the passage that decided me to have flowers on the beautiful Cassandra's bonnet. I chose daffodils because they are funny and expressive, and I wanted to show them sharing Cassandra's experience – curtseying when she curtseys, and getting fat when she eats six ices.

The story of "The Beautifull Cassandra" is so short that in the process of illustrating it I have come to know it virtually by heart. Perhaps, in the prolonged process of negotiations with publishers about my project, I have became *a little* obsessive. (I will concede no more than "a little.") At any rate, my unusually intimate knowledge of this story has made me sensitive to echoes of it that I find elsewhere. And I *do* find echoes.

Until recently, most readers, including Jane Austen's brothers and collateral descendants, seem to have considered her juvenilia as ephemera, squibs tossed off by a fledgling genius on her way to greatness, and left behind. The publication history has been erratic, and critical attention has continued to be directed almost exclusively to the six published novels. But to Jane Austen herself, I'd like to suggest, her juvenilia had almost canonical status. They were milestones in her artistic development, and fondly remembered and alluded to in her later work as well as in her letters. The joke about "The Beautifull Cassandra" as having obtained a place in every library in the kingdom was not entirely laughable to the writer. For her, her juvenilia jostled with *Cecilia* and *Camilla* and *Sir Charles Grandison* as available for reminiscence and allusion.

At fourteen, in 'Love and Freindship', she invented the forgathering of all the personnel of the story in the coach that is driven "from Edinburgh to Sterling & from Sterling to Edinburgh every other day" (105). At thirty-eight, the seasoned author, finding a number of acquaintances who turn out to be travelling together, wrote to Cassandra, "It put me in mind of my own Coach between Edinburgh & Sterling" (*Letters*, 397). The familiar reference can be shared between the sisters as readily as a quotation from Shakespeare. At fifteen, she wrote her parodic "History of England," with the subtitle "by a partial, preju-

"She next ascended a Hackney Coach and ordered it to Hampstead"

diced & ignorant Historian." Doesn't that combination and sequence of adjectives ring a bell? Remember the climactic moment in *Pride and Prejudice*: Elizabeth realizes she has been "blind, *partial, prejudiced, absurd*" (*PP*, 208; my italics). Everyone remembers this great moment. But it is made the greater for the reader who recognizes the touch of self-referentiality, and the suggestion that in this achievement of maturity there is a hint of putting away childish things. The grown-up Elizabeth may not boast of prejudice and partiality as the cheerful young historian could.

There is a similar but more developed relation between "The Beautifull Cassandra" and *Northanger Abbey*, I would suggest. One can trace the footsteps of the one still quietly echoing in the other. Some of the echoes are merely verbal. For instance:

[Cassandra] searched her pockets over again & again; but every search was unsuccessfull. (*MW*, 46)

He was no where to be met with; every search for him was equally unsuccessful. (*NA*, 35)

But there is a set of similar concerns and preoccupations of the twelve-year-old author that the grown-up author cares to develop. Cassandra falls "in love with an elegant Bonnet" in Bond Street (*MW*, 45); Isabella Thorpe confides, "I saw the prettiest hat you can imagine, in a shop window in Milsom-street just now. . . . I quite longed for it" (*NA*, 39). Cassandra "proceeded to a Pastry-cooks where she devoured six ices" (46); in *Northanger Abbey* the narrator laments the delays occasioned to "parties of ladies, however important their business, whether in quest of pastry, millinery, or even (as in the present case) of young men" (*NA*, 44). Cassandra has to cope with an importunate coachman; Catherine with the egregious John Thorpe, who pesters her with questions such as "What do you think of my gig, Miss Morland? a neat one, is not it? Well hung" (*NA*, 46). Cassandra goes on a pointless trip to Hampstead, "where she was no sooner arrived than she ordered the coachman to turn round & drive her back again" (45). John Thorpe likewise goes in for pointless motion. He claims that his horse "*cannot* go less than ten miles an hour," and that he plans to exercise it "four hours every day." "That will be forty miles a day," responds Catherine "very seriously" (*NA*, 46, 48).

Even the ending of "The Beautifull Cassandra" has its echo in the maternal welcome to the wandering offspring. Cassandra comes home, after her day's outrageous doings, to an unconditionally loving mother who gives her a welcoming embrace and no reproaches. John Thorpe likewise arrives unexpectedly at his mother's lodgings with

> the feelings of the dutiful and affectionate son, as they met Mrs. Thorpe. . . . "Ah, mother! how do you do?. . .where did you get that quiz of a hat, it makes you look like an old witch?. . ." And this address seemed to satisfy all the fondest wishes of the mother's heart, for she received him with the most delighted and exulting affection." (*NA*, 49)

Bonnets and hats remain to the fore.

That is, the important concerns, and even some of the episodes and phrasing, are carried forward from "The Beautifull Cassandra" to chapters 4 to 7 of *Northanger Abbey*. But, as the narrator wryly observes, the priorities have changed. Fifteen-year-old Cassandra bestows only a hasty curtsy on the eligible viscount before she and her bonnet hurry on to the more interesting things like ices and trips to Hampstead. But for seventeen-year-old Catherine, and particularly for the more sexually developed Isabella Thorpe, being in "quest . . . of young men" is even more important business than being "in quest of pastry, [or] millinery." Moreover, the narrative has been reconceived in moral terms. Catherine must shed some of the self-indulgent behaviour that is so engaging in Cassandra; and Cassandra's most outrageous behaviour has been relocated in Isabella and John Thorpe.

Both Cassandra and Catherine take a healthy delight in clothes, and their acute attention to bonnets is charming and forgivable. It emphasizes their humanity and makes them sympathetic. But even Cassandra knows when to abandon her bonnet; and Catherine can subordinate her love of finery to more important things. While Mrs. Allen can think only about not tearing her gown, Catherine's mind turns to human company (*NA*, 22). The important motif of dress in this novel draws some tongue-in-cheek moralizing from the narrator. ("Dress is at all times a frivolous distinction, and excessive solicitude about it often destroys its own aim. . ." 73). But Catherine is judged indulgently for lying "awake ten minutes on Wednesday night debating between her spotted and her tamboured muslin" (73). Ten minutes after all are forgivable. But Mrs. Allen, who can think of nothing *but* clothes, and Isabella, who introduces the subject at inappropriate moments, are more severely judged. Isabella's letter to Catherine asking her to intercede with James employs a devastating zeugma that reduces love to the dimensions of a bonnet:

He is the only man I ever did or could love, and I trust you will convince him of it. The spring fashions are partly down; and the hats the most frightful you can imagine. (216)

Her frivolous absorption with surfaces defines her letter as "a strain of shallow artifice" (218). Cassandra was never so harshly judged. Cassandra's delight in pointless motion is similarly transferred to John Thorpe. As Stuart Tave noticed, the mature Jane Austen recurrently marks untrustworthy characters by their false claims about time and space. John Thorpe, who lies about his horse's speed, and Mary Crawford, who reckons time "with feminine lawlessness" (*MP*, 94), are likewise manipulators of truth.[7]

In *Northanger Abbey* the youthful exuberance that informed "The Beautifull Cassandra" has been toned down and channelled; and its excesses are relocated in the unapproved siblings Isabella and John Thorpe. Cassandra, still enchanted by bonnets and motion, stands between the seventeen-year-old Catherine, with her dawning moral responsibility, and Catherine the child, who at ten was "noisy and wild, hated confinement and cleanliness, and loved nothing so well in the world as rolling down the green slope at the back of the house" (*NA*, 14). Jane Austen is delighted by such behaviour, and tolerant of it. She is indulgent towards the enjoyments of youth, as she remembers fondly the *jeu d'esprit* she wrote when she was twelve. But as she brings her later heroines through their rites of passage, she marks both what they carry forward and what they must leave behind.

Notes

1.   "The Beautifull Cassandra" appears on pages 44 to 47 of Chapman's edition of *The Minor Works*.

2.   One of the few attentive readings of "The Beautifull Cassandra" is provided by Ellen E. Martin, "The Madness of Jane Austen: Metonymic Style and Literature's Resistance to Interpretation," *Persuasions*, 9 (1987), pp. 79–80. More recently (and since I wrote this piece), Margaret Anne Doody and Douglas Murray provide commentary and annotation in their edition of *Catharine and Other Writings* (Oxford: Oxford University Press, 1993), pp. 303–4.

3.   *The Beautifull Cassandra*, by Jane Austen, with illustrations and an afterword by Juliet McMaster, was published in 1993 (the year I co-convened the 600-strong conference of the Jane Austen Society of North America at Lake Louise in the Canadian Rockies) by Sono Nis Press, 1745 Blanshard Street, Victoria, BC, Canada, V8W 2J8.

4.   B.C. Southam, *Jane Austen's Literary Manuscripts* (Oxford: Clarendon Press, 1964), p. 16.

5.   Quoted by David Waldron Smithers, "Jane Austen's Visit to Kent," *Kent Companion*, 3, June/August, 1988, p. 7.

6.   Frances Burney, *Cecilia* (1782), ed. Peter Sabor and Margaret Anne Doody (Oxford: Oxford University Press, 1988), p. 890.

7.   Stuart M. Tave, *Some Words of Jane Austen* (Chicago: University of Chicago Press, 1973), pp. 2–5.

4

Hospitality

(Note: This talk was originally delivered as a dinner address to the Jane Austen Society of North America, which was held in Toronto, Canada. Rather than delete mention of the outposts of Empire, I have chosen to retain the few references to the occasion.)

Jane Austen and I are both daughters of the Empire. Her Empire was the Napoleonic one, where the ladies wore their waists under the armpits; and mine is the one on which the sun never sets, the one that used to show as pink on maps of the world. My particular outpost of the Empire, Kenya, was more like Jane Austen's world than is our modern-day democratic society, North America or of modern-day England, because in the early years of this century the British had managed to transpose the nineteenth-century class system into twentieth-century Africa. The whites lived as country gentry, and among themselves preserved a rigid hierarchy. The colonial administrators of my parents' generation know all about Rank, and a fair amount about Blood. They cared who led the way in to dinner, and who sat on whose right, and what it was proper and not proper to say to whom. Lady Catherine de Bourgh would have been thoroughly at home.

On the strength of this affinity between Jane Austen's world and the world I grew up in, I'm going to cull a couple of anecdotes from my family history which I hope will usefully illustrate what I have to say about hospitality in her novels. Both anecdotes predate my birth, but they have become part of my family mythology.

Behold my father in the 'twenties, newly married to my mother, installed as District Commissioner at Mombasa. Not the *Provincial* Commissioner, who was the senior administrator of the province, but a mere subordinate. Mombasa was to be honoured by a state visit from the Duke and Duchess of York (later King George and his queen, now the Queen Mother). They were to stay, of course, in Government House. But the Government House at Mombasa was only just completed; and so at short notice it had to be furnished for the royal visitors.

Of course such things were not done by Commissioners, District or Provincial, but by their wives. Now it happened that Mrs Provincial Commissioner was away in England, so the job devolved on Mrs District Commissioner, my mother. She was young, new to the country and inexperienced, and also four months pregnant (not with me – I was number five). But she flung herself into action. She first denuded our house of all the original paintings (family heirlooms), and hung them with her own hands on the walls of Government House. The furniture went next. Curtains and carpets were borrowed. It was all done just in time.

But on the state occasion at which the royal couple were to lunch with the local officials, my father was told that there wouldn't be room for a mere District Commissioner and his wife. To say that my mother was not disappointed, as Jane Austen would say, "would be to assert a very unlikely thing" (*MW*, 347). But she was also somewhat relieved, and she and my father had cheerfully sat down to eat their lunch off packing cases, when a phone call summoned them to the royal table. There was room after all. They rushed into their glad rags (my mother had some difficulty in getting into her only smart dress, because of her delicate condition) and duly presented themselves, a little flurried, to lunch with the Duke and Duchess. My mother was retiring in the conversation, and didn't mention her exertions with the furniture. Family history records that she and the Duchess had a lively conversation about sharks instead.

I present that anecdote as my positive example of hospitality. My mother (I like to make a heroine of her), if not the mistress of the home where the guests were to be entertained, nevertheless was ready to give what she had for her community's guests, and without receiving any glory. (Her virtue was finally rewarded; but she hadn't done it for a reward.)

Anecdote number two, and the last. Time has advanced. My father is now Provincial Commissioner of Nyanza Province, and is himself to be the host of the important person. My two older sisters, an enterprising eight and six years old, are on the scene. And the honoured guest is the late Aga Khan, who is coming to stay. To my parents the Aga Khan was a politically important and a socially charming man. But to the large population of Ismaili Muslims in Kisumu he was sacred, a descendant of the Prophet. They gathered in silent reverent multitudes outside our garden, and waited, day and night, for only a glimpse of him. If he called on the faithful to give in a worthy cause, they were ready to balance his weight in gold and in diamonds.

My sisters, Anthea and Eleanor, found themselves on terms of domestic familiarity with this god, and saw the chance of capitalizing. Anthea, particularly, at eight, had a sound commercial instinct. She decided to take up the profession of Chaucer's Pardoner, and go into business selling relics. Wouldn't a good Muslim give good money for the Aga Khan's nail clippings, for instance? The nail clippings weren't available, but what about his bath water? Surely selling bathwater to the faithful would be a good commercial proposition.

In the rather primitive plumbing arrangements we had, there was a little pipe that squirted the released bath water into an open drain. Here my sisters squatted when the evening came, with a fine collection of jam jars and tin cans, awaiting the happy moment when the Aga Khan should pull out his reverend plug, and a golden river would come gurgling into their receptacles. (My sisters must have been early practitioners of "trickle-down economics"!)

Well, they never realized their dreams of riches. My mother, the spoil-sport, caught them in the midst of their pots and jars, and emptied them all. So we never did ascertain the market value of a bottle of Aga Khan bathwater.

In this anecdote, my sisters are the negative example, the villains. They were betraying the hallowed rules of hospitality in order to capitalize on their guest.

In Jane Austen's novels we can similarly classify the hosts and hostesses. Some, like that heroine my mother, are ready to give of their time, their space and their substance, even if their means are limited, and without expecting more than civility in return. The Harvilles in *Persuasion* are like that. Their house in Lyme is not large, and they have a bunch of children to accommodate, as well as a resident broken-hearted lover. But when their friend Captain Wentworth brings his party from Uppercross to Lyme, they are eager to have the whole group to dinner. "They seemed almost hurt that Captain Wentworth should have brought any such party to Lyme, without considering it as a thing of course that they should dine with them." Anne, who has been more used to the cold ceremony of Sir Walter and Elizabeth at Kellynch, is delighted and moved by such warmth, by "a degree of hospitality so uncommon, so unlike the usual style of give-and-take invitations, and dinners of formality and display" (*P*, 98). The effects of such warm-heartedness spread like widening ripples in the human community, and almost magically enlarge the capacity of the hosts for hospitality. Anne is at first astonished at the comprehensive invitation when she enters their house, "and found rooms so small as none but those who invite from the heart could think capable of accommodating so many" (98). But presently she recognizes all the ingenious contrivances "to turn the actual space to the best possible account." And in the crisis of Louisa Musgrove's fall from the Cobb, the Harvilles' hospitality is gratefully called upon, and their home even becomes a hospital. It is a kind of analogy, scaled down to the Austen world, to the gospel story of the loaves and the fishes that fed the multitude.

But not all hosts are like the Harvilles. Lady Catherine de Bourgh is more like my sisters. She wouldn't be caught collecting her guests' bathwater, I admit, but she has her own equally self-seeking means of turning them to good account. The chapter in which Elizabeth goes with the Collinses and Sir William and Maria Lucas to her first dinner at Rosings is a marvellous handling of a kind of hospitality in which the host takes all and gives nothing. Well, not quite *nothing*: Lady Catherine provides, to be sure, spacious premises and an elegant meal. But one can hardly call it giving when these conveniences are to be paid for in kind, and at so exorbitant a rate. Mr. Collins, who is less her pastor and guest than her majordomo and head waiter, is employed to make sure everyone pays up, in the right kind of coin. First, the guests must dress in such a way as to mark their social inferiority to their hostess. "Do not make yourself uneasy, my dear cousin," Mr. Collins tells Elizabeth, "about your apparel. Lady Catherine is far from requiring that elegance of dress in us, which becomes herself and daughter. . . . She likes to have the distinction of rank preserved" (*PP*, 160–1). Lady Catherine, when she receives her guests, confirms his perception. "Her air was not conciliating, nor was her manner of receiving them, such as to make her visitors forget their inferior rank" (162). Presently, they are "all sent to one of the windows, to admire the view," – no alternative of *not* admiring it being permitted by her servant, Mr. Collins. When the dinner is served, the guests must keep working. Mr. Collins "carved, and ate, and praised with delighted alacrity; and every dish was commended, first by him, and then by Sir William, who was now enough recovered to echo whatever his son in law said, in a manner which Elizabeth wondered Lady Catherine could bear. But Lady Catherine seemed gratified by their excessive admiration, and gave most gracious smiles" (163). The conversation languishes. There is no meeting of minds, no genuine conviviality, no confirmation of human community. "Maria thought speaking out of the question, and the gentlemen did nothing but eat and admire" (163).

This is not hospitality, but its negation. Lady Catherine turns her guests into servants and customers. They must work for their food, *and* pay for it. If the gentlemen do nothing but eat and admire, it is because they have instinctively settled into the roles she has created for them. They must eat, so that Lady Catherine will have the gratification of making them grateful, and they must admire in order to pay for what they eat. Such fare indeed comes rather expensive. Her guests are obliged to be chanting a perpetual *Te Deum*, a chorus of "We praise thee, O Lady Catherine." This may sound blasphemous, but the scene is not without its suggestion that Lady Catherine credits herself and her rank with some divine attributes. Before her party from the parsonage leaves, they are "gathered round the fire to hear Lady Catherine determine what weather they were to have on the morrow" (166). Apparently she has the power to arrange such matters. And I wonder which, of God and Lady Catherine, her clergyman Mr. Collins most reveres?

As with hosts, so with guests – and it is appropriate that the Latin word *hospes* comprehends both roles. Lady Catherine, as she is the most disagreeable host, is also the most disagreeable guest in the novel. This is her behaviour on her visit to Longbourn:

> She entered the room with an air more than usually ungracious, made no other reply to Elizabeth's salutation, than a slight inclination of the head, and sat down without saying a word. . . .
> "This must be a most inconvenient sitting room for the evening, in summer," [she comments, when she does condescend to converse]. . .
> As they passed through the hall, Lady Catherine opened the doors into the dining-parlour and drawing room, and pronouncing them, after a short survey, to be decent looking rooms, walked on. (351–3)

She systematically reverses the behaviour she requires of her own guests: she is intrusive, overbearing and insulting. She infringes against all the elements of the implied contract between guest and host. She who required so much praise of her own estate of Rosings, at Longbourn abuses the park, and the western exposure of the sitting-room; she refuses, "very resolutely, and not very politely," all offers of refreshment (352); and pointedly tells Elizabeth as she leaves, "I send no compliments to your mother" (358). Such is the behaviour of the Bennets' "noble guest" (352).

A guest also should give as well as take, but without reducing the relation of host and guest to a matter of bargain and sale. Anne Elliot at Uppercross does all of the giving, but little of the taking: she mediates between husband and wife, soothes her hypochondriac sister, nurses her injured nephew, and plays the piano while other people dance. Mrs. Norris, on the other hand, specializes in the taking part of the business:

> "I think *you* have done pretty well yourself, ma'am [Maria says to her in the carriage, when they are on the way home from Sotherton]. Your lap seems full of good things, and here is a basket of something between us, which has been knocking my elbow unmercifully."
>
> "My dear, it is only a beautiful little heath, which that nice old gardener would make me take; but if it is in your way, I will have it in my lap directly. There Fanny, you shall carry that parcel for me – take great care of it . . . it is a cream cheese, just like the excellent one we had at dinner. Nothing would satisfy that good old Mrs. Whitaker, but my taking one of the cheeses. . . ."
>
> "What else have you been spunging?" said Maria, half pleased that Sotherton should be so complimented.
>
> "Spunging, my dear! It is nothing but four of those beautiful pheasant's eggs, which Mrs. Whitaker would quite force upon me; she would not take a denial." (*MP*, 105–6)

If Mrs. Norris were a frequent visitor, one feels, even the stately county seat of Sotherton might be swiftly depleted.

In a memorable moment in *Northanger Abbey*, Henry Tilney tells Catherine on the dance floor at Bath,

> "We have entered into a contract of mutual agreeableness for the space of an evening, and all our agreeableness belongs solely to each other for that time. . . . I consider a country-dance as an emblem of marriage. Fidelity and complaisance are the principal duties of both. . . . In both, it is an engagement between man and woman, formed for the advantage of each." (*NA*, 76–7)

That speech has great resonance in the novels, partly because it is an instance of developed figurative language that Mary Lascelles has told us is rare in Jane Austen. Henry Tilney draws an analogy between marriage and the dance – "such very different things!" as Catherine calls them – that is almost as elaborate as a metaphysical conceit. Other examples of such emblems, again used by the characters rather than by the narrator, are Captain Wentworth's likening of a "character of decision and firmness" to a hazel nut in *Persuasion* (88), and Elizabeth's comparison of the development of social graces with playing the piano in *Pride and Prejudice* (175). All these images provide intense moments in the novels, and are accessible, like all parables, to lengthy analysis. But Tilney's little lecture on the dance as emblematic of marriage is particularly satisfying because it puts in a nutshell (like Wentworth's) what the rest of the novels demonstrate at large: that nothing in the Jane Austen world is insignificant, because every little incident is indicative of a whole set of moral and social and psychological relations; each coming together of the characters is a microcosm for the whole narrative. Whether we are considering a dance, or a marriage, or a journey, or a game of quadrille or speculation, we find that the characters keep illustrating themselves. What they are in small things, they are in large. To the impatient student who asks in exasperation, "Who *cares* if Emma scores off a boring old spinster? Miss Bates had it coming," the answer is, *we* care, because Jane Austen makes us care. The momentary discourtesy to a harmless and vulnerable spinster shakes the world of *Emma* as the slamming down of the guillotine shakes the world of *A Tale of Two Cities*; because in Jane Austen's novels everything matters.

Host and guest, like husband and wife, or like a lady and gentleman in the dance, have entered into a contract of mutual agreeableness; and like all the intricate social contracts in the novels it is one that epitomizes the delicate balance that must be maintained between the will of the individual and the needs of the community.

Jane Austen is far from suggesting that hospitality should be confined to your social equals. "The usual style of give-and-take invitations, and dinners of formality and display" (*P*, 98), such as are in current exchange between Sir Walter Elliot and his fellow snobs, are not the positive model. It is very proper that Mr. and Miss Woodhouse of Hartfield should welcome the shabby-genteel old clergyman's widow and daughter to their home, without expecting to be entertained in return. And Emma, though she has plenty of other faults, is a good hostess. "I hope I am not often deficient in what is due to guests at Hartfield," she can claim with justice (*E*, 170).

But there are nevertheless certain dangers inherent in hospitality that can be extended in only one direction. Emma does at last turn on Miss Bates, and openly exult in her own superiority – though it's not in her in her own home (where she would never have done it, I think). The guest who cannot return hospitality is in a position to trade on his immunity, as the host of such a guest may be tempted to trade on her superiority, and so the delicate balance of giving and receiving, the contract of mutual agreeableness, is violated. And the consequences may be enormous.

Lady Susan, that fierce and funny piece of fiction, is interesting in presenting an extreme case of the infringement of this contract. It is a story that could well carry the subtitle, if Jane Austen went in for such things, "The Nightmare of the Unwelcome Guest" (*MW*, 243). It opens ominously with a letter from Lady Susan to her brother, dated from Langford, the home of the Manwarings, with an announcement that she is coming to stay:

> My dear Brother
> I can no longer refuse myself the pleasure of profitting by your kind invitation . . . of spending some weeks with you at Churchill. . . . My kind friends here are most urgent with me to prolong my stay, but their hospitable & chearful dispositions lead them too much into society for my present situation & state of mind; & I impatiently look forward to the hour when I shall be admitted into your delightful retirement. I long to be made known to your dear little Children. . . . (*Lady Susan*, MW 243)

The second letter from Lady Susan, addressed to her intimate confidante, fills in some of the ugly truths behind the warm professions of the first. She is leaving Langford, it emerges, because she has simply made it too hot to hold her. She has carried on a flagrant affair with her host, Mr. Manwaring, under the nose of his outraged wife. And she has alienated the affections of their daughter's fiancé, the eligible Sir James Martin, and proposes to marry him to her own daughter instead. Now this formidable lady, having destroyed the happiness of one home, prepares to batten on to another.

And she wreaks havoc at Churchill, too. She tyrannizes over her daughter, and parades her lovers before her hostess. And by a specious show of virtue she ensnares her hostess's brother into falling in love with her. Well may his mother lament the "vexation & trouble" caused to the family by "this unwelcome Guest" (263). As the hero finally tells Lady Susan, "you robbed [the family] of it's Peace, in return for the hospitality with which you were received into it" (305).

Though Jane Austen doesn't venture on so extreme a character portrayal in the major novels, we glimpse again that vision of the homeless guest who may fasten on to her hosts like a vampire, making their substance her own, and rendering nothing in return, in Lucy Steele of *Sense and Sensibility*. Sir John Middleton, whose omnivorous appetite for company of any kind makes him a rather tiresomely importunate host, meets the two Misses Steele in Exeter, and discovering they are distant relatives of his wife's, at once invites them to Barton Park. They accept with suspicious alacrity – "Their engagements at Exeter instantly gave way before such an invitation" (*SS*, 118) – and move in at once. They come prepared to pay for their accommodation, but in that debased coin that Mr. Collins offers Lady Catherine, a servile subservience and gushing admiration. And like Lady Susan, they pretend to adore children. "They were delighted with the house, and in raptures with the furniture, and they happened to be so doatingly fond of children that Lady Middleton's good opinion was engaged in their favour before they had been an hour at the Park" (119). Presently Lucy has slithered into a position of false confidence in the household, and is able to get her teeth into Sir John's young cousin, Elinor.

We are made to feel how much is wrong in this kind of relation between host and guest. Sir John invites his guests not so much from genuine warm-heartedness and a desire to extend and confirm the human community as from a need of his own, because he is aware of some vacuum in himself that he needs other people to fill up. And the Misses Steele are also selfishly inclined to hang up their hats in comfortable quarters, and take what is genuine while returning only what is false. Jane Austen can be as astringently critical of undiscriminating hospitality as of unscrupulous self-seeking.

If I were talking about hospitality in Fielding, or Smollett, or Dickens, I would inevitably be referring often to the good cheer and other amenities available in the Inn at Upton, or at the Blue Lion at Muggleton, or at the Maypole, and a character who would necessarily claim my attention would be Mine Host, the Innkeeper, the professional dispenser of hospitality. How many great scenes of conviviality are set in public places on the road, how much generous fare is provided and eaten, how much punch brewed and consumed, how many companies have met and acted themselves out in gatherings where the restraints of home and family don't apply! But Jane Austen is comparatively uninterested in hospitality as a profession. Innkeepers and their wives and servants, such favourite characters with Fielding, scarcely appear. This was not just because as a woman she would have less acquaintance with inns and pubs than riotous Harry Fielding or omnivorous Boz. For her the hospitality that counts happens in the home; the home being an extension of the personality, as Pemberley is of Darcy, it is there that the host most fully manifests himself, and the guest can enter most intricately into a relation with him.

When we come to the physical stuff of hospitality, the creature comforts of clean linen, warm space, attentive service, and particularly, food and drink – such comforts as we have been enjoying tonight – she can't rival Dickens in the sheer quantity of specification; but then, who can? Nevertheless, she valued such things, and paid attention to them, though with an amused sense that a preoccupation with the physical can sometimes lead to a neglect of the moral.

Some people think that Jane Austen's characters never drink anything stronger than tea, and seldom eat much more than Mr. Woodhouse's very thin gruel. (Fortunately, we know better.) Such people might profitably read that wicked little story, "Jack and Alice." The 14-year-old Jane could envisage characters just as boozy as Mr. Pickwick and his associates. At the end of the masquerade party at the Johnsons, we hear, "the Company retired to another room to partake of an elegant & well-managed Entertainment, after which the Bottle being pretty briskly pushed about . . . the whole party . . . were carried home, Dead Drunk" (*MW*, 14). In the major novels, too, there are those who put away a good deal more than the Mr. Woodhouse Special of "a *small* half glass [of wine] – put into a tumbler of water" (*E*, 25): we all remember the enormity committed in the carriage by Mr. Elton after "he had been drinking too much of Mr. Weston's good wine" (*E*, 129).

The character most interested in food is Mr. Woodhouse, who is a kind of glutton in reverse, and spends a lot of his time denying rich delicacies to himself and his friends. He does what he can to dissuade his guests from eating wedding cake (*E*, 19), minced chicken, scalloped oysters, apple tarts, custard (24–5), roast pork (172), and so on; but since Emma assiduously supplies the luxuries he would withhold, the reader is allowed at least a waft of indulgence in the good things, and an assurance that affairs of the palate are not neglected at Hartfield.

Dr. Grant is a glutton more severely treated. We hear at the outset of *Mansfield Park* that "The Dr. was very fond of eating, and would have a good dinner every day" (*MP*, 31). His interest in food and drink is a leitmotif attached to him throughout: he regards the visit of the Crawfords as "an excuse for drinking claret every day" (47), and he gets bad-tempered about some defective apricots, a turkey, and a green goose (54, 215, 111). Perhaps because he cares most that these good things should go down his own gullet, he is condemned as "an indolent selfish bon vivant, who must have his palate consulted in every thing" (111). Jane Austen rather sternly kills him off with an attack of apoplexy after "three great institutionary dinners in one week" (469).

With the cautionary fate of Dr. Grant in mind, I confess to some anxiety about her intentions for poor Arthur Parker in *Sanditon*. Arthur manages to take a considerable interest in food, in spite of being a confirmed invalid, and under surveillance by his spartan sisters:

> "I hope you will eat some of this Toast, [he says gallantly to his visitor, Charlotte Heywood.] I reckon myself a very good Toaster. . . . I hope you like dry Toast." – "With a reasonable quantity of Butter spread over it, very much – said Charlotte – but not otherwise. – " "No more do I – said he exceedingly pleased – We think quite alike there. – So far from dry Toast being wholesome, I think it a very bad thing for the Stomach. Without a little butter to soften it, it hurts the Coats of the Stomach. I am sure it does. – I will have the pleasure of spreading some for you directly – & afterwards I will spread some for myself." . . .but when her Toast was done, & he took his own in hand, Charlotte c ᵈ hardly contain herself as she saw him watching his sisters, while he scrupulously scraped off almost as much butter as he put on, & then seize an odd moment for adding a great dab just before it went into his Mouth. (*MW*, 417–18)

The author who can invent such a scene knows all about the indulgence of the taste buds. And I am inclined to augur well for Arthur, because although he is greedy, he does take pains to look after his guest's toast as well as his own. In this he contrasts notably with Lady Denham, in the same novel (or sad fragment of one). Lady Denham, who like Lady Catherine is very well provided, nevertheless most characteristically asserts herself by gleefully *not* inviting her nephew and niece to stay. "If People want to be by the Sea, why dont they take Lodgings?" she argues. "Charity begins at home you know" (402). Clearly, in her last novel Jane Austen was still pondering the contract of mutual agreeableness that is entered into by host and guest, and the many ways of fulfilling and violating it. The selfish Lady Denham is balanced by the Heywoods, who act as Good Samaritans to the stricken Parkers at the beginning of the novel: "As every office of hospitality & friendliness was received as it ought – as there was not more good will on one side than Gratitude on the other – . . . they grew to like each other in the course of that fortnight, exceedingly well" (*MW*, 371).

There again we have the vision of hospitality as a joyful enlargement of both host and guest. It blesseth him that gives, and him that takes. Tonight we too have had a chance to grow to like each other, in the course of this dinner, exceedingly well. Ladies and gentlemen, for what we have *given*, as well as for what we have received, may the Lord make us truly thankful!

5

"God Gave Us Our Relations": The Watson Family

"God gave us our relations," goes the saying; "but we can *choose* our friends." If Jane Austen didn't invent that proverb, she could have, for the sentiment echoes through her writings. In her work, the relations – the family – are God-given and determined; either a boon or a curse, but in any case part of the essential "given" at the outset of a heroine's story. The family forms the envelope of circumstances, a ready-made set of contingencies for which she can't be held responsible, but which must be a major factor in the choice of the "friends" to whom she turns. God gave Elizabeth the Bennets, but she can and does choose Darcy rather than Collins, and she is richly responsible in that choice.

In *The Watsons*, since it is uncompleted, the focus remains on the family. And of course the family is the central social unit of the world Austen creates. What is Jane Austen's subject? Why, "3 or 4 Families in a Country Village," of course (*Letters*, 401). What does she principally create? – in her own words again, "pictures of domestic life" (*Letters*, 452).[1]

Her titles too focus on relations and the family. One of her juvenile compositions was called "The Three Sisters." According to one Austen family member, her last novel, which we know as the fragment *Sanditon*, was to have been called *The Brothers*.[2] And in the middle of her career comes *The Watsons*. Conveniently for my purposes, *The Watsons* is named not for a central character, like *Emma*; not for a principal place, like *Northanger Abbey* and *Mansfield Park*; not for a prominent theme, like *Sense and Sensibility, Pride and Prejudice,* and *Persuasion*; but for a family. If it was a title selected by its first editor, James Edward Austen-Leigh, rather than by its author, I can still take advantage of his convenient choice.

The family for Jane Austen is the context and battleground for the heroine's moral and psychological testing. And in its combination of

59

intimacy, routine, long-standing and inescapable relationships, love, and exasperation, it forms a testing ground for judgement and charity, the two virtues that she would have associated with the Old and New Testaments. Before I plunge into *The Watsons*, I would like to take a little space to explore this major recurring concern in her novels.

The conflict between judgement and charity forms one of the constant and recurring moral crises for Jane Austen's heroines, particularly for the highly intelligent ones. Since learning to judge correctly is the major moral task,[3] they are going through a constant process of sharpening and refining their perceptions: of correcting their "first impressions," discovering when "sensibility" is not sensible, when "pride" is proper pride, when judgement is "prejudice." To be good is not enough. The successful heroine must learn to be intelligently good; and to be intelligently good one must justly estimate people, one must discriminate. But then there is the dilemma of what one is to do with one's judgement once one has learned to make it. The educated heroine is all too likely to discover, "Use every man after his desert, and who shall 'scape whipping?" And to brandish the whip, to become a castigator and a misanthrope, is no graceful role for a heroine.

Jane Austen spoke of her favourite niece, Fanny Knight, as "one who had rather more Acuteness, Penetration & Taste, than Love" (*Letters*, 408). The same could be said of Jane Austen herself. We are aware, all the time, of the acuteness, penetration and taste at work in the novels, and that is why we read them. And yet we judge her, I think, not deficient in the love: and here I mean love in its large and Christian sense of *caritas*, the Charity that suffereth long and is kind; that thinketh no evil, and rejoiceth not in iniquity. She values this virtue, values it fully, but sometimes perhaps with a wistful sense that it's one that other people are better at than she is.

In the Bennet sisters, Elizabeth and Jane, we have a little allegory of the conflict of judgement and love. Elizabeth has judgement, in its unrefined form as prejudice. We might almost say that Elizabeth does rejoice in iniquity. She admits, "Follies and nonsense, whims and inconsistencies, *do* divert me, I own." And she means to be uncommonly clever in taking decided dislikes (*PP*, 57, 225). She has more acuteness, penetration and taste than love. Jane, on the other hand, has "candour" (in its eighteenth-century sense), "that key word in Miss Austen's vocabulary."[4] Johnson defines *candour* as "sweetness of temper; . . . kindness." To be *candid* is to be "free from malice; not desirous to find fault" – to be very different from Elizabeth, even after her reform. Between them the two sisters epitomize Old Testament judgement and New Testament mercy. And although we judge and sympathize with Elizabeth, not Jane, and would rather be triumphantly right, or even stylishly wrong with her than kindly deluded with Jane, still Elizabeth who prided herself on her discernment must learn to reproach herself for having "disdained the generous candour of my sister" (208).

The same conflict is the basis of that morally loaded incident, Emma's snub of Miss Bates. Emma is another character in whom taste and discrimination are at war with charity. Priding herself on her discernment, she is exasperated by Miss Bates's "universal goodwill" (*E*, 21); and when the moment arrives she can't resist humiliating her. It takes Mr. Knightley to make Emma properly aware how her rampant "Acuteness, Penetration & Taste" have trampled on Miss Bates's "candour and generosity" (*E*, 375).

What, then, is the perceptive heroine to do with her perceptions? If the vigorous activity of the mind so acquaints her with evil, where is she to find the mercy to tolerate it? Must intelligent judgement, so painstakingly arrived at, be simply shelved, and subsumed in an undiscriminating benevolence? That is what Marianne Dashwood supposes is Elinor's principle: "I thought our judgements were given us merely to be subservient to those of our neighbours," she says sarcastically. But Elinor and Jane Austen have already worked out a practical relationship between judgement and mercy. "My doctrine," Elinor explains, "has never aimed at the subjection of the understanding. All I have ever attempted to influence has been the behaviour" (*SS*, 94). One may judge Miss Bates accurately, as Mr. Knightley does, and recognize that she is one in whom "what is good and what is ridiculous are most unfortunately blended" (*E*, 375); but one must nevertheless treat her with courtesy and give her the best of the apple crop. The conduct, but not the judgement, must be regulated.

It is an ongoing moral battle, this reconciliation of judgement with charity, and it clearly occupied Jane Austen herself. In her letters she is both the erring Elizabeth and Emma, armed with the sharp awareness of what is wrong or ridiculous, and the author by whom they are punished for their lack of charity. We see the constant see-saw between her waspish acuteness and her determined benevolence. "I cannot anyhow continue to find people agreable," says the Elizabeth in her author. But, speaks the Knightley, "I like the Mother, ... because she is chearful & grateful for what she is at the age of 90 & upwards" (*Letters*, 129, 342).

In his classic essay, D.W. Harding characterized Jane Austen's position as one of "regulated hatred."[5] We may argue about the phrase and its particular emphasis. Perhaps some would prefer "enlightened candour," or "compassionate judgement." But some such oxymoron does seem appropriate to suggest the constant effort of the moral life to reconcile an acute awareness of evil with a determined practice of generous tolerance. That Jane Austen herself was aware of the conflict is testified by a passage in one of her prayers:[6]

> Incline us oh God! to think humbly of ourselves, to be severe only in the examination of our own conduct, to consider our fellow-creatures with kindness, and to judge of all they say and do with that charity which we would desire from them ourselves. (*MW*, 456)

The principles of the parson's daughter clearly jostled with the shrewd perceptions and sharp judgements of the satiric writer.

For the exercise of this tense moral life, the family is the perfect location. Where but in the intimacy of the family has one so golden and continuing an opportunity for gleaning knowledge and arriving at full and soundly-based judgement? And where but among close relations are the love and forbearance most abundant? – or at least most needed if *not* abundant. The family furnishes to the full both the opportunity for judgement and the urgent need for charity. In the family, if anywhere, we have the best sphere for the regulation of conduct.

Brian Southam finds in *The Watsons* "a failing in generosity and a loss of creative power."[7] I would dispute the "loss of creative power"; but the failing in generosity is perhaps there to the extent that in this fragment Jane Austen's judgement is more to the fore than her charity. Emma Watson is bravely successful in regulating her behaviour; but she has more cause than any other heroine to judge her neighbours, and particularly her family, adversely.

The Watson family is perhaps the most desperately disagreeable milieu that any Austen heroine has to endure. And Emma Watson's plight in it is worse than Elizabeth's among the Bennets or Anne's among the Elliots, because, coming from a sojourn of fourteen years in her aunt's home, she is catapulted into immediate intimacy with a set of strangers. She is an alien by her own fireside. She has had no shared life in which to grow the love that will make candour easy. Neither has she developed those mental calluses that habit brings, whereby she will cease to be chafed by the family bristles and roughnesses. Her situation is most like Fanny Price's at Portsmouth; but

Fanny knows she can go back to Mansfield Park, and besides is no financial burden on her family. Emma Watson has no escape. Her unfeeling brother brutally summarizes her situation,

> "Unluckily [your Aunt] has left the pleasure of providing for you, to your Father, & without the power. – That's the long & the short of the business. After keeping you at a distance from your family for such a length of time as must do away all natural affection among us & breeding you up (I suppose) in a superior stile, you are returned upon their hands without a sixpence." (*MW*, 352)

There is a delicate expression of brotherly affection! And Emma has further cause to dislike these family strangers with whom she is thrust into immediate and embarrassing intimacy. Her sisters are rivals and enemies. Margaret competes for Tom Musgrave's exclusive attention, and Penelope has ruined Elizabeth's happiness by turning Purvis against her. "Rivalry, Treachery between sisters!" Emma exclaims, deeply shocked (316). Her brother is coarse and unfeeling, her sister-in-law vulgar and pretentious. At the end of the fragment we are left with the bleak picture of Emma's taking refuge in her invalid father's room "from the dreadful mortifications of unequal Society, & family Discord – from the immediate endurance of Hard-hearted prosperity, low-minded Conceit, & wrong-headed folly" (361). From such a situation at home, who would not leap at any chance of escape by marrying? Emma's sister, Elizabeth, like Charlotte Lucas, feels she can't afford the luxury of marriage for love. "I should not like marrying a disagreable Man . . . – but I do not think there *are* many very disagreable Men; – I think I could like any good humoured Man with a comfortable Income" (318). But the more "refined" Emma, we know, will have to prove her outstanding moral integrity by refusing even the temptingly eligible Lord Osborne, even in the teeth of her misery at home. The precious liberty to choose your friends must be dearly bought.

I have summarized the pains of Emma's family situation only briefly, but Jane Austen fills in the picture with wonderful specificity, and in the process shows herself acquainted with the fine tuning of family dynamics, and surprisingly modern in many of her perceptions.

She is the first and most prominent author, I think, to specialize in dramatizing an emotion that is very familiar to us in the twentieth century, but which receives only limited attention in earlier literature: family shame. We all remember the convulsions of embarrassment

suffered as children when our parents dressed or behaved inappro-
priately in front of our school friends. And – to bring the record up
to date – most of us cause the same pangs of embarrassment to our
sons, daughters, nephews, nieces, grandchildren. Jane Austen knew,
in advance, how they feel!

The eighteenth-century novel, which reflects a more patriarchal
society than our own, seldom notices this acute if not very exalted
emotion (although Fanny Burney registered something of it with
Evelina among her vulgar Branghton cousins). There, parents or brothers or sisters may be wicked or absurd, but their shortcomings don't
reflect on their relatives in such a way as to make them squirm. To
cause this particular emotion, there must be three parties: A, the sensitive consciousness; B, the erring relative; and C, some third person,
more or less exalted, before whom A feels shame for B. B, the relation, is usually serenely unaware of doing anything wrong.

Dickens, closer to our own time, knew all about family shame, and
dramatizes it most memorably in *Great Expectations*. You will remember how Pip, mediating between his blacksmith brother-in-law and
the stately Miss Havisham, is driven nearly frantic by Joe's bumpkin
maunderings. And when Joe proposes to come and visit Pip and his
new genteel friends in London, Pip is appalled:

> Let me confess exactly, with what feelings I looked forward to Joe's
> coming [writes Pip].
> Not with pleasure, though I was bound to him by so many ties;
> no; with considerable disturbance, some mortification, and a keen
> sense of incongruity. If I could have kept him away by paying
> money, I certainly would have paid money. (Ch. 27)

Jane Austen may be said to have specialized in this kind of "mortification."[8] We remember Elizabeth at the Netherfield ball, agonized
by the displayed absurdities of her mother, her cousin, and even her
father:

> To Elizabeth it appeared, that had her family made an agreement
> to expose themselves as much as they could during the evening, it
> would have been impossible for them to play their parts with more
> spirit, or finer success. (*PP*, 101)

Fanny among the Prices at Portsmouth has many things to suffer; but
the crowning torture is the arrival of Henry Crawford. Even though

she doesn't like him and doesn't want to impress him, to her he is that refined third party whose scrutiny of her family immeasurably increases her sense of its shortcomings. "To her many other sources of uneasiness was added the severe one of shame for the home in which he found her" (*MP*, 400). The fact that such shame is irrational does not mend the matter. "It was soon pain upon pain, confusion upon confusion; for they were hardly in the High Street, before they met her father, whose appearance was not the better from its being Saturday" (401).

Conditions in the Watson family are such as to make this particular pain one of the major trials of the heroine. The relations are certainly not such as to be proud of; Lord Osborne, the third party, though not himself highly discriminating, is of a class to perceive the family's shabbiness in sharp focus; and Emma has a consciousness refined enough to suffer fully the shame of the exposure of the one before the other. Like Pip, she has been educated beyond her station, so that she is intensely aware of her relations' vulgarity; and like Fanny, she has come down in the world; so that she suffers a particular complication of emotions. When Lord Osborne and Tom Musgrave come visiting, and catch the Misses Watson about to sit down to their unfashionably early dinner, Emma,

> having in her Aunt's family been used to many of the Elegancies of Life, was fully sensible of all that must be open to the ridicule of Richer people in her present home. – Of the pain of such feelings, Eliz[abeth] knew very little; – her simpler Mind, or juster reason saved her from such mortification – & tho' shrinking under a general sense of Inferiority, she felt no particular Shame. (345)

The "particular Shame" is Emma's portion, and it is likely to be a recurring emotion when she goes to live with Mr. and Mr. Robert Watson in Croydon. No other novel is set up with quite this emphasis on the trials of a heroine stuck with an alien and uncongenial family to afflict her with complicated embarrassment.

Another aspect of family life to which Jane Austen paid particular attention in *The Watsons* is the one that the family shares with any small and closely-knit community: habit and routine. The many recurring actions and events in our lives, the means by which we structure our time, and come to expect that, say, breakfast will be at eight and lunch at noon, may be felt as a comforting and sustaining ritual, but may also become a maddening monotony. Consider the opening of *The Watsons*:

The first winter assembly in the Town of D. in Surry was to be held on Tuesday Octr ye 13th, & it was generally expected to be a very good one; a long list of Country Families was confidently run over as sure of attending, & sanguine hopes were entertained that the Osbornes themselves would be there. – The Edwardes' invitation to the Watsons followed of course. (314)

The emphasis is on what is recurrent, expected, predictable. The assembly is the first of a series, the participants can be "confidently run over," in advance, "as sure of attending"; and – as the narrator moves in to identify the two families that are to concern us – the invitation of one to the other "followed of course." Even the Watsons' old mare knows the routine, and proceeds to the Edwards' house without guidance, "making only one Blunder, in proposing to stop at the Milleners" (322). Stanton and the town of D form a predictable world. In the opening scene of dialogue, Elizabeth Watson confidently and accurately predicts many of the details of the assembly and the behaviour of those attending it. The Edwardses will go early, and if Mr. Edwards wins at cards will stay late; there will be good soup afterwards in any case; Tom Musgrave will wait in the passage for the Osbornes, but will pay attention to Emma as he does to every new girl. And it's all perfectly accurate. All that is yet to be decided, it seems, is who is to dance with Mary Edwards. As the story advances we are constantly reminded how everything proceeds according to precedent. The Tomlinsons go first, and the sound of their passing carriage is "the constant signal for Mrs. Edwards to order hers to the door" (327). All happens "as usual" (327). Elizabeth has had "a ten years Enjoyment" of the winter assemblies (315), her sisters several seasons; and now Emma, the youngest, she says, will "have as fair a chance as we have all had, to make your fortune" (320). The Watson sisters are considered as a series, and Tom Musgrave apparently expects them to fall for him as regularly as a row of dominoes.

Tom Musgrave, who occupies the role of anti-hero, makes it his business both to observe predictable routines himself and to be acquainted with other peoples'. "You are determined to be in good time I see, as usual," he greets the Edwardses at the ball (327). He knowledgeably declares, the next day, "As to Mrs. Edwardes' carriage being used the day after a Ball, it is a thing quite out of rule I assure you" (340). And he is perfectly acquainted with the usual mealtimes among the Watsons at Stanton. It becomes Emma's task to combat and overthrow his confident expectations, and restore some spontaneity and reality to an existence lived according to rule and precedent. She takes a certain pleasure in disappointing him. When, according to his constant rule, he retires to solitude after the Osbornes have left the ball, Emma assures him – though somewhat against her conscience – that the dancing had been as spirited as ever (340).

It is to be Emma's role, in the local society and in her family as with Tom Musgrave, to break the monotonous and predictable chain of expected occurrences. She is the Cinderella, or the youngest of the twelve dancing princesses. Already at the ball we see the process beginning. She surprises and charms everybody by dancing spontaneously with little Charles Blake. "Emma did not think, or reflect; – she felt & acted," we hear (330). And her action is the more healthy and refreshing for the stultifying social routines that it interrupts. She overthrows Tom's confident expectations by refusing to dance with him, flirt with him, or ride in his phaeton. But after the ball is over, Emma in Stanton must reconcile herself to the trivial round and common task. In the emphasis on ritual recurrence and social routines – the predictable events of the winter assembly, the dreary timetable observed by the Edwards, the early hours kept by the Watsons, the foreseen invitation to Croydon – Jane Austen has established an atmosphere that goes with Emma's stultifying entrapment in her uncongenial family circle. Things in families and small towns can be monotonous, claustrophobic, frustrating. That is one more of the pains of the family when it is viewed as a training ground for marriage.

In the 1960s the psychologist Eric Berne gave our language a new phrase, *Games People Play*.[9] He could have used Jane Austen's characters, particularly those in *The Watsons*, as the case studies. For Jane Austen, like Berne, is alert not only to the routines and rituals in families and small communities, but to their development into dishonest psychological manoeuvring that is conducted according to its own sets of tacitly acknowledged rules. Husbands and wives and family members, because of their intimacy and continual association, are particularly adept and prone to play games with each other, and the games may be more or less destructive. The Edwards, we hear, know when to stop in their ritual sparring about his evenings at the whist club:

"Your Club w^d be better fitted for an Invalid, said M^{rs} E[dwards] if you did not keep it up so late." – This was an old greivance. – "So late, my dear, what are you talking of; cried the Husband with sturdy pleasantry. – We are always at home before Midnight. They would laugh at Osborne Castle to hear you call *that* late; they are but just rising from dinner at midnight." – "That is nothing to the purpose. – retorted the Lady calmly. The Osbornes are to be no rule for us. You had better meet every night, & break up two hours sooner." So far, the subject was very often carried; – but Mr. and Mrs. Edwards were so wise as never to pass that point. (325)

Other players of games are not so forbearing, and their games are more damaging. Tom Musgrave skilfully plays the game called "Flirt" with the Watson family over a number of years, with painful consequences for all other players. Mrs. Robert Watson perpetrates various fictions, which everybody knows to be fictions, but which are effective in the game that Berne might call "The Style to Which I am Accustomed." The object is to put down her in-law relations, and make them properly conscious of her superior status:

> Mrs. Robert exactly as smart as she had been at her own party, came in [to dinner] with apologies for her dress – "I would not make you wait, said she, so I put on the first thing I met with. – I am afraid I am a sad figure." (353)

And later, at dinner, she cries,

> "I do beg & entreat that no Turkey may be seen today. I am really frightened out of my wits at the number of dishes we have already. Let us have no Turkey I beseech you." (354)

There is clearly not a word that is honestly meant to convey its own meaning in such speeches. Essentially they announce, "You are my poor relations, and I'm not going to let you forget it." Elizabeth Watson, cast in the ungracious role of Patsy, has to bring on the turkey, by way of putting on the special show that her sister-in-law expects, but refuses to appreciate.

Margaret Watson is another habitual game-player, though not a very good one; and she early angles for some losing role in which to cast Emma. There is no way for Emma to win in the issue of whose bedroom she is to share:

> "I suppose, said Marg[are]t rather quickly to Emma, you & I are to be together: Eliz[abe]th always takes care to have a room to herself." – "No – Eliz[abe]th gives me half her's." – "Oh! – (in a soft-

en'd voice, & rather mortified to find she was not ill used) "I am sorry I am not to have the pleasure of your company – especially as it makes me nervous to be much alone." (351)

Margaret performs a set of poses, moves, ploys, aimed at getting a pay-off. Reality doesn't get a look in, for games played in life, as Berne shows, are basically dishonest. Emma's instinct to withdraw from Margaret is sound and healthy. She is one who will win by refusing to play.

Berne provides a full set of rules for the game called "Alcoholic." Jane Austen, I think, gives all the material for a cognate game called "Invalid." She might well have coined a new aphorism: "God gave us our diseases; but we can choose our ailments." In the basic tension between judgement and charity that I have identified as a central moral concern in her work, ill health provides a crucial test. Who so deserves our compassion as the sick? On the other hand, who so wears it out? And the devoted attendance exacted by those who fall ill prompts the sneaking suspicion that perhaps they do it on purpose. "Speak roughly to your little boy," advises the Duchess in *Alice*, "And beat him when he *sneezes*; / He only does it to annoy, / Because he knows it teases." Such exasperation with other people's symptoms is familiar in both real and fictional families. "Kitty has no discretion in her coughs," says Mr. Bennet drily of his daughter; "she times them ill" (*PP*, 6). There are other characters who seem to choose their ailments, and do it to annoy. Mrs. Bennet is forever invoking her nerves in order to get extra compassion and attention. Mrs. Churchill in *Emma* is always assumed to be using her ill health as a power play, until by actually dying she is "fully justified," and cleared of all suspicion of having done it to annoy (*E*, 387). The valetudinarian Mr. Woodhouse is a constant tax on Emma's good humour, and it is much to her moral credit that she is more patient with him than most modern daughters would be.

Jane Austen herself had her own experience of parents who play "Invalid."

My mother continues hearty [she wrote to Cassandra from Steventon], her appetite & nights very good, but her Bowels are still not entirely settled, & she sometimes complains of an Asthma, a Dropsy, Water in her Chest & a Liver Disorder. (*Letters*, 39)

For one who eats and sleeps well, that is quite a list of complaints, and Jane's patience is clearly tried, although she stops short of the

witticism that she would employ of someone less nearly related.[10]
Health and ill health are a major issue in the Watson family.[11] Emma
Watson's brother Sam, who is clearly to be the hero of a sub-plot, is
a surgeon, and is prevented from attending the ball because "just now
it is a sickly time at Guilford" (321). Her sister Penelope is trying to
make a match with "rich old Dr. Harding" before he expires of asthma (317). Her uncle Turner was an invalid who died, and her father
is another, and also fated to die soon.

The presentation of Mr. Watson shows a tension between judgement and compassion that is not fully resolved. Some critics have
found him to be one of the few admirable characters in the work.[12]
We know that he is "a Man of Sense and Education" (361), and that
he has the correct views about the proper way to deliver a sermon
(343–4). And Emma and the hero Howard demonstrate their virtue
by being solicitous for his comfort. So far compassion reigns. But the
invalid in the family is subject to sharp judgement, too. A father of
four girls who needs babysitting by one of them, even on the night
of a ball, calls for great filial self-sacrifice. And what business has
such a father to tell them, of an eligible young clergyman, "By the
bye, he enquired after one of my Daughters, but I do not know which.
I suppose you know among yourselves" (344). He begins to make
Mr. Bennet look like a truly solicitous parent. Mr. Bennet *did* pay that
crucial visit to Netherfield; but when Lord Osborne visits at Stanton,
Mr. Watson is not about to exert himself to promote this eligible
acquaintance. A message of excuse is sent to Osborne Castle, we are
told, "on the too-sufficient plea of Mr Watson's infirm state of health"
(348). The plea may be sufficient; but we have just heard Mr. Watson
testily exclaim, "I cannot return the visit. – *I* would not if I could"
(348). There he declares himself responsible, and must be judged
accordingly. On one occasion he causes his daughters severe and
avoidable embarrassment. When Elizabeth and Emma are just recov-
ering from the humiliation of Lord Osborne's arriving simultaneously with the early dinner service, and the visit is proceeding
pleasantly, Nanny arrives with the querulous message, "Please
Ma'am, Master wants to know why he be'nt to have his dinner" (346).
There is only so much one can forgive a father, even one who is "a
little peevish under immediate pain" (348). The invalid Mr. Watson
presents in a vivid form the moral testing that is a constant condition of family life.

In the Watson family, it sometimes seems, charity begins anywhere
but at home. It is one of the distressing aspects of Emma's sojourn

among the strangers who are her brothers and sisters (348) that she must learn how quickly familiarity breeds contempt. Robert Watson, when visiting at Stanton, refuses to put fresh powder in his hair when he dresses for dinner. "I think there is powder enough in my hair for my wife & sisters," he declares, when his wife reproaches him (353). But when company arrives, in the person of Tom Musgrave, he swiftly makes excuses: "You cannot be more in dishabille than myself. – We got here so late, that I had not time even to put a little fresh powder in my hair" (357). Jane Austen has a sharp sense of the dual identity adopted by those who are one person within the family, and another before those they want to impress. Margaret is an extended study in such a person. She even has two voices, one for the family, and one for company. Emma, as the new sister, initially gets the benefit of the company voice:

> On meeting her long-absent Sister, as on every occasion of shew, [Margaret's] manner was all affection & her voice all gentleness; continued smiles & a very slow articulation being her constant resource when determined on pleasing. –
> She was now so "delighted to see dear, dear Emma" that she could hardly speak a word in a minute. – "I am sure we shall be great friends" – she observed, with much sentiment, as they were sitting together. (349)

But presently, Emma hears Margaret address Elizabeth, on domestic matters, "in a sharp quick accent, totally unlike the first" (351); and Emma herself, after a few days of Margaret's acquaintance, is soon reduced to the same status of mere sister, and finds "the continuance of the gentle voice beyond her calculation short" (361). It is not surprising that she should come to be relieved even by the company of Tom Musgrave, because his presence produces the relative graciousness of company manners among family members who otherwise bicker and quarrel. Emma has already learned that "a family party might be the worst of all parties" (358).

However, the picture is not unrelievedly bleak. Even among the Watsons there are moments of spontaneous and joyful communion. Small units within the family group may find themselves a precious sanctuary. Elizabeth and Jane Bennet, and Fanny and Susan Price, like Jane and Cassandra Austen, form a congenial alliance within their larger families; and so do Emma and Elizabeth Watson. These two are able to enjoy the full pleasure of family intimacy, as Emma cheer-

fully gives her sister a detailed account of everything that happened
at the ball:

> As their quietly-sociable little meal concluded, Miss Watson could
> not help observing how comfortably it had passed. "It is so delight-
> ful to me, said she, to have Things going on in peace & good-
> humour. . . . Now, tho' we have had nothing but fried beef, how
> good it has all seemed." (343)

But even in this mood Elizabeth has to admit that this family accord
is very rare. "I wish everybody were as easily satisfied as you – but
poor Marg[are]t is very snappish, & Penelope owns she had rather
have Quarrelling going on, than nothing at all" (343). Some relations,
perhaps, we might choose even if God hadn't already given them to
us. But in *The Watsons* most of them give the heroine every reason to
choose *other* friends.

As I approach my conclusion I can't resist the temptation to consider, briefly, why *The Watsons* remained a fragment, and what its
shape would have been if it were finished. For Emma's place in the
family is to test and qualify her for the moral and emotional victory
that we expect of a Jane Austen heroine.

Critics have found fault with Emma Watson as heroine because she
is too good: her judgements are sound from the outset, they say, and
so close to her creator's that there is no room for moral growth, or for
that irony at her expense which is one of the delights of Jane Austen's
fiction, and one of the triumphs of her art.[13] But those who argue thus
take the erring heroines, Catherine, Marianne, Elizabeth, and Emma
Woodhouse as the essential Austen model. They forget that Elinor,
Fanny and Anne are also heroines. These ones have less to learn,
because they have the right principles from the beginning; but each
has a significant progress nonetheless. Fanny Price, for instance, may
be morally static, but she is socially mobile, and must learn to assert
herself in society in order to make her goodness effective. Emma
Watson's progress is to be comparable; and like Fanny's it will be a
social rather than a moral journey.

Emma's shortcoming is also a virtue. She is "refined," as Elizabeth
tells her in the first scene (318). From her advantaged home with her
rich uncle and aunt she brings a moral fastidiousness into a circle that
cannot afford to be fastidious.[14] She accepts Elizabeth's comment on
her refinement as a criticism: "If my opinions are wrong, I must correct them – if they are above my situation, I must endeavour to con-

ceal them" (318). Here is the pointer for Emma's progress, and the central thematic statement of the novel that is to be. The irony at Emma's expense – and there *is* irony – is aimed at her social hypersensitivity. When Tom Musgrave is interrupted in his interesting anecdote of what Lord Osborne and Howard have said about her, anyone else would simply prompt him to go on. But "Emma, tho' suffering a good deal from Curiosity, dared not remind him" (359). We can smile as she pays the price for being refined. Snobbery, as all the fuss about the Osbornes suggests, is a major satiric target. And the conflict of feeling with propriety, like that of sense and sensibility in the earlier novel, is to be thematically central. As Lucy Steele's unfeeling calculation is an extreme version of Elinor's "sense," so Mrs. Edwards, the "judge of Decorum" (334), is a parody of Emma's excessive concern with proper behaviour. Other characters will also have to overcome the social punctilios that are too apt to govern Emma. Sam Watson will win Mary Edwards when he conquers his own social diffidence; and she will respond to his love when she learns to recognize her feeling for him in spite of her parents' disapproval. The hero, Mr. Howard of the "unexceptionable . . . Manners" (335), will have an associated trial. An excessive deference to the wishes of his patroness Lady Osborne will initially inhibit his love for Emma, but he too will learn to follow the dictates of his own heart rather than of society. (I'm convinced, you see, that *Lady* Osborne, the "handsome" dowager [329], is Emma's rival, and not *Miss* Osborne as Chapman assumes.[15] Miss Osborne will be too busy jilting Tom Musgrave to enter deeply into a relation with Howard.) In endorsing strong and authentic feeling rather than prudence and propriety, *The Watsons* would have been one of the most Romantic of Jane Austen's novels.

As I read it, we have no falling-off in creativity in *The Watsons*. In its thematic structure, as in its evocation of the family, this fragment suggests that it could have been part of a beautiful and successful novel, if not always a comfortable one. Then why did Jane Austen abandon it?

The usual biographical answer is derived from Fanny Lefroy: "Somewhere in 1804 she began 'The Watsons,' but her father died early in 1805, and it was never finished."[16] The domestic frustrations and the economic difficulties following on her father's death are usually cited as the reason for abandoning a work which was in any case depressing and too "low" in its setting.[17] But I believe her father's death itself, and its inevitable link in Jane Austen's mind with Mr. Watson's death, is the major reason. We know from her other works that Jane Austen was chary of representing death. Mr. Dashwood dies before the action of his novel begins, and Dr. Grant after it is over. Mrs. Churchill dies in the course of the action, but off-stage; and after all we had never met her. In her completed fiction, in fact, Jane Austen never "kills" a developed character. Mr. Watson would have been the exception. He is a prominent figure in the story – the heroine's sensible but selfish father – and he is to die in the middle of it, possibly in a dramatized scene. And while Jane Austen was working herself up to this scene – and it would have been *hard* work for her – her own father died, suddenly and unexpectedly. For one who had been musing along the lines, "God gave us our relations, but we can choose our friends," there must have been a surge of guilt, strong though irrational. With the god-like authority of an author, she had *given* her heroine a father, and planned to take him away. It must have seemed as though that god-like power had slipped nightmarishly from her fiction to her life when her own father was removed. No wonder she closed that book, and never opened it again.

And so, for reasons that belong to Jane Austen as daughter rather than to Jane Austen as artist, Emma Watson is never to escape her family, but must stay immobilized among her God-given relations. But *we* may choose to project how *she* would choose her friends.

Notes

1.	I preserve the spelling and punctuation of R.W. Chapman's edition of the letters as of the works.
2.	See Chapman's note (*MW*, 363).
3.	Susan Morgan has explored this process at large in *In the Meantime: Character and Perception in Jane Austen's Fiction* (Chicago: University of Chicago Press, 1980).
4.	The phrase is Q.D. Leavis's, from her 1941 article "A Critical Theory of Jane Austen's Writings (I)." See *A Selection from 'Scrutiny,'* compiled by F.R. Leavis, 2 vols (Cambridge: Cambridge University Press, 1968), II, 21.
5.	"Regulated Hatred: An Aspect of the Work of Jane Austen," *Scrutiny*, VIII (1940), pp. 346–62.
6.	I am indebted to my colleague Bruce Stovel for bringing this passage in the "Prayers" to my attention.
7.	*Jane Austen's Literary Manuscripts* (Oxford: Clarendon Press, 1964), p. 63.
8.	"Mortification" is a word that Stuart Tave connects with Elizabeth's moral development. *Some Words of Jane Austen* (Chicago: University of Chicago Press, 1973), p. 116 ff.

9.   *Games People Play: The Psychology of Human Relationships* (New York: Grove Press, 1964).

10. George Tucker, who takes a more charitable view of Jane's mother than I do, discusses Mrs. Austen's hypochondria in *A Goodly Heritage: A History of Jane Austen's Family* (Manchester: Carcanet New Press, 1983), pp. 72–3.

11. John Wiltshire, in his impressive book on *Jane Austen and the Body* (Cambridge: Cambridge University Press, 1992), might well have explored this fragment as thoroughly as he explores *Sanditon*.

12. Marvin Mudrick finds that "Mr. Watson is the only figure . . . who aspires, in outline at least, toward the tragic." *Jane Austen: Irony as Defense and Discovery* (Berkeley and Los Angeles: University of California Press, 1952), p. 147.

13. See especially Mudrick, pp. 141, 197, 151, and Southam, pp. 68–70.

14. I have developed this argument more fully in "Emma Watson: Jane Austen's Uncompleted Heroine," in *Critical Reconstructions: The Relationship of Fiction to Life*, ed. Robert Polhemus and Roger B. Henkel (Stanford: Stanford University Press, 1994), 212–30.

15. In the edition I use Chapman quotes from the *Memoir*: "much of the interest of the tale was to arise from Lady Osborne's love for Mr. Howard, and his counter affection for Emma, whom he was finally to marry." But he adds a note to "Lady Osborne": "Doubtless a slip for *Miss Osborne*. Lady O. was 'nearly fifty' (p. 329)" (363). I hope it's not only because I'm past fifty myself that I dispute this assumption. We likewise hear that "Of the females [including Miss Osborne], Ly. Osborne had by much the finest person; – tho' nearly 50, she was very handsome, & had all the Dignity of Rank" (329). We may remember that another widow of about the same age, Emma's aunt, has just married the dashing Irish Captain O'Brien.

16. "Is it Just?" *Temple Bar*, 67 (1883), p. 277.

17. James Edward Austen-Leigh had suggested that Jane Austen became aware "of the evil of having placed her heroine too low, in such a position of poverty and obscurity." *Memoir of Jane Austen*, 2nd edition (1871), p. 296.

6

"Acting by Design" in *Pride and Prejudice*

"I meant to be uncommonly clever in taking so decided a dislike to him, without any reason," Elizabeth Bennet admits of Darcy in one of her moments of self-knowledge and confession (225).[1] She *meant* to be clever. It is a phrase that makes clear a refinement of the theme of *Pride and Prejudice*. Elizabeth is not only a misguided heroine who makes mistakes and learns the error of her ways: but she *wilfully* makes mistakes, almost according to a programme she has laid down for herself. Her meaning to be clever connects her with Trollope's characters, who characteristically "teach themselves to believe" this or that, and with James's Isabel Archer, who consciously forms herself as though she were a work of art. As T.S. Eliot puts it in "The Hollow Men,"

> Between the idea
> And the reality
> Between the motion
> And the act
> Falls the shadow.

The nineteenth-century novel does not, by and large, deal with hollow men. But it certainly suggests a movement in that direction. Austen and Trollope and James are alike interested in the shadow that falls between impulse and action, the interval wherein the mind takes its decision, I will do or be this and not that, because *this* is appropriate to the person that I intend to make of myself. It is the movement towards not just self-realization, but self-creation, that fascinates such authors.

Often enough the model for the self-creator is literary. The Quixote theme of the character who takes romantic fiction as the precedent for life, as we have seen, is prominent in Austen's writings, from the father in *Love and Freindship* who rumbles, "You have been studying

Novels I suspect" (*MW*, 81), to Catherine Morland's gothic fantasies and Elinor Dashwood's reliance on the conventions of romantic poetry and sentimental fiction.

Emma Woodhouse, the imaginist, is the most inventive Quixote of all, even though the Quixote theme in this novel is not so clamorously to the fore as it is in *Northanger Abbey*. Emma is not only a self-creator, but she creates roles for the people who surround her too, and does all she can to make them live the roles she has cast them in. It is from her reading, not her experience, that she has become convinced of certain rules of existence: for instance, that a child of unknown parents must be of noble birth (*ergo*, that Harriet Smith, Highbury's princess in disguise, is worthy of Mr. Elton); that a man who rescues a woman from physical danger must simultaneously fall in love with her and gain her affections (therefore, that Mr. Dixon and Jane must be in love, because he once saved her from falling out of a boat); and that love is blind (hence, that Mr. Knightley can't be in love with her, because he so evidently sees her faults). With these kinds of preconceptions, Emma sets about her task of marrying off the people around her and making them live happily ever after; and as in *Don Quixote*, much of the comedy of the novel arises from the inconsistency between the benevolent fictions she endeavours to enact and the stubborn stuff of life that resists them – just as the windmills resist the construction the Don seeks to impose on them.

Pride and Prejudice has a place in this pattern. Its heroine is a self-creator, too, and she is one who is not always successful in the enactment of her designs. Unlike Emma, but like James's Isabel Archer, it is her self rather than others that she uses as her primary material, though like Emma she is fortunate in being unsuccessful in the creation of her destiny. It is the besetting sin of the heroine that she means to be clever; and she is moreover surrounded by other characters who similarly distort reality by subordinating feeling to calculation.

Of all the completed novels,[2] *Pride and Prejudice* is the closest to being what Northrop Frye calls a Menippean satire,[3] a satire on eggheads and diseases of the intellect. It is not ungoverned passions that threaten the happiness of the heroine, but ungoverned opinions, and the society at large is subject to a kind of cancer of the mind whereby ratiocination is in danger of usurping the proper functions of the heart. Lucy Steele, as the heroine's antagonist in *Sense and Sensibility*, is a caricature of what Elinor represents, an appalling example of the triumph of prudence over feeling. But the spirit of Lucy Steele seems to preside over the characters and action of *Pride and Prejudice*, where it is a truth universally acknowledged that eligible young bachelors are the rightful property of the unmarried girls of the district. The feelings of either party are not to be taken into account, any more than they are by Mrs. Bennet in the famous opening scene. "You must know that I am thinking of his marrying one of them," she tells her husband, in trying to persuade him to call on Mr. Bingley. Her syntax is indicative – the proposition of Bingley's marrying one of her daughters is subordinate to her *thinking* and her husband's *knowing*: feeling doesn't get a look in. "Is that his design in settling here?" her husband asks, parodying her mode of calculation (4). Bingley in fact is innocent of designs, as is Jane, but there are designers enough about them almost to ruin their happiness.

The prudential marriage motive is of course a major issue in this novel,[4] as has often been pointed out. From the opening scene onwards we have constantly before us examples of how money, status, patronage, and "an establishment" figure overwhelmingly in the calculations of who is to marry whom, and love scarcely has a place among the considerations. Marriages are planned, projected in advance, and the behaviour of the principals is adapted to the successful completion of the plan. The issue of the propriety of manifesting feeling, so fully canvassed in *Sense and Sensibility*, is here canvassed again between Charlotte Lucas and Elizabeth. "In nine cases out of ten," argues Charlotte, "a woman had better shew *more* affection than she feels" – the better to catch her man by encouragement. "Your plan is a good one," Elizabeth acknowledges, "when nothing is in question but the desire of being well married" (22) – and that is of course the case with Charlotte herself, who marries Mr. Collins "from the pure and disinterested desire of an establishment" (122). Likewise Miss Bingley plans to entrap Darcy, who is already marked out from birth by Lady Catherine as the rightful property of his cousin; and Mr. Collins, before being snapped up by Charlotte, is ready to marry any one of the five misses Bennet, sight unseen: "This was his plan of amends – of atonement – for inheriting their father's estate; and he thought it an excellent one, full of eligibility and suitableness" (70).

To complement this pattern of prudence and planning in marriage, another manifestation of the domination of head over heart is the repetition of situations where calculation takes the place of spontaneity. Elizabeth's sin of prejudice, the judgement that precedes due process, is not only a manifestation of her "quickness" (5), the cleverness of a "headstrong" girl (110), it is also part of a pattern of prejudgement and premeditation, the mental activity that pre-empts feeling and immediate response. Along with "prejudice," a number of words with the same prefix have a special resonance in this novel: "prepossession," "preference," "premeditation," "precipitance," "previous study." They testify to the same short-circuiting of organic emotional processes. Mr. Collins, for instance, not only marries according to plan; he lives and loves (or thinks he does) according to plan, and even pays compliments by the same method. Mr. Bennet, drawing him out, asks whether his elegant verbal courtesies "proceed from the impulse of the moment, or are the result of previous study?" Collins has at his fingertips a whole aesthetics of the art of flattery, including the concept of *ars celare artem*:

> They arise chiefly from what is passing at the time, and though I sometimes amuse myself with suggesting and arranging such little elegant compliments as may be adapted to ordinary occasions, I always wish to give them as unstudied an air as possible. (68)

Charlotte, with her theory that a woman should do what she can to secure a man first, as "there will be leisure for falling in love as much as she chuses" afterwards (22), is in many ways a perfect match for him, as she too can work at giving her calculations as unstudied an air as possible: during his brief and successful campaign, when she sees him approach Lucas Lodge, she "instantly set out to meet him accidentally in the lane" (121). In this world where calculation displaces spontaneity, even a cough can be considered as a piece of strategy:

> "Don't keep coughing so, Kitty, for heaven's sake! Have a little compassion on my nerves. You tear them to pieces."
> "Kitty has no discretion in her coughs," said her father; "she times them ill."
> "I do not cough for my own amusement," replied Kitty fretfully. (6)

If in this case we believe her, it's only because we know Kitty hasn't the wit to cough with calculated artistry.

We are recurrently shown the tendency of the brain to usurp the functions of the other faculties, the physical as well as the emotional. Miss Bingley, who wants to impress the intellectual Darcy, suggests a reform in the conduct of balls: "It would surely be much more rational if conversation instead of dancing made the order of the day."

"Much more rational, . . . I dare say," concedes her brother, "but it would not be near so much like a ball" (55–6). For once the rational is to be kept within proper bounds. The character in the novel who is most genuinely spontaneous and impulsive, Bingley, is firmly put in his place. His manner of moving to the district is characteristic: "he was tempted by an accidental recommendation to look at Netherfield House. He did look at it and into it for half an hour, was pleased . . . and took it immediately" (16). But when he intimates that he would leave it as quickly Darcy is severe: "When you told Mrs. Bennet this morning that if you ever resolved on quitting Netherfield you should be gone in five minutes, you meant it to be a sort of panegyric, of compliment to yourself – and yet what is there so very laudable in a precipitance which must leave very necessary business undone . . . ?" (49). Bingley's impulsive sensibility must be made to serve Darcy's cooler sense, and it is one of Darcy's faults that he takes advantage of Bingley's "ductility." Elizabeth is partly justified in her impatience at "that want of proper resolution which now made him the slave of his designing friends" (133). Even Darcy becomes subject to a more skilled designer than himself, Mr. Bennet, who calculates with satisfaction that he will now not have to pay off his debt on the price of Wickham: "these violent young lovers carry everything their own way. I shall offer to pay him tomorrow; he will rant and storm about his love for you, and there will be an end of the matter" (377).

"Every impulse of feeling should be guided by reason" (32). In *Sense and Sensibility* such a sentiment might have proceeded from the narrator, but in *Pride and Prejudice* it is put into the mouth of Mary Bennet, that specialist in "thread-bare morality" (60). Mary is another of the characters who remind us how the moral climate has changed since the previous novel. Here the danger is not that the impulse of feeling may elude the guidance of reason, or at least by some mental activity that would claim the name. Mary, "who . . . in consequence of being the only plain one in the family, worked hard for knowledge and accomplishments" (25), is a salient example of one who so subordinates her feelings to her mind that the feelings have atrophied, and she is Jane Austen's version of those women that D.H. Lawrence was appalled by, all head and no body. By the time we hear her drawing a "useful lesson" about the irretrievability of female virtue from the moral disgrace of her youngest sister, we, like Elizabeth, have ceased to be amused (289). But although Mary is a caricature, we need to remember that she, like Elizabeth, is clearly her father's daughter.

Mr. Bennet is Jane Austen's Walter Shandy, a man with a set of hobby-horses, mental constructs that he has substituted for the reality that surrounds him. His feelings are seldom described, but his mental operations have the force of passions. His attitude is carefully accounted for. We are to suppose that since his emotional life has been a disaster, he has retreated to a cerebral irony, whereby all the troubles and disappointments of life are to be viewed as mere amusements. His "conjugal felicity," by the time we know the Bennets, has been reduced to the kind of satisfaction we see him deriving from his verbal barbs at his wife's expense in the first scene.

> To his wife he was very little otherwise indebted, than as her ignorance and folly had contributed to his amusement. This is not the sort of happiness which a man would in general wish to owe to his wife; but where other powers of entertainment are wanting, the true philosopher will derive benefit from such as are given. (236)

Like Walter, another "true philosopher," he can even contemplate the death of a child with equanimity, as long as it gives him the opportunity for a *bon mot*. "Well, my dear," he tells Mrs. Bennet when the news comes that Jane is confined at Netherfield, after being sent out in the rain to dine with the Bingleys, "if your daughter should have a dangerous fit of illness, if she should die, it would be a comfort to know that it was all in pursuit of Mr. Bingley, and under your orders" (31).

He has deliberately set aside the natural preference of a father for his offspring, in favour of a clinical lack of bias: "If my children are silly I must hope to be always sensible of it," he announces coolly (29). There is a searing quality about his wit and his lack of compassion. In the face of Jane's genuine unhappiness when Bingley abandons her, he can respond only with the critical satisfaction of a spectator at a play: "Next to being married, a girl likes to be crossed in love a little now and then. It is something to think of, and gives her a sort of distinction among her companions" (137–8).

He can successfully separate his personal interest from his aesthetic appreciation of Wickham's roguery when he considers the matter of the price Wickham sets on himself as a husband for Lydia: "Wickham's a fool, if he takes her with a farthing less than ten thousand pounds. I should be sorry to think so ill of him, in the very beginning of our relationship" (304). For Mr. Bennet is a connoisseur, a spectator and a critic of the kind dear to Browning and James. "For what do we live, but to make sport for our neighbours, and laugh at them in our turn?" he asks, not expecting an answer (364). Such a question looks forward to Ralph Touchett's in *The Portrait of a Lady*: "What's the use of being ill and disabled and restricted to mere spectatorship at the game of life if I really can't see the show when I've paid so much for my ticket?" (ch. 15) Mr. Bennet's stance of intellectual detachment is sometimes exposed almost as a negation of itself, a moral idiocy. As in *Love and Freindship*, where acute sensibility to the pains of others is finally shown to be an elaborate kind of selfishness, in *Pride and Prejudice* we see Mr. Bennet's wit and acuity as a kind of obtuseness. When he tries to share a joke about the rumour of Darcy's courtship with Elizabeth, even she, his disciple, is unable to participate: "It was necessary to laugh, when she would rather have cried. Her father had most cruelly mortified her, . . . and she could do nothing but wonder at such a want of penetration" (364).

The judgement on Mr. Bennet for neglecting his responsibilities as husband and father is clear enough, but the reader is very ready to forgive him. For it is in large measure the sins of Mr. Bennet and his favourite daughter, their overweening intelligence and relish for the absurd, that make *Pride and Prejudice* such delightful reading. He in particular is our on-stage spectator and critic, articulating and sometimes creating for us our delight in the people and incidents around him. Mr. Collins in himself is a fine creation, but it is Mr. Collins as savoured and drawn out by Mr. Bennet who becomes immortal.

Elizabeth, to her lasting glory, has style, and much of her style is an inheritance from her father. "She had a lively, playful disposition," we hear at the outset, "which delighted in any thing ridiculous" (12). In fact, so far as she is one of the Quixotes in Jane Austen's novels, she behaves not so much according to the model of romance as according to the model set by her father. It is because she wants to live up to her position as his favourite daughter that she means to be clever. After she has read and absorbed Darcy's letter, and so come to know herself, she is able to recognize the exact nature of her failing.

I meant to be uncommonly clever in taking so decided dislike to him, without any reason. It is such a spur to one's genius, such an opening for wit to have a dislike of that kind. (225–6)

Spurs to one's genius and openings for wit are likely to be items coveted by a devoted daughter of Mr. Bennet. And as the process of Catherine Morland's and Emma's education involves their discarding romantic models of experience, so Elizabeth learns by gradually sloughing off the influence of her father's aesthetic detachment.

At the outset it is strong. She comes on as delighting in the ridiculous, she accepts the title of "a studier of character" (42) and announces "Follies and nonsense, whims and inconsistencies *do* divert me, I own, and I laugh at them whenever I can" (57). Like her father, she is a vehicle for much of the reader's appreciation in taking on the examination and elucidation of character, as she does of Bingley's and Darcy's during her stay at Netherfield. She also becomes the critic and exponent of her own character (not always a reliable one), and the traits she chooses to emphasise bear perhaps more relation to a model derived from her father than to the truth. "I always delight in overthrowing . . . schemes, and cheating a person of their premeditated contempt," she tells Darcy when she expects him to despise her taste (52). It is the same delight manifested by Mr. Bennet when he refuses to call on Bingley, and subsequently visits him on the sly. To be whimsical and unpredictable is his mode also. And in her as in her father we see that interpenetration of emotional with intellectual response, so that mental operations have the force of strong feeling. "You take delight in vexing me," Mrs. Bennet accuses her husband, with unusual perspicacity (5). Similarly Elizabeth is glad to be "restored . . . to the enjoyment of all her original dislike" towards the Bingley sisters (35). By a characteristic process, her emotion becomes subordinate to her consciousness of the emotion.

Elizabeth takes pains to live up to her father and share his attitudes. When Mr. Bennet is joking about Jane's being jilted, Elizabeth enters into the spirit of his irony: at his suggestion that Wickham "would jilt you creditably," she replies, "Thank you, Sir, but a less agreeable man would satisfy me. We must not all expect Jane's good fortune" (138). She takes up his proposition in her letter to her aunt, in which she humorously announces that Wickham *has* jilted her; but here she is able to make a sensible qualification:

> I am now convinced, my dear aunt, that I have never been much in love; for had I really experienced that pure and elevating passion, I should at present detest his very name, and wish him all manner of evil. By my feelings are not only cordial towards *him*; they are even impartial towards Miss King. . . . There can be no love in all this. My watchfulness has been effectual; and though I should certainly be a more interesting object to all my acquaintance, were I distractedly in love with him, I cannot say that I regret my comparative insignificance. Importance may sometimes be purchased too dearly. (150)

The passage shows her propensity to snatch up an emotional subject and cunningly encase it in an intellectual web. She had been enough in love with Wickham, at one time, to have "her head full of him" (not her heart, we notice). But such emotion as she has felt is successfully analysed an dissected, and proves to have been little more than an idea, a mere opinion. Now like her father she can mock love by her parodic terminology – "that pure and elevating passion," "distractedly in love" – and presently her desertion by Wickham is imagined as a spectacle for others, wherein she is to figure as the "interesting object." However, her mental health is such that she will not be seduced by this attraction, and she sensibly concludes "Importance may sometimes be purchased too dearly." Though she was ready to participate in her father's savouring of the aesthetic pleasure in the spectacle of the jilted lady, she will not surrender her happiness in order to have the satisfaction of providing the spectacle. This is comedy, after all, and a light, bright and sparkling one at that.

Elizabeth's misjudgement of the relative merits of Darcy and Wickham is in large measure a result of her aesthetic stance. Darcy offends her by saying she is not handsome enough to tempt him; Wickham wins her allegiance by telling her a story. His version of his youth and blighted prospects has the verbal embellishment of romantic fiction:

> His estate there is a noble one. . . . I verily believe I could forgive him any thing and every thing, rather than his disappointing the hopes and disgracing the memory of his father. . . . I have been a disappointed man, and my spirits will not bear solitude. (77–9)

The satisfying fiction, along with Wickham's professional delivery, charms Elizabeth, and she believes it because she wants to. As her father takes life to be a spectacle, Elizabeth will accept a fiction as life. She leaves Wickham with her head full of him, and insists "there was truth in his looks" (86). Subsequently she is to elaborate on his story, and construct from it her own version of the fable of the virtuous and idle apprentices.

After Darcy's letter Elizabeth cannot be in concert with her father. The education about the errors of prejudice and first impressions goes with a discarding of attitudes she had imbibed from him. Some readers have seen this moral awakening as a disappointing taming of a vivacious heroine. But it is a necessary part of her detaching herself from her father and becoming her own person. Now she urges the unsuitability of Lydia's going to Brighton, and is exasperated by Mr. Bennet's irresponsible detachment. Though she "had never been blind to the impropriety of her father's behaviour as a husband," we hear it is only now that her judgement overcomes her partiality and loyalty: "she had never felt so strongly as now, the disadvantages which must attend the children of so unsuitable a marriage, nor ever been so fully aware of the evils arising from so ill-judged a direction of talents" (236–7). The failure in sympathy between father and daughter persists until the final fortunate culmination. He becomes the painful reminder of her own follies by continuing to assume her "pointed dislike" of Darcy, and by his revival of her prejudice: "We all know him to be a proud, unpleasant sort of man," he says of the man she proposes to marry (376).

Of course it is not only Mr. Bennet who is to blame for his daughter's misguided following in his footsteps. Elizabeth is responsible, and very clearly elects her own path. There is an emphasis not just on her mistakes, but on her wilful choice of them. If she goes astray, she does so very consciously, even though she is unaware of the full extent of her wandering. In discussing Jane's behaviour with Charlotte, Elizabeth insists that Jane, unlike the husband-hunting girl that Charlotte posits, has no "plan," "she is not acting by design" (22). It is one more of the points of contrast between the sisters by which Jane Austen defines Elizabeth's character; for Elizabeth by contrast *is* acting by design, though to an extent she does not herself recognize. "Design" is another word that recurs in the novel with pointed frequency, and is often connected with the pattern of planned matches. Mr. Bennet asks if marrying one of the Bennet girls is Bingley's "design in settling here" (4). Wickham pursues Georgiana Darcy to Ramsgate, "undoubtedly by design" (202). Mr. Collins admits during his proposal that he came to Hertfordshire "with the design of selecting a wife" (105), and congratulates himself after his marriage that he and his wife "seem to have been designed for each other" (216). Except in the case of Jane, Elizabeth is prone to attribute "design" to others – she sees through Miss Bingley's "designs" on Darcy (170), and considers Bingley the slave of his "designing friends" (133). Less clear-sightedly, she angrily accuses Darcy of proposing to her "with so evident a design of offending and insulting me" (190). But she often accuses others of faults she does not recognize in herself.

If Elizabeth acts by "design," the word connotes not just a preconceived plan of action, but an aesthetic structure. Her style is I think in some senses a design, a deliberately adopted set of responses by

which she projects herself among her acquaintance. Her wit and vivac-
ity are no doubt innate, but the manifestation of them again shows
that discontinuity between stimulus and reaction that signals a chosen image. Her style, delightful though it is, is in some senses *other*
than herself, and it is the artificially adopted part of her style that she
has ultimately to recognize as extraneous and to discard. When she
discovers the extent to which she has been "blind, partial, prejudiced,
absurd," she connects the discovery with the self-image she has created: "I, who have prided myself on my discernment! – I, who have
valued myself on my abilities! who have often disdained the generous candour of my sister, and gratified my vanity, in useless or blame-
able distrust" (208). We judge her, and she judges herself, not only
for her "prepossession and ignorance," but because, as she says, she
has *courted* prepossession and ignorance (208), as she has *encouraged*
prejudices (226), and been *determined* to hate Darcy (90).

It is Darcy, in fact, who is most clear-sighted about the artificial
aspect of Elizabeth's style. In the playful discussion between them at
Netherfield when they spar on the subject of each other's characters,
Darcy develops within the comic context of the fatal flaw, a kind of
comic hamartia that is this novel's version of Hamlet's "vicious mole
of nature":

> "There is, I believe, in every disposition a tendency to some par-
> ticular evil, a natural defect, which not even the best education can
> overcome."
> "And *your* defect is a propensity to hate every body."
> "And yours," he replied with a smile, "is wilfully to misunder-
> stand them." (58)

Darcy has hit off her flaw quite accurately, and shows himself in this
case to be a more effective studier of character than Elizabeth the specialist. It is the wilful elements in Elizabeth's misunderstandings that
are most clearly judged, morally speaking – as they are most enjoy-
ably savoured, aesthetically speaking. Darcy is appreciative of her
style, and attracted by it, even while recognizing some of its manifestations as mere verbal play that by no means conveys reality. When
Elizabeth hears his final self-reproaches, and offers the confident
advice, "You must learn some of my philosophy. Think only of the
past as its remembrance gives you pleasure," Darcy again recognizes
a front, and staunchly argues, "I cannot give you credit for any philosophy of the kind" (369). He is right, of course – that philosophy is

being preached by one who not long before was taking a solitary walk in order to "indulge in all the delight of unpleasant recollections" (212). He again shows his perspicacity about her adopted style at Rosings, where he tells her, "I have had the pleasure of your acquaintance long enough to know, that you find great enjoyment in occasionally professing opinions which in fact are not your own" (174). In context we hear that "Elizabeth laughed heartily at this picture of herself"; but in fact her "opinions," the strength of which is part of her attraction, take a hard beating in the course of the novel. They come back, as an appropriate nemesis, to haunt her after she has, as she thinks, safely buried them. After her engagement, when Jane reminds her how she dislikes Darcy, Elizabeth breezily dismisses the proposition; "*That* is all to be forgot. . . . This is the last time I shall ever remember it myself" (373). But her father reminds her, when she asks for his consent to the marriage, that she had "always hated him." "How earnestly did she then wish that her former opinions had been more reasonable, her expressions more moderate!" (376). She at last wryly admits to Darcy "we have both reason to think my opinions not entirely unalterable" (368).

It is part of the pattern of the novel that Elizabeth, the studier of character, the clever girl who prides herself on her discernment, should constantly and surprisingly emerge as less astute than the relative dullards who surround her. Such is her wit and charm that the reader nearly always takes her side against others; but we are to recognize too that she is guilty of the faults of which she accuses them. When Jane hesitatingly suggests "one does not know what to think" about Wickham's wrongs at Darcy's hand, Elizabeth patronizingly contradicts her, "I beg your pardon; – one knows exactly what to think" (86). Such confidence is Elizabeth's comic hubris, as her tendency wilfully to misunderstand is her comic hamartia. Recurrently, the fools and clowns who surround her show up the failings she thought fell to their share alone. Mr. Collins is absurd when he asserts that young ladies always refuse a proposal at the first asking, but in the event Elizabeth is what she assures him she is not – "one of those young ladies (if such young ladies there are) who are so daring as to risk their happiness on the chance of being asked a second time" (107). Her sharp prejudice against Darcy and decided preference for Wickham, attitudes she takes such pride in as spurs to her genius, are enlarged and parodied in the collective attitudes of that least astute of communities, Meryton, whose gossipy views go through just such an evolution as Elizabeth's: after Wickham's elopement with Lydia,

"All Meryton seemed striving to blacken the man, who, but three months before, had been almost an angel of light" (294). Gossip is to Meryton what the more elaborate fictions she chooses to believe in are to Elizabeth. Even Mrs. Bennet, the mother whom Elizabeth and most other people would least like to resemble, is recognizable not as a contrast to but as a caricature of Elizabeth. The reformed Elizabeth is pained that her mother keeps calling the man she loves "that disagreeable Mr. Darcy" (her own epithet), and she is faintly ashamed of Mrs. Bennet's *volte face* after his proposal: "Such a charming man! – so handsome! so tall! – Oh, my dear Lizzy! pray apologise for my having disliked him so much before. I hope he will overlook it" (378). Both the dislike and its reversal are expressed in terms characteristic of Mrs. Bennet, but their substance is reminiscent of the reversal of Elizabeth's own feelings. We may even see in Mrs. Bennet's propensity to "fanc[y] herself nervous" (5) an exercise of the fictive imagination that is parallel to Elizabeth's meaning to be clever.

We are recurrently shown that, while the best-laid plans of such people as Elizabeth and Darcy are apt to go agley, they may be rescued from the dilemmas that their designs land them in by random or ill-intentioned actions of others. It is Lydia's thoughtless letting slip the fact of Darcy's presence at her wedding that leads to Elizabeth's finding out Darcy's part in the transaction, and so her determination to thank him, and so his proposal. It is Lady Catherine's ill-judged expedition to frighten Elizabeth out of marrying Darcy that extracts her avowal that she wouldn't refuse him, and hence Darcy's renewed hope, and hence his renewed offer. The two of them, conscious of dangers overcome, quests achieved, and an approaching ending that will allow them to live happily ever after, playfully discuss this matter of the outcome's moral consonance with the action. "What becomes of the moral?" speculates Elizabeth. "The moral will be perfectly fair," Darcy cheerfully reassures her (381).

In the last chapter of *Northanger Abbey* the narrator draws attention to "the tell-tale compression of the pages," the signal "that we are all hastening together to perfect felicity," and speculates about the moral, "whether the tendency of this work be altogether to recommend parental tyranny, or reward filial disobedience" (*NA*, 250, 252). But in *Pride and Prejudice* it is appropriately the central characters themselves who playfully discourse on their own experience as a story with a moral, an aesthetic structure.

The outcome of the story is fortunate, sparkling, and if Elizabeth has had to abandon some of her stylish fictions, she has yet been allowed to retain much of her style. But in her undoubted successor in the next novel, Mary Crawford in *Mansfield Park*, we are shown in more sombre terms the consequences of the disjunction of style from principle. Elizabeth is triumphant, but we have seen her come close to disaster because of her tendency to interfere in her own responses, to subordinate feeling and the due process of judgement to a smart stylishness, and to project an image of herself that is distinct from the real self. Although her style is what attracts us and Darcy, it is also clear that in acting by design she almost comes to grief.

Notes

1. This essay was first published in *The Novel from Sterne to James: Essays on the Relation of Literature to Life*, by Juliet and Rowland McMaster (London: Macmillan, 1981), pp. 19–35.
2. The fragment *Sanditon* is likewise a satire of mental attitudes and projections. See B.C. Southam, *"Sanditon:* the Seventh Novel," in Juliet McMaster (ed.) *Jane Austen's Achievement* (London: Macmillan, 1976), 1–26.
3. See Northrop Frye, *The Anatomy of Criticism* (Princeton: Princeton University Press, 1957), pp. 309ff.
4. See especially Mark Schorer, "Pride Unprejudiced," *Kenyon Review* 18 (Winter 1956), pp. 85ff.

7

The Secret Languages of *Emma*[1]

When I teach Jane Austen, I give my students mean little reading tests, by way of training them to read for detail. There's one question that helps me make sure that my students are alert to the many layers of meaning in the characters' speech. I quote Emma speaking to Harriet: "The service he rendered you was enough to warm your heart" (342), she says. I ask my students to explain the misunderstanding that results from this speech. As we all remember, in this case Emma says one thing and Harriet hears another. Emma *says* (and here as elsewhere I offer what you might call a free translation), "The service Frank Churchill rendered you in chasing away the gipsies was enough to warm your heart." But Harriet *hears* "The service Mr. Knightley rendered you in asking you to dance was enough to warm your heart." And as we all know, this little confusion over who rendered what service is the source of great travail and sorrow. This is one simple instance of what is going on all the time throughout the novel: characteristically a speech has not one meaning, but often two, and sometimes more. And that is what makes *Emma* endlessly rereadable.

Nearly all the characters make speeches that contain a covert as well as an overt meaning. If Emma sometimes deals in the coded message, she is a mere babbling infant in comparison with Frank Churchill, who makes it his métier to load his speech with secrets that only the alerted listener or reader can understand. Mrs. Elton, who is a parody of Emma in her speech as in other ways, makes a bustle and parade of being in on a secret: "Mum! a word to the wise," she says with heavy-handed discretion, when she has heard of Jane Fairfax's engagement. "I mentioned no *names*, you will observe. . . . We do not say a word of . . . a certain young physician from Windsor. – Oh! no" (454). Even Miss Bates, gabby old Miss Bates, who can never keep a secret for the life of her, has secret communications embedded in her endless chattering. We readers, like the characters, must comb out the significant elements in all these speeches, and decode them, if we are to understand what is going on.

Jane Austen's novels, as we know, are populated largely by leisured people, people whose main business is not to go to work, or to create things, or to make money, but to get along with each other in their society. Social converse among them is not incidental, not merely the activity for a coffee break, but their main activity. *Emma* presents social intercourse – conversation – raised to an art form, a profession. The people judge each other according to how good at it they are. Their speech is not simply a transparent medium of communication, or a commodity for practical use: it is a vocation, and capable of a high degree of development and refinement. Conversation with the right interlocutor, for Emma, is like conquering a new computer program for the expert, or pumping iron for the athlete. And Emma particularly needs such workouts, because at home with her father she gets very little vigorous verbal exercise.

Speech has its different genres, as literature has. "Conversation" is not a word Jane Austen uses lightly, and not all speech qualifies. Back in *Northanger Abbey* she made the distinction about John Thorpe's discourse: "All the rest of his conversation, or rather talk, began and ended with himself and his own concerns" (*NA*, 66). "Conversation," unlike mere "talk," must go somewhere, must, through a process of verbal exchange and enlargement, refine a topic and advance it. So Emma, to improve Harriet's mind, plans "a great deal of useful reading and conversation," but finds it easier to settle for "chat" instead (69). We hear also of other genres of discourse in Highbury: the "quiet prosings" of Mr. Woodhouse's chosen companions, Mrs. Goddard and company (22); the "comfortable talk" of Mr. Woodhouse and his daughter Isabella (100); the "sighs and fine words" of the courting Mr. Elton; the "every day remarks, dull repetitions, old news, and heavy jokes" at the Coles' dinner party (219); and the more satisfactory "uninterrupted communication of all those little matters on which the daily happiness of private life depends" (117) that goes on between Emma and Mrs. Weston.

In a society that places such emphasis on the quality of verbal communication, speech habits are regarded as an essential constituent of identity. Highbury has two step-children – young people who belong to it and yet belong elsewhere too – Frank Churchill and Jane Fairfax. And in the talk and speculation on what these relative strangers are like the issue swiftly becomes one of how they speak. What sort of young man will Frank Churchill be? Either "conversible," or "a chattering coxcomb," assumes Mr. Knightley. "My idea of him," says Emma, "is, that he can adapt his conversation to the taste of every body" (150). If so, then he will be "a puppy," argues Mr. Knightley jealously (150). They disagree on this, but not on the proposition that speech maketh man. Similarly, the issue with Jane Fairfax is not whether she is good, or beautiful, or talented, but whether she talks enough. Jane Fairfax is "reserved" – "disgustingly, . . . suspiciously reserved," as Emma thinks (169). Speech is the articulation of the self, and nearly all of the self that surrounding characters can perceive. It follows that a highly reserved person is incompletely present, and so cannot inspire strong feeling. "One cannot love a reserved person," declares Frank Churchill of Jane – disingenuously of course (203). But Emma shrewdly introduces a qualification: "Not till the reserve ceases towards oneself; and then the attraction may be the greater" (203). It is one of the comments that must have made Frank Churchill suspect that Emma was on to him and his secret love. Estimation of character must be largely determined by the quality and quantity of what the character says.

The discerning people of Highbury have high standards in speech, and become expert critics of each other's discourse. Emma perceives Miss Bates's talk as a genre so characteristic that she can even parody it. She imagines Mr. Knightley married to Jane Fairfax, and being thanked all day long for it:

> "'So very kind and obliging! – but he always had been such a very kind neighbour!' And then fly off, through half a sentence, to her mother's old petticoat. 'Not that it was such a very old petticoat either – for still it would last a great while – and, indeed, she must thankfully say that their petticoats were all very strong.'" (225)

With her keen ear for speech, Emma can parody Mr. Elton too: "He . . . will suit Harriet exactly; it will be an 'Exactly so,' as he says himself" (49). Nor does *Mrs.* Elton escape, "with her Mr. E., and her *caro sposo*" (279). Parody implies an intimate knowledge of the work parodied, and Emma has become an expert mimic and critic. Mr. Knightley, too, has a good ear; and one of the absorbing scenes of the end of the novel consists of his reading Frank Churchill's long letter of explanation; and delivering a three-page lecture in practical criticism on it (444–8). The discriminating members of Highbury society have a virtually professional expertise in each other's language.

Their expertise in language manifests itself in the word games they play. They take language apart, and put it together again. Mr. Elton's charade separates the syllables of *courtship,* and then rejoins them in order to deliver his secret message. Mr. Weston's conundrum, his "one thing very clever" in the game at Box Hill, is his reduction of Emma's name to the two letters M and A, to convey the compliment that she is "perfection" (370–1). In the game of alphabet, properly played by children, but taken over by sophisticated adults for their own devious purposes, the words *blunder* and *Dixon* are disassembled to their component letters and then reconstructed in order to convey a "covert meaning" (349). Here I want to play a similar game. I shall be taking apart some of the characters' speeches, their secret languages, and putting them together again in order to illuminate their covert meaning.

I'll start with Emma's speech – and that should please her, because she loves to be first. Emma, we know, is an "imaginist" (335). She constructs narratives about the people she knows, and she takes steps to make them live her stories. She constantly interprets reality, so as to make it conform to her constructed version of it. In the realm of language, this activity takes the form of over-interpreting other people's speech. She often assumes an innuendo, a secret message, that isn't there; and while she is assuming a non-existent secret message, she is likely to miss the one that *is* there.

I make the excuse for Emma that if she is addicted to covert meanings in what she says, and especially in what she hears, it is partly because she has been starved at home for complex discourse. With all her talent for conversation and ingenious speculation, she is stuck with Mr. Woodhouse. "Conversation," in the exacting sense of the word that implies advancing a subject by a verbal exchange between speakers, is beyond him. On their first evening alone together after the departure of Miss Taylor, and in spite of Emma's bracing words of consolation, "when tea came it was impossible for him not to say exactly as he had said at dinner, 'Poor Miss Taylor!'" (8). If he is sedentary in his life, he is even more so in his speech, which characteristically goes nowhere. When it snows at the Randalls dinner party, "'What is to be done, my dear Emma? – what is to be done?' was Mr. Woodhouse's first exclamation; and all that he could say for some time" (126). He is like a record stuck in a groove.

Emma's other talking companion, Harriet, is not much better. "If Harriet's praise could have satisfied her, she might soon have been comforted," we hear (231). But Harriet exemplifies the principle that words of praise or agreement from the undiscriminating are completely devalued. In Highbury there are a number of yea-sayers who are willing to suppress their own identities in order to get along with people; and it avails them very little. "To be sure. Yes" is Harriet's formula for agreement, used three times on two pages (30–1); Mr. Elton says "Exactly so" (42, 44, 48); Isabella Knightley says "Very true, my love" (113). And small thanks they get for their agreeableness, any of them. For genuine conversation, for a verbal tennis match of Wimbledon quality, the kind of opposition that raises the quality of the game, Emma needs more seeded players. Emma is starved for lack of competent verbal opposition. That is one reason Mr. Knightley is so valuable to her.

Being so overqualified in her exchanges with Harriet, Emma varies the game by trying some virtuoso tactics. She drops direct and explicit speech, and moves into a layered discourse that does two things at once. When she proceeds to detach Harriet from Robert Martin, she doesn't talk directly and say "Robert Martin isn't good enough for you." Instead she pretends to assume Harriet knows this already. She says, "When Mr. Martin marries, I wish you may not be drawn in . . . to be acquainted with the wife, who will probably be some mere farmer's daughter, without education" (31). Emma has a secret agenda, and she disguises it; and Harriet can't argue on these mysterious grounds. When Robert Martin's proposal arrives, Emma tries to dictate the answer without *appearing* to do so. "*You* need not be prompted to write with the appearance of sorrow for his disappointment," she says disingenuously. Harriet, who isn't very good at following this verbal double-dealing, tactlessly translates: "You think I ought to refuse him, then" (52). *Dumb* Harriet! To put in direct terms just the instruction that Emma claims she is scrupulously *not* giving! Here we see Emma at her worst, using a language of implication to lie with. "Not for the world . . . would I advise you either way," she says loftily (53). *Liar!*

Emma gets more practice in developing levels of meaning in her speech with Mr. Elton, when he comes courting. He absurdly overdoes his language of implication: "There was a sort of parade in his speeches which was very apt to incline her to laugh," we hear (82). His over-emphasis is one reason she cannot see *herself* as "a principal" in the courtship (49). But she takes up this discourse of indirection with a certain zest, proud of being, as she thinks, an adept at it. The language of courtship in this society must be guarded, oblique, particularly in its early stages. The man must send out signals without absolutely committing himself. If the woman returns the signals, he has received "encouragement," and can proceed accordingly. If she doesn't, he can withdraw without loss of face, because there has been no direct declaration. Mr. Elton takes pains to send all the right signals. A lover, according to the code, must admire his ladylove in all she does. Mr. Elton is quite ready to do this, or at least to *say* he does. Emma's current enterprise is to improve Harriet. Mr. Elton is ready with the praise.

> "You have given Miss Smith all that she required," said he; "You have made her graceful and easy. She was a beautiful creature when she came to you, but . . . the attractions you have added are infinitely superior to what she received from nature. . . . Skilful has been the hand." (42–3)

Poor chap, he could hardly lay it on any thicker. But even though Emma recognizes the code very well, she misreads its terms. Elton emphasizes the "you" in his praise; but the emphasis that she hears is on "she." Both are so intent on the code they are *speaking* that they don't pay proper attention to the code they are hearing. Emma entirely mistranslates Mr. Elton's secret language. But so does he hers.

One last attempt he makes to interpret Emma's signals the way he wants to understand them. In the carriage coming back from Randalls on that snowy night, he seizes his opportunity and gabbles his proposal. Emma is silent with chagrin. "Allow me to interpret this interesting silence [he continues]. It confesses that you have long understood me" (131). By the time people take on interpreting each other's silences, we are fully aware that the secret languages are being over-translated.

Interpreting silence is an occupation that Emma takes up in her relation with Jane Fairfax. Jane is so "reserved," so cagey and noncommittal in all her pronouncements, that Emma comes to assume she has something to conceal: and of course she is quite right. Jane is *most* reserved, Emma finds, "on the subject of Weymouth and the Dixons" (169). This is a shrewd discovery. But Emma picks up on the wrong element of the package, the Dixons rather than Weymouth: "[Jane] seemed bent on giving no real insight into Mr. Dixon's character, or her own value for his company. . . . It did her no service however. Her caution was thrown away. Emma saw its artifice, and returned to her first surmises" (169). She too proceeds to interpret the interesting silences, hearing a secret language. But again it is the *wrong* secret language.

Where Jane Fairfax, having a secret to conceal, takes refuge in silence and reserve, Frank Churchill specializes in a display of openness that is really an elaborate disguise. And all this is enacted in his speech. His name, "Frank," is his first disguise. Though Jane Austen uses the adjective "frank," in the familiar sense of open and candid, in her earlier work,[2] in *Emma* the only "Frank" that appears is the name.[3] Frank's name is an epitome of himself and his language. At first he seems frank and open to both the reader and the surrounding characters. As we learn more we discover he has not been "frank" at all, but has practised an elaborate and deliberate deceit. But finally, when we have followed his language through to the end, we discover that his ultimate pronouncement is truthful, and "Frank" is not a misnomer after all. To follow through this process we need to peel off his secret languages, layer by layer, from his direct speech.

Frank is important to Emma in providing her with the witty and freighted conversation that she has so notably lacked in her communications with her father and Harriet. In dealing with Mr. Elton she was getting into training for following through the intricacies of a language of implication. In her relation with Frank Churchill she sees a virtuoso at work, someone who skilfully manages a multi-layered discourse, which includes different secret languages for different hearers, and who rejoices in his facility as well. His first move is to disarm suspicion by discreet praise. He doesn't plaster people with flattery, as Lucy Steele does in *Sense and Sensibility*; he's more subtle than that. For instance, he wins over Mrs. Weston by praising Emma. And likewise he wins over Emma by praising Mrs. Weston, with a flattering insinuation that Emma can take credit for the virtues of her governess. "He got as near as he could to thanking her for Miss Taylor's merits" (192). Emma needs no "additional proof of his knowing how to please" (191). He is a master of the art of informed compliment.

Just as he uses this art to disarm and blind Emma, he uses gentle abuse as another front. He quickly picks up the fact that Jane Fairfax's reserve has made Emma suspicious. When Emma asks how well he knew Jane at Weymouth, he hedges, and Emma exclaims, "Upon my word! you answer as discreetly as she could do herself" (200). Thereafter he proceeds to live up to his name, "Frank." Or at least to *appear* to. As he has discreetly praised, now he discreetly blames. He abuses Jane's pale complexion, her outré hairdo, her languid dancing. He says Jane looks "Ill, very ill – that is, if a young lady can ever be allowed to look ill. . . . – A most deplorable want of complexion" (199). While Emma staunchly defends Jane's complexion, she is, of course, quite pleased to hear some deviation from Mr. Knightley's uniform praise of her; and, feeling privileged and preferred, she is completely fooled. (Much later, when Frank is rhapsodizing over his fiancée's complexion, Emma reminds him of those comments, and he laughs gleefully: "What an impudent dog I was!" [478]. He enjoyed his successful deception.)

Frank doesn't tell outright lies. His preferred mode is to speak a speech that in context deceives, but is in fact technically true. Remember the dinner at the Coles, for instance. The intriguing news is spreading that Jane Fairfax has just received a piano from a mystery donor. Emma proceeds to speculate about it with Frank. Being the mystery donor himself, he is naturally nervous, but outwardly cool. "Why do you smile?" she asks him. "Nay, why do you?" he responds cagily. He is determined to follow, not to lead.

"You may *say* what you chuse [she persists] – but your countenance testifies that your *thoughts* on this subject are very much like mine."

Frank must be in a sweat. No wonder he thinks she is on to him. But he covers himself cautiously:

"I rather believe you are giving me more credit for acuteness than I deserve. I smile because you smile, and shall probably suspect whatever I find you suspect." (216)

Such delightful deference to her deductive powers is irresistible to Emma, and presently she spills the beans about her suspicions on Mr. Dixon. Frank – as one imagines, with a sigh of relief – can enjoy his immunity from suspicion. And he delightedly acquiesces, pretending to be utterly convinced:

"Now I can see [the piano] in no other light than as an offering of love."

There was no occasion [for Emma] to push the matter further. The conviction seemed real; he looked as if he felt it. (219)

As we know and he knows, the piano *is* an offering of love. Frank Churchill is "Frank" after all, although Emma is still completely deceived. He has managed to come full circle through deception to literal truth: and he clearly rejoices in the fancy verbal footwork involved.

Now I would like to consider the piano scene at the Bateses for a moment, because it furnishes Frank with his best opportunity for the spectacular display of his virtuoso's talent in secret languages. The scene follows on one of the most passionate *unwritten* scenes in Jane Austen. It is the morning after the Coles' party. Miss Bates and Mrs. Weston – "one voice and two ladies"! (235) – have walked into the street to persuade Emma and Harriet to come and hear the piano. Meanwhile, back at the Bateses, as we deduce, Frank is having his first moments alone, or almost alone, with Jane since he gave her the piano. The piano was a Valentine's gift, remember: it arrived on February 14.[4] He has told her the gift was from him. Her feelings must be tumultuous, if conflicting. Frank – dare we guess it? – has kissed her. In any case, we have enough evidence that on the re-entry of the company the two have sprung guiltily apart. Old Mrs. Bates, most accommodating of chaperones, is peacefully "slumbering"; Frank is "most deedily occupied" in mending her spectacles (a fine cover-up). And Jane, who is not nearly so good as Frank at concealing her feelings or her guilt, is "standing with her back to them, intent on her pianoforté" (240) – or so Emma mistakenly supposes. Even Emma can see that Jane is deeply disturbed. She can't yet play the piano: "she had not yet possessed the instrument long enough to touch it without emotion," Emma explains to herself (240). Whatever went on between Frank and Jane in their precious private moments together, Jane is still vibrating.

In this *tense* situation, Frank Churchill has enough to do. Deeply in love, he must carry on his love scene with Jane, though covertly. Deeply intriguing, he must carry on his speculation with Emma, also covertly. And as for the company at large, he must divert suspicion. This is what he says of the Irish melodies that have been sent along with the instrument:

> "Very thoughtful of Col. Campbell, was not it? – He knew Miss Fairfax could have no music here. I honour that part of the attention particularly; it shews it to have been so thoroughly from the heart. Nothing hastily done; nothing incomplete. True affection only could have prompted it." (242)

One needs to be an interpreter of truly United Nations quality to translate these secret languages. But let me try. To Jane Frank says, "Jane, I gave you the piano and the music that goes with it because I love you, and I think about you all the time." To Emma he says, "Watch me embarrass Jane Fairfax by talking pointedly about Colonel Campbell as the donor, when she knows, as you and I know, that it was Dixon's guilty love that prompted the gift." And for the company at large, he simply confirms the proper assumption that the gift was from avuncular Colonel Campbell.

We know that the two girls, at least, receive the secret messages:

> Emma wished he would be less pointed, yet could not help being amused; and . . . on glancing her eye towards Jane Fairfax she caught . . . with all the deep blush of consciousness . . . a smile of secret delight. (243)

Clearly Frank has managed his secret transmissions very successfully.

Though Jane understands Frank's secret language very well, she doesn't use such codes herself; or at least not usually. Her covert communications are the involuntary ones, the reliable body language of blushes and secret smiles, rather than deliberate and verbal. But at Box Hill she finds her covert tongue, and delivers the coded message as skilfully as Frank. He has been carrying on – in code – their lovers' quarrel of the day before. Apparently à propos of the Eltons, but for her ears meaning himself, he says "How many a man has committed himself on a short acquaintance, and rued it all the rest of his life!" (372). In other words, he wants out of the engagement. "Such things do occur, undoubtedly," she begins. But "she was stopped by a cough" (373). Don't miss that cough! Her body is declaring her again. Jane Fairfax, cold fish though Emma has always thought her, is fighting back her tears. When she has "recovered her voice," she resolutely delivers her secret message to Frank: "it can be only weak, irresolute characters . . . who will suffer an unfortunate acquaintance to be an inconvenience, an oppression for ever" (373). In other words, "Get lost, Frank!"

Emma has been listening avidly to this exchange. And what does she hear? Another language altogether. Frank's apparently light-hearted undertaking, "I shall go abroad for a couple of years – and when I return, I shall come to you for my wife," is really intended for Jane. Bitterly disappointed in love, he signals, he will take to European travel, like a cynical Childe Harold. But Emma has her own translation: "Would not Harriet be the very creature described? . . . He might even have Harriet in his thoughts at the moment" (373).

In her converse with Elton and Frank Emma has learned about secret languages, different levels of meaning, and she thinks she has become adept at separating the layers. She applies her skill to Mr. Knightley's speech. But Mr. Knightley is not a good subject for the exercise.

So far as is possible with such a volatile medium as language, and among beings as complicated as Austen's characters, Mr. Knightley says what he means and means what he says, with no overplus of innuendo and no shortfall of concealment. He is like his own estate, Donwell Abbey, which "was just what it ought to be, and looked what it was" (358). Emma knows this of him, and his reliability in language is from the first a reason for her lasting trust and respect for him. She describes to Harriet his "downright, decided, commanding sort of manner" (34). She notes and appreciates the contrast between her father's elaborate and ceremonial courtesies and Mr. Knightley's "short, decided answers" (57). When Mrs. Weston suggests that *he* might have given the piano to Jane Fairfax, Emma is confident and accurate in rejecting the suggestion. "Mr. Knightley does nothing mysteriously," she declares (226). And she is right.

Occasionally we see the two of them acting together as a team, and using language effectively in a crisis. For instance: Mr. Woodhouse, on his single excursion from home, faces a snowfall, and becomes almost catatonic:

> While the others were variously urging and recommending, Mr. Knightley and Emma settled in it a few brief sentences: thus –
> "Your father will not be easy; why do not you go?"
> "I am ready, if the others are."
> "Shall I ring the bell?"
> "Yes, do."
> And the bell was rung, and the carriages spoken for. (128)

Language may be put to other and more glorious uses; but unless it works at this simple level of usefulness, it is unlikely to be effective for more complex and decorative purposes. This little scene, which puts the two principal characters in a relation through their "few brief sentences," as they cope with a situation involving a third, shows them as essentially compatible partners. It is like the scene on the Cobb in *Persuasion*, where Anne's prompt thinking and speaking in a crisis reawakens Wentworth to her being the only woman he can love.

Mr. Knightley has no hidden agendas. While Emma is befuddling Harriet with unspoken assumptions about whether Robert Martin is good enough for Miss Woodhouse's friend, Mr. Knightley can be quite open and outspoken on the delicate matter of female friendship: "I do not know what your opinion may be, Mrs. Weston, . . . of this great intimacy between Emma and Harriet Smith, but I think it a bad thing" (36). No need to translate or interpret *that* speech. It says what it means and means what it says.

All this is not to say that Mr. Knightley is incapable of using language playfully or figuratively. A simple unvarying one-to-one relationship between word and referent, signifier and signified, is neither attainable nor desirable. Mr. Knightley can use humour and irony very effectively when he chooses. One of the funniest speeches in the novel, to my ear, is the one he delivers from horseback, when he is outside Miss Bates's window. It is late in the piano scene that I've discussed, after the reader has been following through Frank Churchill's devious verbal gambits and misleading compliments. Half the gentlefolk of Highbury are assembled in order to hear the new piano and discuss the dinner and dance at the Coles'. And kind gushing Miss Bates loudly calls to Mr. Knightley out of her window, so that their exchange is necessarily somewhat public.

"Oh! Mr. Knightley, what a delightful party last night; . . . Did you ever see such dancing? – Was not it delightful? – Miss Woodhouse and Mr. Frank Churchill; I never saw anything equal to it."

"Oh! very delightful indeed [he calls back]; I can say nothing less, for I suppose Miss Woodhouse and Mr. Frank Churchill are hearing every thing that passes. And (raising his voice still more) I do not see why Miss Fairfax should not be mentioned too. I think Miss Fairfax dances very well; and Mrs. Weston is the very best country-dance player, without exception, in England. Now, if your friends have any gratitude, they will say something pretty loud about you and me in return; but I cannot stay to hear it." (245)

In this awkward situation, in which most people would be thoroughly embarrassed, Mr. Knightley manages to pick up the social and complimentary mode of Miss Bates and Frank Churchill, parody it effectively, hand out further praise where it is due, relieve his feelings on the Emma–Frank pairing, and bow out while the last word is his; and all without giving offence.

As the novel amply demonstrates, "Seldom, very seldom, does complete truth belong to any human disclosure" (431). Even Mr. Knightley can't be clear and direct in all he says. No subject is so apt to cloud and distort communications as love. People expect and assume secrecy and indirection in the expression of love. But even on that subject Mr. Knightley tries to be clear and exact. Mrs. Weston suspects him of being in love with Jane Fairfax. Instead of asking him outright if this is the case, she discusses the matter with Emma, and so the suspicion grows. They listen to him for clues to this attachment, exchange glances, nudge and nod. Mrs. Weston presses Emma's foot, Emma "returned her friend's pressure with interest" (287). And all the while Mr. Knightley is trying his best to tell the exact truth. "I know how highly you think of Jane Fairfax," Emma says, guilefully leading him on, because "little Henry was in her thoughts." "Yes," he says, "any body may know how highly I think of her" – disarming all speculation, one would suppose. But Emma, not satisfied, wants "to know the worst at once," and suggests he may admire Jane more than he knows himself. This is as far as she can go in plain speaking. But he can go further, and does so, promptly. He is concerned to put an end to such hinting and speculation. "Miss Fairfax, I dare say, would not have me if I were to ask her – and I am very sure I shall never ask her" (287). This, surely, should be clear enough. But Mrs. Weston is still not satisfied. Some people won't be convinced, even by the most direct and declarative language.

Mr. Knightley is of course more reticent about whom he *does* love. Emma, at least, is surprised when she finds out. And yet he has been disarmingly frank about this too. In a very early scene he agrees with Mrs. Weston about Emma's beauty, and avows without disguise, "I love to look at her" (39). As for her personality, he also declares, "I love an open temper" (289). But in the subject of love, frankness puts all the interpreters off the scent.

For in spite of his openness, his steady pursuit of the principle of saying what he means and eschewing disguise, Emma misreads Mr. Knightley, and most crucially in the matter of his love for herself. (It is her saving touch of humility that she does not see it.) She misreads him because she over-interprets. All her training with the Eltons and the Frank Churchills of her world have made her too avid an interpreter, so alert to secret languages that she can't hear the direct and overt language. And this fault in her, her tendency to over-interpret, comes very close to ruining her happiness.

I spent some time on the piano scene in considering Frank Churchill's language, and Emma's powers of interpretation. Now I'd like to focus on the proposal scene as the example for Mr. Knightley's and Emma's language, and their mutual powers of interpretation.

You will remember that when Emma and Mr. Knightley get together in the shrubbery on that turbulent day, with the summertime reasserting itself after the "cold stormy rain" (421), he thinks *she* is in love with Frank Churchill, and she thinks *he* is in love with Harriet. Hardly a propitious context for a proposal from one to the other. Mr. Knightley, insecure and depressed, does some over-interpreting of his own. As they discuss Frank's engagement to Jane, Emma, painfully aware how she has exposed herself and misled Harriet, confesses, "I seem to have been doomed to blindness" (425). But the secret language that Mr. Knightley *hears* may be translated, "I fell in love with him, not knowing he was engaged." "Abominable scoundrel!" Mr. Knightley explodes (426). He is fierce against Frank, tender towards Emma, inarticulate in his syntax, but clear in his body language: he takes her arm and presses it.

For all his explosive and disconnected syntax, however, we hear "Emma understood him" (426). And presently, speaking as clearly and directly as she can, she has set his mind at rest about her feelings for Frank. She cannot be *completely* clear, however. This is what she says:

> "No one, I am sure, could be more effectually blinded [by Frank Churchill's behaviour] than myself – except that I was *not* blinded – that it was my good fortune – that, in short, I was somehow or other safe from him." (427)

Her stumbling sentence structure signals a secret, which the reader can translate though Mr. Knightley can't. "In short, I was safe from him because I was already in love with you," she reveals involuntarily, though *he* can't yet understand as we can. "Prepossession" is almost a woman's only defence from a confident man's persistent courtship – as with Fanny Price and Henry Crawford.

Once Mr. Knightley is enlightened as to Emma's being heartwhole – at least so far as Frank is concerned – there is no obstacle to his own declaration, and he at once moves in that direction. But this is where *Emma*'s over-interpretation almost ruins everything. Mr. Knightley says he envies Frank Churchill. That puts the ball in her court. Emma *ought* to say, "Oh? In what way do you envy him?" – and then he could proceed with his declaration. But Emma has already projected that he is about to blurt out, "Emma, I'm in love with Harriet! I've told John and Isabella about it, and they're furious. What shall I do?" (Not that Mr. Knightley would ever be guilty of such hackneyed language; but Emma and I are doing our translation in advance!) When Mr. Knightley persists, and says, "I must tell what you will not ask," Emma is sure he is "within half a sentence of Harriet," and eagerly cries, "Oh! then, don't speak it, don't speak it!" (429).

"Oh, Emma!" we feel like shouting at her, "for God's sake, shut *up*, and just *listen*. *Listen* to what the man is saying, not what you *think* he's saying! He isn't talking a secret language now!"

For in fact, as we all remember, she has silenced him. She has stopped him from saying the very words she most wants and needs to hear. This to me is the most crucial moral climax in the novel. We know Mr. Knightley loves Emma. We know she loves him. But does she *deserve* him? Everything depends on her thoughts and words of the next moments. Hanging in the balance is her happiness, and Mr. Knightley's. Shall it be shipwreck, or sunny sailing in blue seas?

What does she think? Just what she ought, of course:

> Emma could not bear to give him pain. He was wishing to confide in her – perhaps to consult her; – cost her what it would, she would listen. She might assist his resolution, or reconcile him to it; she might give just praise to Harriet. (429)

Hurray, Emma, you've done it! You've just earned Mr. Knightley! In that brief piece of reflection Emma atones for all her sins of over-interpretation, and of selfishness and self-aggrandisement, all her unwarrantable manipulation of Harriet, her unkind cut at Miss Bates. We know enough of Emma's powers to be sure that she could put a spoke in the wheel of a Harriet–Knightley match, as she had prevented a Harriet–Robert Martin match. But she is not going to do that. For Mr. Knightley's sake, for Harriet's sake, she is ready to face the pain of hearing he loves Harriet, and the difficulty of encouraging him to be happy with the orphan girl of his choice. At last she is ready to listen, and to hear what he actually has to say. She is willing to make a sacrifice, and for that very reason she is saved from having to make it.

Well, we all know what happens. She bravely reopens the conversation. She hears the declaration of love she had suspended – and it is a declaration of love for *her*, not for Harriet. So she can live happily ever after. And she *earned* that happiness.

Even if all the secret languages, the multi-layered discourse of the many busily intriguing characters, had been only there as a build-up to this scene, with its zigzags of misunderstandings and misinterpretations, they would have been worth it. As it is, though, they are delightful – intriguing in the other sense – in themselves. Speech has been developed as an art form capable of immense refinement, a profession, indeed, worth devoting a lifetime to. As we watch the characters at their business of talking, sending their signals covert and overt, we as readers receive an elaborate training in complex articulation and ingenious interpretation. We also become aware, as we follow the intricacies of Frank's deceptive frankness or Emma's over-interpretation, of the dangers of *over*-reading.

Notes

1. This paper was first delivered at the annual meeting of the Jane Austen Society of North America in Ottawa, in October 1991.
2. In *Sense and Sensibility*, for instance, we hear of "an easy and frank communication of her sentiments" (127); and in *Pride and Prejudice* Lady Catherine memorably boasts, "My character has ever been celebrated for its sincerity and frankness" (*PP* 353).
3. See *A Concordance to the Works of Jane Austen*, by Peter L. DeRose and S.W. McGuire, 3 vols. (New York: Garland, 1982), under "frank."
4. Jo Modert establishes this submerged but significant date for Frank's gift of the piano in "Chronology within the Novels," in *The Jane Austen Companion*, ed. J. David Grey, A. Walton Litz and Brian Southam (New York: Macmillan, 1986), p. 57.

Part II

Love in Jane Austen's Novels
A Preface to Chapters 8–11

Note: Three of the next four essays were part of an 80-page monograph called Jane Austen on Love, *which was published in 1978 in the English Literary Monographs Series, at the University of Victoria in Canada. Although not widely distributed, that little book has done well in its way, and parts of it have been anthologized, for instance in the Modern Critical Interpretations series under the general editorship of Harold Bloom. It has been out of print for some time now, so I am glad of the chance to give it a new lease of life in this volume of my essays.*

The last essay, on the "Women in Love," is new; and its addition to the others will mark some progress in my thinking on feminist issues.

A graduate student in my course on the novel some years ago – she was better read though less guarded than many of her contemporaries – produced this critical comment after rereading the chapters on Marianne's desertion by Willoughby in *Sense and Sensibility*: "Oh, Mrs. McMaster, I just cried and cried."[1] And a male colleague of mine once admitted that he found Elizabeth Bennet more sexually stimulating than the centre-fold of *Playboy*. I cite these two not altogether academic responses to Jane Austen's work as evidence for what will be my main arguments in the following chapters: that Jane Austen, knowing satirist and beautifully controlled comic artist though she is, is far from deficient in feeling; and that, notwithstanding her spinsterhood and her vaunted determination not to stray in subject-matter beyond the limits of her own experience, she is acutely awake to sex, and quite able to convey sexual feeling even though she may not take us into bedrooms.

Her novels are centrally concerned with courtship, and their culmination is marriage: for such a novelist Charlotte Brontë's contention that "the Passions are perfectly unknown to her,"[2] and Lawrence's strictures on her as an old maid "knowing in apartness,"[3] are serious charges. Yet the charges continue to reverberate – in the comic count of the total sixteen kisses in the six novels (none of them between a man and a woman), and in the popular conception of her as a writer whose most passionate encounters are conversations at a tea party or a walk to the vicarage.[4] Even many of her admirers are ready to admit that though she is a great novelist, it is not to Jane Austen that we should go if we want to be deeply moved: she is great for other reasons. I am ready to admit numbers of reasons for which she is a great novelist; but I find no need to apologise for her in the area of her main concern. My contention is that her subject was love, and she knew her subject.

Notes

1. Contrast Annabella Milbanke on another novel: she wrote on reading *Pride and Prejudice* on its first emergence: "It is not a crying book, but the interest is very strong, especially for Mr. Darcy." The woman who was susceptible to Mr. Darcy two years later married Lord Byron. See Marghanita Laski, *Jane Austen and her World* (London: Thames and Hudson), p. 86.
2. Letter to G.H. Lewes, 12 January 1848. See *Jane Austen: The Critical Heritage*, ed. B.C. Southam (London: Routledge & Kegan Paul, 1968), p. 128. I shall be returning to Charlotte Brontë's charges in Chapter IX.
3. See "Apropos of *Lady Chatterley's Lover*" (1930).
4. See, for instance, Marjorie Proops: "Jane, the spinster daughter of a country Tory parson, . . . ignored sex. At any rate, she threw a discreet veil over it. . . . She was a deeply religious woman and the physical consummation of love appeared to be outside her comprehension." *Pride, Prejudice and Proops* (London, 1975), pp. 11–12. Marjorie Proops can hardly be considered an expert on Jane Austen (she calls Darcy D'arcy, and thinks Jane Fairfax married Willoughby); but her silly little book is an interesting compendium of the popular modern clichés about Jane Austen.

8

The Symptoms of Love[1]

I'll begin by quoting Shakespeare's Rosalind, when she rebukes Orlando for looking so unlike a lover. The proper marks of a lover, she insists, are:

> A lean cheek, which you have not; a blue eye and sunken, which you have not; . . . a beard neglected, which you have not – but I pardon you for that; . . . . Then your hose should be ungartered, your bonnet unbanded, your sleeve unbuttoned, your shoe untied, and everything about you demonstrating a careless desolation. But you are no such man: you are rather point-device in your accoutrements.
> (*As You Like It*, III, ii)

A lover, according to Rosalind, wears a uniform, by which you may know him. Rosalind has set herself up as an expert on the subject of love, and she cheerfully undertakes its diagnosis and cure.

For the moment I want to emulate Rosalind, and take it upon myself to explore some of the traditional scholarship on love, and some of the dramatizations of it, because Jane Austen, like Shakespeare in his comedies, makes love and the conventions surrounding it her subject. It is not just an emotion among others, it is a topic for debate, and for informed and playful commentary. Before I come to a consideration of love in her novels, I will undertake a swift consideration of the Renaissance convention of love as Jane Austen inherited it. The subject, after all, has its own intrinsic interest.

Robert Burton's *Anatomy of Melancholy*, Dr. Johnson said, "was the only book that ever took him out of bed two hours sooner than he wished to rise."[2] Jane Austen is likely at least to have browsed in the favourite book of her favourite author; but she need not have known *The Anatomy of Melancholy* to have been familiar with much of the lore it contained. Many of the conventions and physical aberrations discussed in the fascinating section on Love Melancholy are still with us, as commonplaces of the behaviour of the lover. But I use Burton as my textbook, as he usefully collects the copious information on the subject.

111

Love melancholy is sexual desire considered as a disease. "They that are in love are likewise sick," Burton states categorically (658).[3] The love malady has its physical causes and symptoms, its proper treatment and cure; and, if untreated, it is acknowledged as likely to end in death or the madhouse. "Go to Bedlam for examples," says Burton succinctly.

To speak first of its causes. The person of a sanguine temperament, whose blood predominates over the other humours of his body, is the most likely to fall victim to the love disease. A rich diet, strong wines, and a leisurely life, which promote the flux of blood, are apt to add to the predisposition to love. "Lascivious meats" and "Noble Wine first of all," says Burton, promote desire, and he adds one of his catalogues of inflammatory foods: "Honey mixtures, exquisite and exotick Fruits, Allspices, Cakes, Meat-broths, smoothly powerful Wine . . . who would not then exceedingly rage with lust? . . . Inflammation of the belly is quickly worked off in venery, Hierome saith. After benching, then comes wenching" (663–4). Hence the modern lecher's refrain, "Have some Madeira, m'dear."

Sanguinity, youth, idleness and a rich diet create the predisposition to love. But the infection itself strikes from the sight of the beloved. When Phebe, Shakespeare's love-sick shepherdess, quotes Marlowe, "Who ever lov'd that lov'd not at first sight?" she is presenting the orthodoxy of the day. (By the way, Phebe, like another zealous advocate of first attachments, Marianne Dashwood, marries not her first love but her second.) Love happens all at once, it strikes like a thunderbolt, and it happens on the sight of the beloved. The meeting of the eyes is the crucial moment: from one pair of eyes to the other streaks a beam, or a ray, something that is conventionally represented as having a physical force, like Cupid's arrow; and then the victim is a goner. "Angry Cupid, bolting from her eyes, / Hath shot himself into me like a flame," moans Volpone. "Even so quickly may one catch the plague?" Olivia wonders in *Twelfth Night*; "Methinks I feel this youth's perfections / With an invisible and subtle stealth / To creep in at mine eyes" (I, v). "The more [the lover] sees her," moralizes Burton, "the worse he is; the sight burns, . . . the rays of Love are projected from her eyes" (677). This love, "first learned in a lady's eyes," is an infection that proceeds, Burton says, through the vital spirits to the liver, heart, and finally the brain, so that it preoccupies appetite, passion and reason.[4] "The heart, eyes, ears, and all his thoughts are full of her," Burton explains. The progress to Bedlam has begun.

And now we come to the symptoms. On first taking the infection the lover stands bemused, she sighs; she is struck speechless, or if she speaks she speaks disconnectedly. The signs of falling in love become so formalized, in fact, that in one play Marston simply supplied the stage direction, "[*Isabella falls in love*],"[5] and left it to the actor to represent the condition to the audience's satisfaction. (Burton usually generalizes about the lover as masculine, the beloved as feminine. But in the drama one finds both sexes producing like symptoms.)

Things go from bad to worse. The lover is sleepless. His pulse is uneven. After his indulgence in food and drink that made him prone to take the infection, he fasts. His total absorption in his love makes him affect solitude; his infected reason makes his speech fragmentary; his interrupted respiration makes his breath come in gasps and sighs. Not surprisingly, he becomes pale and thin. Pallor is the badge of love – "Let everyone that loves be pale, for lovers 'tis the proper colour," Burton lays it down. Jacques Ferrand, author of a learned seventeenth-century work on *Erotomania*, further explains, "We must not understand by this word pale a simple decoloration or whiteness of the skin . . . but rather a mixed colour of white and yellow; or of white, yellow and green."[6] Viola is therefore quite accurate in describing the state of her "sister" who died of love:

> She pin'd in thought,
> And with a green and yellow melancholy
> She sat like Patience on a monument,
> Smiling at grief. (*Twelfth Night*, II, iv)

Those last lines, by the way, are among the tags from Shakespeare that Catherine Morland commits to memory (*NA*, 16).

It is necessary to distinguish between two forms of the love disease, the sanguine and the melancholic.[7] If the lover's suit is successful, his sanguine symptoms will continue, and he will blush and sing and be gay, and though he will be irrational in the idolatry of his beloved, his will not be a dangerous case for the physician. But the lover whose love is scorned turns from sanguine to melancholic; his blood corrupts to melancholy; and his sleeplessness and fasting wreak havoc with his constitution. Chaucer's Squire, with his embroidered tunic and cheerful music-making, is a classic example of the sanguine lover; but Arcite, in the Knight's Tale, is the pattern for the melancholic lover:

His slep, his mete, his drynke, is hym biraft,
That lene he wex and drye as is a shaft;
His eyen holwe, and grisly to biholde,
His hewe falow and pale as asshen colde,
And solitarie he was and evere allone,
And waillynge al the nyght, makynge his mone;
And if he herde song or instrument,
Thanne wolde he wepe, he myghte nat be stent.
So feble eek were his spiritz, and so lowe,
And chaunged so, that no man koude knowe
His speche nor his voys, though men it herde. (1361-71)

In Jane Austen's novels, Mr. Elton is the type of the sanguine lover, with his fine display of symptoms, his blushing, sighing, and the charade on courtship, his own version of the classic lover's "ballad made to his mistress' eyebrow." Among the minor characters, Captain Benwick, at least before his cure, is Jane Austen's Arcite: he has "a melancholy air," we hear, "just as he ought to have, and drew back from conversation" (*P*, 97). The major character who displays all the classic symptoms of love melancholy is Marianne. The few paragraphs describing her condition after Willoughby's departure can stand as a parallel to the description of Arcite. In fact Marianne may well have had some such precedent in mind, for she does it all quite correctly. I quote selectively:

She was awake the whole night, and she wept the greatest part of it. She got up with an headache, was unable to talk, and unwilling to take any nourishment. . . . When breakfast was over she walked out by herself, . . . indulging the recollection of past enjoyment and crying over the present reverse for the chief of the morning . . . She played over every favourite song that she had been used to play to Willoughby, . . . and sat at the instrument gazing on every line of music that he had written out for her, till her heart was so heavy that no farther sadness could be gained. . . . She spent whole hours at the pianoforté alternately singing and crying; her voice often totally suspended by her tears. . . . Such violence of affliction . . . sunk within a few days into a calmer melancholy. (*SS*, 83)

According to the prosperity or ill success of his love, the lover's symptoms will vary. The careless desolation in dress, for instance, which Rosalind cites as the proper uniform of the lover, belongs to the melancholic phase of the disease. Had Rosalind had *The Anatomy of Melancholy* to hand, though, she might have been consoled to read, "let them be never so clownish, rude and horrid, Grobians and sluts, if once they be in love, they will be most neat and spruce" (753). We, as an audience knowledgeable in the scholarship on love, can appreciate that Orlando is point-device in his accoutrements because his love is in fact a very prosperous one. He sees his beloved every day, though he does not know it. It is the kind of happy irony that Jane Austen enjoyed as much as Shakespeare.

The symptoms in the classic lover's behaviour are manifold. If he really wants to do the thing properly he will wear a broad-brimmed hat over his eyes, and carry his arms folded. It is thus that the "Inamorato" is represented in the frontispiece to *The Anatomy of Melancholy*. So in *Love's Labour's Lost* Moth advises Don Armado that if he wants to convince discriminating wenches that he is in love, he must appear "with your hat penthouse-like o'er the shop of your eyes; with your arms crossed on your thin-belly doublet like a rabbit on a spit" (III, i). Hence Berowne, another of Shakespeare's experts on love, calls Cupid "Regent of love-rhymes, lord of folded arms" (III, i). Compulsive versifying is also among the symptoms. "I do love, and it hath taught me to rhyme," admits Berowne.

The lover becomes particularly sensitive to the name of his beloved. Orlando packs Rosalind's name into every other line of verse, and carves it on all the trees; Cesario assures Olivia he will

> Halloo your name to the reverberate hills,
> And make the babbling gossip of the air
> Cry out "Olivia!" (*Twelfth Night*, I, v)

On the other hand the lover may become reticent about the name, and be unable to pronounce it, though he thinks it all the time. (Jane Austen's heroines usually belong in the latter category.)

The picture of the beloved is likewise sacred, and may prompt all the behavioural symptoms displayed on the first sight. By showing a picture the crafty physician may often diagnose a love malady, even if the patient is anxious to keep his love a secret. Proteus, in *The Two Gentlemen of Verona*, resolves to content himself with a picture *instead* of its original. He tells Sylvia,

> Madam, if your heart be so obdurate,
> Vouchsafe me yet your picture for my love. . . .
> To that I'll speak, to that I'll sigh and weep. (IV, ii)

But the lover will dote not just on the portrait of the beloved, but on any image – such as a likeness perceived in the countenance of a relative; or any relic – such as a lock of her hair; or even, like Harriet Smith, the stub of a pencil or a piece of court plaister. When we hear, in an early chapter of *Emma*, that Mr. Knightley has preserved a reading list that Emma drew up when she was fourteen, we may draw our own conclusions (*E*, 37).

The lover's total absorption in his love makes him hypersensitive to the presence or approach of the loved one. "A lover's eyes will gaze an eagle blind," says Berowne. "She looks out at window still to see whether he come," says Burton. An updated Burton would include among his examples Elizabeth Bennet at the window of Longbourn, descrying before anyone else the figure of Darcy, and Anne Elliot in Bath, who can pick Wentworth out in a crowd at the far end of the street.

The physician who undertakes to cure a patient of the love disease can most easily treat the physical symptoms. His cures will correspond with the causes. To remedy the lover's sanguinity, bleed him; – the treatment of love was frequently a pretty gory business; to remedy his inflammatory rich diet, starve him, substituting a vegetable diet of "Cowcumbers, Melons, ... Lettice" for the spicy foods; to remedy idleness, exercise him. A sixteenth-century French doctor, André du Laurens, advises briskly, "Take away idleness, take away bellie cheere, and quaffing of strong drinkes, and without doubt lecherie will fall stark lame."[8] One can easily imagine why many a patient felt the cure was worse than the disease. And indeed this rather rigorous treatment, added to the symptoms of the melancholic lover, can bring the patient close to death's door. At this point, Burton advises humanely, "If they be much dejected and brought low in body, and now ready to despair through anguish, grief, and too sensible a feeling of their misery, a cup of wine . . . is not amiss" (768).

But there are other cures, which have their different advocates. "I profess curing [love] by counsel," says Rosalind. The cure by good counsel involves the forceful representation of the irrationality of the patient's passion and of the defects of his beloved. But physicians admit that it seldom works. It is a sign that Elizabeth is not very far gone with Wickham that she takes her aunt's advice in such good part – "a wonderful instance," we hear, "of advice being given on such a point, without being resented" (*PP*, 145). More efficacious is what Burton calls the "contrary passion," or driving out one nail with another, and he quotes Ovid to the effect that "a new love thrusteth out the old" (776). But that can mean out of the frying pan, into the fire – like Romeo cured of Rosaline by Juliet, or Harriet Smith cured of Robert Martin by Mr. Elton. "The last and best Cure of Love-Melancholy," admits Burton at last, "is, to let them have their desire" (798). This may sound more like a total surrender to the disease than a treatment, but the wise physician is ready to consider marriage a prescription in order to free the lover from his pathological and irrational state of mind. Conjugal love is right and reasonable; and is offered as a sovereign cure to make "amantes no more amentes" – lovers no more lunatics. So the physician and the comic dramatist unite in the final prescription of marriage, and many a successful case history, like many a romantic comedy, ends in a celebration of Hymen.

Jane Austen, like Shakespeare, both made fun of the love convention and used it. The earlier works, particularly, are full of high-spirited satire of all the commonplaces of love. Mr. Adams in "Jack and Alice" is "of so dazzling a Beauty that none but Eagles could look him in the Face." Alice is overpowered by "the Beams that darted from his Eyes," and instantly falls in love (*MW*, 13). In 'Evelyn' the deserted Maria is "so much grieved at [her husband's] departure that she died of a broken heart about 3 hours after" (*MW*, 189). And the two heroines of "Love and Freindship" between them neatly fulfil the prognosis of the uncured love disease – Laura runs mad and Sophia dies (after imprudently fainting on the wet grass) (*MW*, 102). The young Jane is showing that she really shares Rosalind's unromantic doctrine: "Men have died from time to time and worms have eaten them, but not for love" (*As You Like It*, IV, i). All this is cheerful and playful. But Jane Austen is ready to take love and its accepted conventions seriously too, to create her own Juliets and Cleopatras. In Marianne Dashwood she presents a girl who is so locked in to the convention that she almost dies in conforming to it; and our sympathies are fully engaged with Fanny Price and Anne Elliot, who suffer long and poignantly from the pangs of despised love.

The novels can be read as commentaries on the various controversies within the subject of love. Like the question of whether people can die of love, the convention of love at first sight and the issue of love's blindness come in for extended consideration, both within single novels and from one novel to another.

Marianne Dashwood is an ardent believer in the exclusive authenticity of first attachments, and a practitioner of love at first sight. Her practice and her principles are questioned and overthrown in *Sense and Sensibility*, and they are at issue too in the other works. In "Jack and Alice," Lady Williams condoles with Alice on "the Miseries, in general attendant on a first Love," and having experienced them herself, sensibly determines never to have a first love again (*MW*, 16). Isabella Thorpe, who does all her Love and Friendship by the book, assures Catherine, "So it always is with me; the first moment settles every thing. The first day that Morland came to us last Christmas – the very first moment I beheld him – my heart was irrecoverably gone" (*NA*, 118). But Isabella's heart proves to be more recoverable than she claims. *Pride and Prejudice*, with its theme of the unreliability of First Impressions, continues to reject the love at first sight convention in the main plot, but in the subplot of Bingley and Jane we have something close to the romantic pattern: "Oh! she is the most beautiful creature I ever beheld!" exclaims Bingley at the first ball (*PP*, 11); and all might have proceeded simply to swift marriage, but for outside interference. If the early novels value sense above sensibility, and a love based on esteem rather than instantaneous passion, *Persuasion* returns to something like the romantic ideal. Anne and Wentworth don't fall in love quite at first sight, but once acquainted, they are "rapidly and deeply in love" (*P*, 26). And Anne's first love is to be also her only love.

"Love is blind" is a proposition that is similarly debated. Cupid's blindness is supposedly communicated to the lover, who, on being smitten by the arrow, loses his power to see the defects of his beloved. Marianne, a vigorous adherent to the doctrine, "honoured her sister for [her] blind partiality" in not seeing Edward's shortcomings (*SS*, 19). *Emma* includes a prolonged exploration of the question of judgement and partiality in the lover. Emma's own conviction that love is blind is the source of many of her blunders: If Mr. Elton can talk of Harriet's "ready wit" he *must* be in love; on the other hand, since Mr. Knightley proves himself so thoroughly cognizant of her own faults, he must be in love with someone else. We are often invited to judge the state of a character's feelings by the degree of his appreciation for a lady's performance. Edward admires Elinor's drawings "as a lover, not as a connoisseur" (*SS*, 17); we are apprised of Colonel Brandon's rational passion for Marianne by the fact that at her piano recital "he paid her only the compliment of attention" (35). Emma is at last alerted to the real direction of Mr. Elton's attentions when he keeps "admiring her drawings with so much zeal and so little knowledge as seemed terribly like a would-be lover" (*E*, 118). "What you do / Still betters what is done," he would be understood to say, like some drawing-room Florizel (*The Winter's Tale*, IV, iv). And when Sir Walter Elliot is so impressed by Mrs. Clay's judicious use of Gowland's Lotion that he quite loses sight of her freckles, we know that he is far gone indeed.

Though Shakespeare and his contemporaries used the love convention, they were also so aware of its conventionality that they sometimes sought to express love in unconventional terms: so they created what we might call the anti-convention convention. "My mistress' eyes are nothing like the sun," declares this revolutionary in the realm of love. He rejects the convention in order to achieve a new immediacy, a greater authenticity in his expression. *Sense and Sensibility*, I think, is an extended essay in this genre. Marianne's is the conventional love, conceived at first sight, prompting heady joys and excessive manifestations, leading to desperation and almost to death. Elinor's is the love that is restrained in its expression, and hence it is invested with that pent-up energy that Shakespeare and Wyatt achieve in their anti-Petrarchan lyrics. It is a dangerous game to play, for it may come about that Marianne's histrionic displays capture our sympathy instead of Elinor's intense reticence. But it *can* succeed. In the novels at large, I think, Jane Austen does achieve a kind of muted intensity that can be as moving as more overtly passionate novels. But I shall have more to say of this in the next chapter.

We hear of Mrs. Dashwood at the beginning of *Sense and Sensibility* that "No sooner did she perceive any symptom of love in [Edward's] behaviour to Elinor, than she considered their serious attachment as certain" (17). Mrs. Dashwood is only one of a number of characters in the novels who are on the lookout for symptoms of love. And the symptoms are there all right, external signs, legitimate evidence that may be perceived and interpreted by the attentive observer. It is one of the conveniences of the love convention that it externalizes emotion, and so enlarges the action, the working out of a love between two people, beyond the principals.

The accurate diagnosis of love is of major import in the plots of Jane Austen's novels. Consider *Pride and Prejudice*, for example. Bingley and Jane fall in love, and Bingley makes no secret of his admiration. When Jane is convalescing at Netherfield, "He was full of joy and attention. The first half hour was spent in piling up the fire, lest she should suffer from the change of room. . . . He then sat down by her, and talked scarcely to any one else. Elizabeth . . . saw it all with great delight" (54). Elizabeth later speaks as a skilled diagnostician of love:

"I never saw a more promising inclination. He was growing quite inattentive to other people, and wholly engrossed by her. . . . At his own ball he offended two or three young ladies, by not asking them to dance, and I spoke to him twice myself, without receiving an answer. Could there be finer symptoms? Is not general incivility the very essence of love?" (141). Mrs. Bennet is exultant, perceiving by such signs that Bingley is almost caught. But Darcy has been on the watch too. "I observed my friend's behaviour attentively; and I could then perceive that his partiality for Miss Bennet was beyond what I had ever witnessed in him" (197). Darcy regards Bingley's attachment to a girl of such connections as scarcely short of an illness, and he takes on the task that in Burton's day would have been the physician's, a cure of the malady by good counsel: "I readily engaged in the office of pointing out to my friend, the certain evils of such a choice. – I described, and enforced them earnestly" (198). However, as a man of honour Darcy does not proceed with detaching Bingley from Jane without attempting to ascertain first that the lady will not be seriously wounded by the rupture. He brings his diagnostician's eye to bear on Jane too:

> Your sister I also watched. – Her look and manners were open, cheerful and engaging as ever, but without any symptom of peculiar regard, and I remained convinced from the evening's scrutiny, that though she received his attentions with pleasure, she did not invite them by any participation of sentiment. (197)

Elizabeth at first rejects his claim to have taken pains to deduce Jane's feelings, but presently remembers that his testimony is corroborated by Charlotte Lucas, who had noted Jane's apparent serenity with uneasiness. Indeed, Bingley would not have been cured by Darcy's good counsel alone, but the assurance of Jane's indifference does end his courtship; at least until his physician, who has meanwhile been smitten by the same malady, prescribes the final cure – "to let them go together" and be married.

So the love of Jane and Bingley, which in itself would be a matter private to themselves, radiates outwards, by means of the external signs of love, to become a matter hotly at issue between the novel's two main characters. And the moral judgement on Darcy and Elizabeth must depend to some extent on their skill as diagnosticians of love.

The novels abound with such characters. Mrs. Jennings in *Sense and Sensibility* is one of the liveliest, though not always the most discriminating. "She was full of jokes and laughter, and before dinner was over had said many witty things on the subject of lovers and husbands." "She was remarkably quick in the discovery of attachments, ... and this kind of discernment enabled her soon after her arrival at Barton decisively to pronounce that Colonel Brandon was very much in love with Marianne Dashwood" (SS, 34, 36). As coming in the fourth chapter, that's an early and accurate diagnosis.

In her benevolent enterprise, once her daughters are off her hands, "to marry all the rest of the world" (36), Mrs. Jennings is a precursor of Emma, the character in all the novels who most prides herself on her skill in the diagnosis, cure, and promotion of love. She even contemplates "a Hartfield edition of Shakespeare," where she intends to add a long note of qualification to the proposition that "The course of true love never did run smooth" (E, 75). She presides, of course, mainly over Harriet's love life: she cures her by "good counsel" of her love for Robert Martin, talks her into love with Mr. Elton (and then finds she can't talk her out again so quickly), and benignly tolerates her symptoms of love for Frank Churchill. Besides that, she is quick to discover Jane Fairfax's illicit passion for Mr. Dixon (Mr. Dixon, after all, admired Jane's piano-playing more than his fiancée's – nothing could be clearer!). Emma gets it all wrong, of course. She misreads the symptoms, but the symptoms are there, and Mr. Knightley is attentive enough to discover something of the secret love of Jane and Frank.

Some of the women in the novels are put to the pain of diagnosing the symptoms in the men they love themselves. Fanny must watch Edmund's growing love for Mary Crawford, and Anne Elliot must speculate on the degree of attachment between Wentworth and the Musgrove girls: "Other opportunities of making her observations could not fail to occur. Anne had soon been in company with [them] often enough to have an opinion ... that Captain Wentworth was not in love with either. They were more in love with him; yet there it was not love. It was a little fever of admiration; but it might, probably must, end in love with some" (P, 82). Anne's skill is such that she can make these minute discriminations accurately.

For a character like Marianne, falling in love is as immediate and perceptible as for a figure in Renaissance comedy. The process is, after all, laid down in advance. When Willoughby rescues her, and carries her off, sprained ankle and all, to her home, she blushes profusely, is unable to speak, and, as soon as she casts an eye on his manly beauty, she is convinced that "of all manly dresses a shooting-jacket was the most becoming" (SS, 43). But other heroines do not have such ready access to their own emotions. Elizabeth and Emma are unconsciously in love with Darcy and Knightley before they ever detect themselves in the fact, and both even imagine themselves in love with other men. Everyone knows that even the best doctors are poor practitioners in their own cases, and so with such patients it is the reader who must become the diagnostician.

We, like Mrs. Jennings and the others, must read for symptoms. It is one of the great pleasures of reading the novels – much more fun than combing for clues in a detective novel. Emma, reflecting on the iniquities of Mrs. Elton in a long soliloquy, thus takes her own pulse: "Oh! what would Frank Churchill say to her, if he were here? How angry and how diverted he would be! Ah! there I am – thinking of him directly. Always the first person to be thought of! How I catch myself out!" (*E*, 279). The close reader, however, by looking back to the beginning of the soliloquy, will note that the "first person to be thought of" was actually Mr. Knightley, not Frank Churchill at all.

So it is with Elizabeth, in singling out Darcy as an object of prejudice. In observing other lovers she is shrewd enough: when she meets Bingley in Derbyshire she can see the symptoms of his lasting feeling for Jane: "Sometimes she could fancy, that he talked less than on former occasions, and once or twice pleased herself with the notion that as he looked at her, he was trying to trace a resemblance" (*PP*, 262). But it is left to the reader to make the proper interpretation of the same symptom in Elizabeth when she meets Lady Catherine, "in whose countenance and deportment she soon found some resemblance of Mr. Darcy" (162).[9] In learning to read such signs the reader becomes a latter-day anatomist of love, and at least as well qualified to edit a new edition of Burton as Emma to edit the Hartfield edition of Shakespeare.

The modern reader on the lookout for symptoms might at first glance suppose that Jane Austen is above the rather quaint Renaissance conception of love as a physical state. Burton's disquisitions on sanguinity, diet, and the state of the liver seem rather far-fetched for useful application to nineteenth-century novels. But the Renaissance physiology of love is still perceptible, even if only in a vestigial form. Mr. Elton, well wined and dined at the Randalls dinner, is equally well primed for love-making: "two moments of silence being ample encouragement for Mr. Elton's sanguine state of mind, he tried to take [Emma's] hand again" (*E*, 131). "Sanguine" is a term used here in a sense Burton would surely have approved. The randy Alice Johnson, who finds herself "somewhat heated by wine (no very uncommon case)," is of a bright red complexion, and suffers from a "disordered Head & Love-sick Heart" (*MW*, 15). The view that amorousness is determined by physical makeup is partly confirmed by the physique of Jane Austen's most susceptible girls. Notice that the ones who are likely victims of seducers are robust: Lydia is "stout, well-grown, . . . with a fine complexion" and "high animal spirits," the largest of the Bennet girls although the youngest (*PP*, 8, 45). Georgiana Darcy, Wickham's other intended victim, is "tall, and on a larger scale than Elizabeth; and, though little more than sixteen, her figure was formed, and her appearance womanly" (*PP*, 261). The Bertram girls, both susceptible to the charms of Henry Crawford, are "tall, full-formed, and fair" (*MP*, 44). And Marianne, who resembles Colonel Brandon's fallen first love, is taller than Elinor, with a complexion "uncommonly brilliant" (*SS*, 46).

Burton's strictures on diet, too, still reverberate. It is surely no accident that Mr. Woodhouse is equally opposed to a rich diet and to matrimony! And Emma's present of arrowroot to Jane Fairfax, reminiscent of Burton's vegetable diets, is cruelly though unintentionally appropriate. No wonder Jane should resent a remedy of love contributed by her rival. Mrs. Jennings may well have used *The Anatomy of Melancholy* as her Home Doctor volume, for when Marianne has been deserted by Willoughby she presses Elinor to take her a glass "of the finest old Constantia wine." Elinor pleads that as Marianne has already fallen asleep she may drink it herself. After all, she reflects, "its healing powers on a disappointed heart might be as reasonably tried on herself as on her sister" (*SS*, 197–8). As Burton directed, if the lover is much dejected, "a cup of wine . . . is not amiss."

The quickened pulse and consequent variation in complexion are further useful signs for the diagnostician, both in *The Anatomy of Melancholy* and in Jane Austen's novels. Burton cites one shrewd physician who was able to discover his patient was in love, and with whom, "by his Pulse and Countenance, . . . because that when she came in presence, or was named, his pulse varied, and he blushed besides" (723). We may reach similar conclusions by observing the same signs in the novels. When she sees Willoughby in London, Marianne's face is first "glowing with sudden delight," then "crimsoned over," and presently she is "looking dreadfully white." Well may Elinor warn her lest she "betray what you feel to every body present" (*SS*, 176–7). In the later novels the signs are presented more subtly. When Edmund recounts his father's praises to a blushing Fanny – "Nay, Fanny, do not turn away about it – it is but an uncle"

– the reader is aware of the irony of Edmund's missing a sign, for Fanny is "distressed by more feelings than he was aware of" (*MP*, 198). Anne at the beginning of *Persuasion* "hoped she had outlived the age of blushing" (49), but it is among the signs of her emotional regeneration and her physical rejuvenation that she is later to regain her "bloom" and the ability to blush. After the concert in Bath, where she was approached by Wentworth and overtly courted by Elliot, Mrs. Smith plays the role of the physician: "'Your countenance perfectly informs me that you were in company last night with the person, whom you think the most agreeable in the world. . . .' A blush overspread Anne's cheeks. She could say nothing" (194). The men blush too, though more frequently they "colour." There is one nicely veiled hint of Mr. Knightley's feelings when Emma suggests he may be in love with Jane Fairfax: "Mr. Knightley was hard at work upon the lower buttons of his thick leather gaiters, and either the exertion of getting them together, or some other cause, brought the colour into his face" (*E*, 287). Here he is blushing not at the mention of Jane Fairfax, but because it is Emma who suggests he is in love. Emma herself could hardly be expected to read this sign, but the reader is invited to. Emma works on such symptoms in her own misguided way. When Harriet has a cold, she tries to raise Mr. Elton's sensibility by this suggestive description of her condition: "a throat very much inflamed, with a great deal of heat about her, a quick low pulse, &c." Mr. Elton can only reply with the exasperating comment, "A sore-throat! – I hope not infectious" (109). After Elton's insult to Harriet at the ball, Emma draws the satisfaction that at least Harriet will have been cured of her love for him. "The fever was over, and Emma could harbour little fear of the pulse being quickened again" (332). What Emma doesn't know is that Harriet's volatile pulse has already been quickened again, by Mr. Knightley's stepping forward to save her from Mr. Elton's insult. So Jane Austen takes over a convention, uses it, shows how her characters use it, and makes her reader aware of its intricacies.

Though the gloomy prognosis of death or madness is not often fulfilled in Jane Austen's realistic novels, she does often show how a disappointed passion can have serious physical consequences. Marianne is a classic case of love melancholy. "It was many days since she had any appetite, and many nights since she had really slept; and . . . the consequence of all this was felt in an aching head, a weakened stomach, and a general nervous faintness" (*SS*, 185). In her illness at Cleveland, which is almost fatal, her pulse is "lower and quicker than ever!" and she is feverish and delirious (311). Men who are crossed in love, like Edward Ferrars, Colonel Brandon, and Captain Benwick, generally give themselves away by showing "oppression of spirits" (*SS*, 50, 90; *P*, 97). Even Mr. Knightley loses his physical vigour when he supposes Emma is about to marry Frank Churchill, and prompts the sad comment from his nieces and nephews, "Uncle seems always tired now" (*E*, 465). But the women are more definitely debilitated. Anne loses her bloom as well as her spirits when she breaks her engagement; Fanny's sick headache has as much to do with Edmund's attentions to Mary Crawford as with her picking roses in the sun; Jane Fairfax in Frank's absence suffers from "a weakened frame and varying spirits" (*E*, 166), and after their quarrel she is actually a case for the doctor. "Her health seemed for the moment completely deranged – appetite quite gone – . . . Her spirits seemed overcome" (389). Hers is a malady that Burton would recognize as being beyond any treatment but the last and final cure of marriage, which happily is forthcoming. As Mrs. Elton says knowingly, "Upon my word, Perry has restored her in a wonderful short time! . . . We do not say a word of any *assistance* that Perry might have; not a word of a certain young physician from Windsor. [That is, Frank.] – Oh! no; Perry shall have all the credit" (*E*, 454). As for Frank himself, he claims – and means to be believed – that if Jane had refused him, "I should have gone mad" (437). Fortunately however the same sovereign remedy keeps him out of Bedlam.

The time-honoured convention of the force of the eyes, the exchange of looks between lovers, remains a strong influence in the novels. We hear much of the attractive power of the heroine's eyes on the hero – Catherine's "sparkling eyes" as she accepts Tilney's invitation to dance (*NA*, 75); "the beautiful expression of her dark eyes" that overcomes Elizabeth's other disadvantages in Darcy's estimation (*PP*, 23; Mary Crawford's "lively dark eye" that so charms Edmund, until he learns "to prefer soft light eyes to sparkling dark ones" [*MP*, 44, 47]); and Emma's "true hazle eye" that makes Mr. Knightley "love to look at her" (*E*, 39). A good deal of significant action in the novels takes the form of exchanges of glances between lovers or would-be lovers. When Mr. Elton presents his charade, which prays conventionally, "May its approval beam in that soft eye!" Emma knows there are signs to be read, but misreads them: "There was deep consciousness about him, and he found it easier to meet her eye than her friend's" (*E*, 71). One longs to alert Emma to this clear sign that he is courting her, not Harriet. In other places, however, Emma can manage the *coup d'oeil* with some finesse – as at the ball with Mr. Knightley, where "her eyes invited him irresistibly to come to her" (330).

In *Persuasion* there is a whole history of looks between lovers. The estrangement between Anne and Wentworth is emphasized by their failure to meet each other's eyes: "Her eye half met Captain Wentworth's" – or – "*Once* she felt that he was looking at herself" (*P*, 59, 72). Only at Lyme, where she begins to recapture his attention, does she receive "a glance of brightness" (104) from him; their continuing misunderstanding in Bath is signalled again by their failure to manage glances: "As her eyes fell on him, his seemed to be withdrawn from her" (188); but at the last he places his letter of proposal before her "with eyes of glowing entreaty" (236). "A word, a look will be enough to decide," he writes. And when they meet, in Union Street, Anne is able to give him the right look (238, 239). The progress of their relation is marked by averted eyes, intercepted glances, and at last the full exchange of loving looks.

In dress we have Marianne again as the conventional model, demonstrating the careless desolation of the melancholy lover: "To her dress and appearance she was grown . . . perfectly indifferent" (*SS*, 249) – unlike Miss Steele who, always in hope to catch the next beau, is point-device in her accoutrements. There are no broad-brimmed melancholy hats in evidence; but Harriet is able to see in "the very sitting of his hat, . . . proof of how much [Mr. Elton] was in love!" (*E*, 184).

Mr. Elton, who much enjoys the trappings of a lover, is likewise a heavy sigher. Even Emma, delighted as she is at his promising attachment to Harriet, becomes almost exasperated: "He does sigh and languish, and study for compliments rather more than I could endure as a principal" (*E*, 49). And the attentive reader who attunes his ear to sighs may gather almost as much as the one on the lookout for dialogues of eyes or quickenings of pulse.

It is of course *de rigueur* that the dedicated lover, like Chaucer's Squire, should "sleep namoore than dooth a nyghtyngale." Marianne, we hear, "would have thought herself very inexcusable had she been able to sleep at all the first night after parting from Willoughby" (*SS*, 83). Isabella Thorpe proudly exclaims to Catherine, "Oh! Catherine, the many sleepless nights I have had on your brother's account!" (*NA*, 118). So when Elizabeth after her visit to Pemberley "lay awake two whole hours" (*PP*, 265) trying to determine what are her feelings for Darcy, the reader could tell her the answer there and then, on the basis of the insomnia alone.

Shakespeare's pastoral lover, Silvius, makes unsociability and the courting of solitude a definitive symptom of love:

> . . . if thou hast not broke from company
> Abruptly as my passion now makes me,
> Thou hast not lov'd. . . . [*Exit*] (*As You Like It*, II, iv)

So Elizabeth lays it down, "Is not general incivility the very essence of love?" (*PP*, 141). It takes Marianne several days, after Willoughby's departure, to bring herself to walk with her sisters "instead of wandering away by herself" (*SS*, 85); and indeed it is on one such solitary ramble that she contracts her putrid throat. Julia Bertram, when Henry Crawford has chosen her sister to play opposite him in the production of *Lovers' Vows*, sits apart "in gloomy silence, wrapt in such gravity as nothing could subdue" (*MP*, 160); and she and Fanny, both watching the amorous adventures of the Crawfords, are "two solitary sufferers" (163). Fanny and Anne Elliot, both of whom are divided from their men through most of the action, are alike also characterized by their loneliness: for Anne, as for Fanny, "her own thoughts and reflections were habitually her best companions" (*MP*, 80). Indeed, the noticeable need of the heroine at times of stress to withdraw, and cope with her feelings in private, is Jane Austen's characteristic adaptation of the conventional lover's penchant for solitude. As Jane Fairfax says feelingly, after she has quarrelled with Frank, "Oh! Miss Woodhouse, the comfort of being sometimes alone!" (*E*, 363).

Viola in *Twelfth Night* is able to discover that Olivia has fallen in love by the fact that "she did speak in starts distractedly" (II, ii). Broken and confused speech is likewise a reliable symptom of love in Jane Austen's novels. Darcy's feelings for Elizabeth are deducible from his unconnected sentences and relapses into silence when he calls at the parsonage in Hunsford (*PP*, 177ff). Mr. Elton is again a model lover when he looks at Emma's painting and "sighed out his half sentences of admiration just as he ought" (*E*, 69). This is a specimen of Mr. Knightley's syntax when he believes Emma to have loved and lost Frank Churchill: "Her arm was pressed again, as he added, in a more broken and subdued accent, 'The feelings of the warmest friendship – Indignation – Abominable scoundrel!'" (426). Even Tilney can be inarticulate: on his visit to the Allens after his proposal, he "talked at random, without sense or connection" (*NA*, 243).

The time-honoured relation between the lover and the picture of his beloved is the basis of many a subtle incident involving pictures in Jane

Austen's fiction. An early instance, in 'Evelyn', is the sad story of Rose Gower, who after losing her fiancé at sea, seeks "to soften her affliction by obtaining a picture of her unfortunate Lover" (*MW*, 185). The same incident recurs, with subtle expansion to include the question of constancy in men and women, in *Persuasion*, where Benwick's picture, painted for Fanny Harville, is to be reframed for his new fiancée, Louisa Musgrove. Elizabeth at Pemberley re-enacts the classic lover's reaction to the portrait, but in a movingly updated version. She wanders through the gallery until she finds what she is looking for, Darcy's portrait:

> At last it arrested her – and she beheld a striking resemblance of Mr. Darcy, with such a smile over the face, as she remembered to have sometimes seen, when he looked at her. She stood several minutes before the picture in earnest contemplation. (*PP*, 250)

Burton would have signed her up for emergency treatment at once.

The complex muddle over Mr. Elton's admiration of Emma's portrait of Harriet shows that Emma has got her conventions confused. Mr. Elton is determined to be a conventional lover, and Emma is determined to read the conventional signs. But he is flashing the "Everything you do is perfect" sign, while Emma is receiving the "Lover doats on portrait" message. Hence she takes Harriet to be his object, not herself. It is a beautiful play with the love convention.

The sound of the name of the beloved can be almost as dangerous as his picture or his actual presence. Elinor helps Marianne in her extremity by avoiding the mention of Willoughby: "Her carefulness in guarding her sister from ever hearing Willoughby's name mentioned, was not thrown away" (*SS*, 214). Catherine, as she is expelled from Northanger Abbey, stammers to Eleanor Tilney "'her kind remembrance for her absent friend.' But with this approach to his name ended all possibility of restraining her feelings" (*NA*, 229). Such reaction being the convention, sharper ladies than Catherine become self-conscious about the matter. Mary Crawford writes to Fanny in Portsmouth, "Of [your cousin Edmund], what shall I say? If I avoided his name entirely, it would look suspicious" (*MP*, 416). Naturally, our suspicions are simultaneously raised and confirmed. And Emma, always taking her own pulse to measure her love for Frank Churchill, goes through this palpitating soliloquy:

> Am I unequal to speaking his name at once before all these people? Is it necessary for me to use any roundabout phrase? . . . No, I can

pronounce his name without the smallest distress. I certainly get better and better. – Now for it. . . . Mr. Frank Churchill writes one of the best gentlemen's hands I ever saw. (*E*, 297)

The reader can smile knowingly as Emma waits in suspense to feel the symptoms of a disease she doesn't have. Except for Mr. Elton's charade, the lover's inclination to versify is not abundantly demonstrated in Jane Austen's novels. In fact Elizabeth pointedly suggests that writing poetry is the cure of the love, rather than its symptom. "I wonder who first discovered the efficacy of poetry in driving away love!" she says (*PP*, 44), anticipating the unromantic view of her descendant, Thackeray, who similarly suggested, "when a gentleman is cudgelling his brain to find any rhyme for sorrow, besides borrow and to-morrow, his woes are nearer at an end than he thinks for" (*Pendennis*, ch. 15). But an indulgence in music is still a proper activity for a lover, and Marianne, in playing over all the songs she has sung with Willoughby, is like that other orthodox lover, Orsino in *Twelfth Night*, who exclaims, "If music be the food of love, play on"! (I.i).

"But," says Burton, as he is struggling to an end of his section on Symptoms, "I conclude there is no end of Love's Symptoms, 'tis a bottomless pit" (761). Emma, another expert on the subject, likewise acknowledges, "There may be a hundred different ways of being in love" (*E*, 49) – though she is confident that she is mistress of them all.

I proceed then to the cures. Blood-letting, as Wordsworth's leechgatherer testifies, is no longer fashionable, but dieting has not quite disappeared: as I have said, Mr. Woodhouse undertakes to cure all and sundry before they ever sicken by a steady diet of coddled eggs and gruel. The cure by good counsel is attempted on Catherine Morland by her mother, on Bingley by Darcy, on Harriet by Emma (more than once), and on Anne by Lady Russell. It never works. The cure of the contrary passion is confirmed as more successful. Mrs. Jennings professes this cure and almost quotes Burton – "one shoulder of mutton, you know, drives another down" (*SS*, 197); and indeed her prescription is successful, as Marianne is ultimately cured of Willoughby by Brandon. A "second attachment," we know, would be "the only thoroughly natural, happy, and sufficient cure" (*P*, 28) for Anne's wounded heart, but that she manages to resuscitate the first attachment. And successive attachments are the only treatment for Harriet's almost chronic state of lovesickness: "The charm of an object to occupy the many vacancies of Harriet's mind was not to be talked away. [Mr.

Elton] might be superseded by another . . . but nothing else . . . would cure her" (*E*, 183–4). However, with Burton, Jane Austen finally prescribes the treatment of marriage, and a highly acceptable one it is. She, like Shakespeare, writes romantic comedies, after all.

A number of modern critics have shown us Jane Austen as the novelist of "regulated hatred," as the bitter satirist, as a writer with almost tragic reach. I have preferred for the moment to dwell on her affinities with Shakespearean comedy, because Jane Austen is a novelist who also celebrates joy and consummation. For all her restraint in depicting sexuality, she can reach like Shakespeare to delight – exuberantly, jubilantly – in the joy of love requited. "O coz, coz, coz, my pretty little coz," exclaims Rosalind in her happiness, "that thou didst know how many fathom deep I am in love!" (IV, i). We find similar jubilant, sparkling passages in the novels. "I am happier even than Jane," says Elizabeth; "she only smiles, I laugh" (*PP*, 383). Or, when Wentworth agrees to escort Anne home in Bath: "There could be only a most proper alacrity, a most obliging compliance for public view; and smiles reined in and spirits dancing in private rapture" (*P*, 240). How many fathom deep they are in love!

Jane Austen's romantic comedies are close to Shakespeare's not just in their playful treatment of the conventions of love, but sometimes in the deliberate choice of situations through which to explore the intricate pains and pleasures of love. As I shall show in more detail in later chapters, Elizabeth Bennet is a descendant of Beatrice in *Much Ado*: both of them single out their men for pointed abuse before a happy reconciliation. Fanny Price is a latter-day Viola, constrained to the painful task of being the go-between in the suit of the man she loves for another woman. And Emma Woodhouse, who takes on the arrangement of other people's love lives while her own is in jeopardy, is a version of Rosalind.

"I believe in a true analogy between our bodily frames and our mental," says Captain Harville (*P*, 233) – a proposition which Anne, and Jane Austen too, accept. From the old conception of the humours, the theory that character derives from physical constitution, Jane Austen inherited a sense that love is not just a state of mind, but a state of body. To the intelligent observer its signs are as definite and palpable as a rash or a high temperature. For us moderns, who use what we call intuition to divine the state of each others' hearts, she would have a tolerant compassion – we are so many Mrs. Dashwoods and unreformed Emmas, relying on inspired guesses that may just as likely be wrong as right. And those outward and visible signs of love serve her purpose as a novelist, too. The artist must deal in appearances, and the visible symptoms of love – its language, as it were – are a fine ready-made set of terms by which to communicate its reality. Jane Austen writes for a reader who is "in the lore / Of deep love learned to the red heart's core."[10] The phrase is Keats's, but the sentiment fits. As her characters are scholars of love, so must we be.

Notes

1. This was originally delivered as the address at the annual meeting of the Jane Austen Society in Chawton, Hampshire, on 16 July 1977. A version of the paper is published in the society's annual Report.
2. James Boswell, *Life of Johnson*, Oxford Standard Authors Edition (London: Oxford University Press, 1961), p. 438. Entry under 1770.
3. *The Anatomy of Melancholy* was first published in 1621, and was revised and enlarged in several subsequent editions. I use the edition of Floyd Dell and P. Jordan-Smith (London: Tudor Publishing, 1927), which helpfully translates the many Latin quotations.
4. See André du Laurens (Burton's "Laurentius"): "Love therefore having abused the eyes, as the proper spyes and porters of the mind, maketh a way for itselfe smoothly to glaunce along through the conducting guides, and passing without any perseverence in this sort through the veines unto the liver, doth suddenly imprint a burning desire to obtaine the thing, which is or seemeth worthie to bee beloved, setteth concupiscence on fire, and beginneth by this desire all the strife and contention: but fearing herselfe too weake to incounter with reason, the principal part of the minde, she posteth in haste to the heart, to surprise and winne the same: whereof when she is once sure, as of the strongest holde, she afterward assaileth and setteth upon reason, and all the other principall powers of the minde so fiercely, as that she subdueth them, and maketh them her vassals and slaves." *A Discourse of the Preservation of the Sight: of Melancholic Diseases; of Rheums, and of Old Age*, trans. Richard Surphlet (London, 1599). Reprinted, Shakespeare Association Facsimile no. 15. London, 1938. p. 118. For ease of reading, I have not retained the Renaissance "u" in place of "v," or "v" in place of "u."
5. See *The Insatiate Countess*, II, i.
6. Jacques Ferrand, *Erotomania, or a Treatise discoursing of the Essence, Causes, Symptomes, Prognosticks, and Cure of LOVE or Erotique Melancholy* (Oxford, 1640), p. 121.
7. See Lawrence Babb, *The Elizabethan Malady* (East Lansing: Michigan State College Press, 1951), p. 134.
8. Du Laurens, p. 123.
9. The symptom of searching a relative's countenance for a likeness to the beloved is elaborated in an interesting scene in *The Watsons*. Here

the likeness becomes a subject of debate between the girl and her parents, who try to discourage her love by denying the resemblance:

The discussion led to more intimate remarks, & Miss Edwardes gently asked Emma if she were not often reckoned very like her youngest brother. – Emma thought she could perceive a faint blush accompany the question, & there seemed something still more suspicious in the manner in which Mr E. took up the subject. – "You are paying Miss Emma no great compliment I think Mary, said he hastily – . . . . Mr. Watson! . . . Well, you astonish me. – There is not the least likeness in the world." (*MW*, 324)

10. *Lamia*, II. 189-190. Keats took the story of *Lamia* from the Love Melancholy section of *The Anatomy of Melancholy* (see p. 648); so he was himself steeped in the lore of love.

9
Surface and Subsurface[1]

I take the metaphor of my chapter title from Charlotte Brontë's memorable criticism of Jane Austen:

> She does her business of delineating the surface of the lives of genteel English people curiously well; there is a Chinese fidelity, a miniature delicacy in the painting: she ruffles her reader by nothing vehement, disturbs him by nothing profound: the Passions are perfectly unknown to her; she rejects even a speaking acquaintance with that stormy Sisterhood; . . . Her business is not half so much with the human heart as with the human eyes, mouth, hands and feet; what sees keenly, speaks aptly, moves flexibly, it suits her to study, but what throbs fast and full, though hidden . . . – *this* Miss Austen ignores.[2]

It is the original and recurring objection to Jane Austen. Mark Twain (who apparently so missed violence in the novels that he thought she shouldn't have been allowed to die a natural death![3]), complained that her characters are automatons which can't "warm up and feel a passion."[4] And even her admirers defended her in terms which to her detractors are damningly faint praise. George Henry Lewes announced, "First and foremost let Jane Austen be named, the greatest artist that has ever written, using the term to signify the most perfect mastery over the means to her end. There are heights and depths in human nature which Miss Austen has never scaled nor fathomed, there are worlds of passionate existence into which she has never set foot; . . . Her circle may be restricted, but it is complete."[5] Elizabeth Barrett Browning was all too ready to accept this view: the novels, she said, are "perfect as far as they go – that's certain. Only they don't go far, I think."[6] "Perfect," for Elizabeth Barrett as for Robert Browning, is a term of opprobrium. It means the reach doesn't exceed the grasp.

In the twentieth century Jane Austen certainly does not want for discriminating critics who make large claims for her significance, but again we who are her admirers have taken our stand on her appeal to the head rather than the heart. Ian Watt quotes Horace Walpole's dictum that "this world is a comedy to those that think, a tragedy to those that feel," and acknowledges "Jane Austen's novels are comedies, and can have little appeal to those who, consciously or unconsciously, believe thought inferior to feeling."[7] We have to a large extent conceded Charlotte Brontë's point, and agreed that Jane Austen's business is indeed with the head and not with the heart – we simply don't find her reaction as devastating a piece of criticism as she evidently meant it to be: valuing as we do the activity of the mind and the application of the intellect. We admire the unruffled surface, and have a properly Augustan reservation about the virtues of the kind of "vehemence" and "profundity" that Brontë misses.[8] I myself have just been demonstrating Jane Austen's intellectual savouring of the love convention, and her affinities with Shakespearean comedy.

And yet . . . do we really need to concede as much as we do? In our heart of hearts (and I use the phrase designedly) don't we know that a *full* reading of a Jane Austen novel is a very *moving* experience, as well as an intellectually delectable one? – that the moment of reconciliation when Mr. Knightley *almost* kisses Emma's hand is fraught with passion, just as is the occasion when Mr. Rochester crushes Jane Eyre to his breast in the orchard at Thornfield, while a violent midsummer storm is brewing?

How is it done? Well, deep reservoirs may have unruffled surfaces as well as shallow ones: if unruffled surface is what we admire, then we need not look beyond it – and we can delight in the fidelity with which the surface of the lives of genteel English people is delineated; but if we do indeed value the dramatization of deep emotion, that too is there, and the more visible, if not more obvious, for the apparent tranquillity.

Charlotte Brontë, accused on one occasion of equivocation, vindicated herself vigorously: "I would scorn in this and every other case to deal in equivoque; I believe language to have been given us to make our meaning clear, and not to wrap it in dishonest doubt."[9] I suspect Jane Austen would consider such a declaration somewhat crude. The naïve Catherine Morland in *Northanger Abbey* has something similar to say of General Tilney's white lies: "Why he should say one thing so positively, and mean another all the while, was most unaccountable! How were people, at that rate, to be understood?" (*NA*, 211). And Catherine's education is to involve the realization that language need not always be interpreted literally.

Of course novelists and dramatists have traditionally made capital out of a discrepancy between the profession and the reality, and many a comic scene has been built around it. Here is Becky Sharp, justifying herself to Jos Sedley when he has come to visit her in her disreputable lodgings: she has just stowed the brandy bottle, the rouge-pot, and the plate of broken meats in the bed.

> "I have had so many griefs and wrongs, Joseph Sedley, I have been made to suffer so cruelly, that I am almost made mad sometimes. . . . I had but one child, one darling, one hope, one joy, which I held to my heart with a mother's affection . . .; and they – they tore it from me – tore it from me;" and she put her hand to her heart with a passionate gesture of despair, burying her face for a moment on the bed.
> The brandy-bottle inside clinked up against the plate which held the cold sausage. Both were moved, no doubt, by the exhibition of so much grief. (*Vanity Fair*, ch. 65).

Becky pours out her wrongs and her griefs; the brandy bottle and the rouge-pot tell a different story. Sometimes Thackeray even provides a direct translation of the subsurface meaning. In another memorable scene between the same pair, when they nervously await the event of Waterloo in Brussels, Becky tells Jos:

> "You men can bear anything. . . . Parting or danger are nothing to you. Own now that you were going to join the army and leave us to our fate. I know you were – something tells me you were. I was so frightened, when the thought came into my head (for I do sometimes think of you when I am alone, Mr. Joseph!), that I ran off immediately to beg and entreat you not to fly from us."
> This speech might be interpreted, "My dear sir, should an accident befall the army, and a retreat be necessary, you have a very comfortable carriage, in which I propose to take a seat." (ch. 31)

I have indulged in this little digression on Becky Sharp because she provides a convenient contrast to the usual process in Jane Austen. Becky's speech is a gush of emotion; Becky's meaning is totally a product of that energetic brain of hers, and one can almost hear the whirr and click of a calculating machine in action. Jane Austen's characters, on the other hand, conduct apparently rational conversations with each other on subjects of general interest, while simultaneously their *hearts* are deeply engaged. She is not particularly interested in the exposure of the hypocrite who uses social forms as a mask for his true motivation.[10] Nor is Charlotte Brontë, by the way – it is notable that in the proposal scene in *Jane Eyre* Jane declares explicitly, "I am not talking to you now through the medium of custom, [or] conventionalities" (ch. 23). Jane Eyre and Lucy Snowe have to maintain a proud reticence, or burst through the barriers of convention in order to express their feelings, and when they do burst through they mean all they say; Becky Sharp and Blanche Amory are socially perfectly at ease in the display of emotion, but they mean something different. But Jane Austen's characters succeed in expressing themselves not in spite of custom and convention, but *through* them; and they mean not something different from what they say, like Thackeray's, nor all they say, like Charlotte's, but far more than what they say. So when Elinor receives Edward after their estrangement, actually believing him to be married to Lucy Steele, we can gather enough of the agonized state of her feelings by hearing merely that "she sat down again and talked of the weather" (*SS*, 359).

And here we come to her powerful use of understatement in emotional scenes. It is her frequent practice to bring a situation to a crisis, to lead you to the point where you expect some climactic exclamation of the "Great was her consternation . . . !" type, and then to report instead some apparent commonplace of behaviour or polite converse. There is a breath of a pause, a kind of hiatus between cause and effect (which I indicate typographically by a double stroke) that we learn to perceive and savour. "No sooner had Fatima discovered the gory remains of Bluebeard's previous wives, // than she made an appointment with her hairdresser" – I must invent a gross example to attune the ear and eye to Jane Austen's refined and delicate use of this device.

For instance:

Elizabeth Bennet has at last realized that Darcy is the man she loves, but just when she has come to believe that he will never approach her again. Her mother calls her to the window to see the arrival of Mr. Bingley. "Elizabeth, to satisfy her mother, went to the window – she looked, – she saw Mr. Darcy with him, and // sat down again by her sister" (*PP*, 333).

Mary Crawford, in spite of her prejudice against younger brothers, has fallen in love with Edmund Bertram. She is engaged in a game of Speculation when the gentlemen's conversation turns on the eligibility of Thornton Lacy as a gentleman's residence: "Thornton Lacey was the name of [Edmund's] impending living, as Miss Crawford well knew; and // her interest in a negociation for William Price's knave increased" (*MP*, 241).

Anne Elliot has steeled herself to speak to Mrs. Croft of her brother, Captain Wentworth, brave in the knowledge that Mrs. Croft knows nothing of the previous engagement:

"Perhaps you may not have heard that he is married," added Mrs. Croft. [Anne] // could now answer as she ought. (*P*, 49)

Again and again Jane Austen indicates a severe emotional shock by this kind of understatement. She is not *avoiding* the presentation of strong feelings; she is presenting them by indirection. It is not because her characters have no feelings that they talk of the weather and make polite responses in such moments. Words would not carry the full weight of what they feel in any case. They observe the social forms, but not at the expense of crushing themselves. For what they feel they *can* express, but they can seldom express it directly or fully: to spill out the words and feelings, regardless of decorum, is to lose the intensity, to be emotionally shallow. (That is what Jane Austen tried to suggest in *Sense and Sensibility*, when Elinor hears the man she loves is married, and *Marianne* goes into hysterics.) Her people speak in a succinct code, where A expresses not only A, but B and C as well.

I would like to examine, in some detail, a few passages of dialogue, and to show how polite conversation, conducted on matters of apparently general import, and within the bounds of decorum, can be informed with a subsurface level of intense personal emotion. One thing is said on the surface; but below the surface are implied the individual's ecstasies and agonies. In this way I hope to mine some of that rich and primitive ore which Charlotte Brontë misses.[11]

I will confine myself to the last three novels, partly for convenience (one has to stop somewhere), but also because I think this is an aspect of Jane Austen's art which she developed and refined, and used with best effect later in her career. Lucy Steele's bitchy insinuations in *Sense and Sensibility* are relatively crude examples of a character's ability to suggest more than is stated, compared with Frank Churchill's elaborate *doubles entendres*, or with the kind of oblique communication that constantly goes on between Anne Elliot and Captain Wentworth, where, though they seldom speak to each other, each constantly understands the full import of the other's speech better than their interlocutors do. In my selection of passages I deliberately choose situations that parallel Charlotte Brontë's characteristic one, where the protagonist is forced to look on while the man she loves is courting an unworthy rival: a Blanche Ingram or a Ginevra Fanshawe, a Mary Crawford or a Louisa Musgrove. In such situations Jane Austen puts her reader on stage, as it were, since we become with the protagonist spectators who are intimately aware of unspoken implications in the exchanges we witness.

My first extract is from the famous excursion to Sotherton in *Mansfield Park*. Mary Crawford, Edmund and Fanny, the trio who are so constantly associated, have begun to wander in the little "wilderness" of the park. Mary has just heard that Edmund is to take orders, and has had all her prejudices against younger brothers renewed. "A clergyman is nothing," she declares. Edmund defends his vocation.

> "A clergyman cannot be high in state or fashion. He must not head mobs, or set the ton in dress. But I cannot call that situation nothing, which has the charge of all that is of the first importance to mankind, individually or collectively considered, temporally and eternally – which has the guardianship of religion and morals, and consequently of the manners which result from their influence." (92)

Mary remains unconvinced: "One does not see much of this influence and importance in society," she argues. And how can a clergyman be so influential when one "scarcely sees [him] out of his pulpit"?

Edmund tries to explain that preaching is not a clergyman's only business, and to enlarge on and explain his previous claim:

> "A fine preacher is followed and admired; but it is not in fine preaching only that a good clergyman will be useful in his parish and his neighbourhood, where the parish and neighbourhood are of a size capable of knowing his private character, and observing his general conduct. . . . And with regard to their influencing public manners, Miss Crawford must not misunderstand me, or suppose I mean to call [clergymen] the arbiters of good breeding, the regulators of refinement and courtesy, the masters of the ceremonies of life. The *manners* I speak of, might rather be called *conduct*, perhaps, the result of good principles; the effect, in short, of those doctrines which it is their duty to teach and recommend; and it will, I believe, be every where found, that as the clergy are, or are not what they ought to be, so are the rest of the nation."

"Certainly," said Fanny with gentle earnestness.

"There," cried Miss Crawford, "you have quite convinced Miss Price already." (93)

There is a touch of irony at Fanny's expense here. We see her as Mary sees her, as an insignificant good little thing; and she is still too much Edmund's creature, and his echo. Nevertheless, she is, with the reader, the spectator who sees more of the game than the contestants. The dispute between Edmund and Mary is a fundamental one. It is the dispute between principle and style.[12] For her, as for her histrionic brother, who believes he would preach splendid sermons (341), preaching is all there is of a clergyman, because that is all that *appears*; it is the part of his profession that can be done with distinction and applause. But Edmund refuses to divorce status from function; he de-emphasizes the preaching, and insists on the practice: he is Jane Austen's version of Chaucer's poor parson. Edmund takes his stand on moral ground, Mary on aesthetic. So far they are distinguished in their general discussion on the duties and the status of clergymen.

However, the issue between them is personal and private too. In reply to Mary's gay, "There, . . . you have quite convinced Miss Price already," Edmund urges,

"I wish I could convince Miss Crawford too."
"I do not think you ever will," said she with an arch smile; "I am just as much surprised now as I was at first that you should intend to take orders. You really are fit for something better. Come, do change your mind. It is not too late. Go into the law."
"Go into the law! with as much ease as I was told to go into this wilderness."
"Now you are going to say something about law being the worst wilderness of the two, but I forestall you; remember I have forestalled you." (93–4)

Mary maintains her gay and even frivolous tone, but there is more at issue here, as all three know, than a general dispute on the merits of various professions. Edmund's underlying argument might be translated thus: "Respect the calling I have chosen," he pleads, "because I want to marry you." Mary's underlying answer goes, "Well, I'm interested in your offer; but you must do something I think is worthy of *me*." They are neither of them fully conscious of this set of implications, but that is essentially the issue under discussion. That "Come, do change your mind. It is not too late," for all its playfulness, has its undertow of urgency.

In spite of Mary's trite witticism about law and the wilderness, Jane Austen evidently intends her readers to understand the wilderness emblematically. It was Mary who led the way into this wood, with its "serpentining" pathways, and Edmund enters it much as the Redcrosse Knight, accompanied by his Una, enters the Wandering Wood in which he encounters the female monster, Error. Related symbolism is unobtrusively developed elsewhere in the novel. Mary is the temptress, the siren, who plays the harp and sings. In another significant little scene involving the same trio, Edmund stands at the window with Fanny, who is like the figure of duty urging him to look up at the stars, while Mary goes to the piano to take part in a glee. He and Fanny agree to go out on the lawn to stargaze, but he finds himself unable to resist the music: "as it advanced, [Fanny] had the mortification of seeing him advance too, moving forward by gentle degrees towards the instrument, and when it ceased, he was close by the singers, among the most urgent in requesting to hear the glee again" (113). This Odysseus has neglected to have himself tied to the mast. Our last glimpse of Mary is to be of her attempt to lure Edmund back to her, with "a saucy playful smile," as he says, "seeming to invite, in order to subdue me" (459). But this time he is able to say Get thee behind me, Satan.[13]

To return to the Sotherton scene: after Mary's sally about the wilderness, Edmund admits he can never achieve a witticism, and "a general silence succeeded." Fanny, as she so often is, has been the most acute sufferer as the witness of this veiled courtship, and presently she indicates her pain:

"I wonder that I should be tired with only walking in this sweet wood; but the next time we come to a seat, if it is not disagreeable to you, I should be glad to sit down for a little while."

"My dear Fanny," cried Edmund, immediately drawing her arm within his, "how thoughtless I have been! I hope you are not very tired. Perhaps," turning to Miss Crawford, "my other companion may do me the honour of taking an arm."

"Thank you, but I am not at all tired." She took it, however, as she spoke, and the gratification of having her do so, of feeling such a connection for the first time, [here one might mark another hiatus //] made him a little forgetful of Fanny. "You scarcely touch me," said he. "You do not make me of any use. What a difference in the weight of a woman's arm from that of a man! At Oxford I have been a good deal used to have a man lean on me for the length of a street, and you are only a fly in the comparison." (94)

Now, that hardly sounds like D.H. Lawrence. Lawrence unkindly called Jane "old maid."[14] And she certainly doesn't expatiate on what he calls "That exquisite and immortal moment of a man's entry into the woman of his desire."[15] But nevertheless, Edmund registers, and within the bounds of polite converse, expresses the thrill he feels at this physical contact with Mary.

There is again an emblematic quality in this threesome – Edmund between his two women, the one needing his arm, the other consenting to take it temporarily. It is a recurring triangle. Later in the novel, Fanny is the chosen witness for another such scene: this one is literally a courtship, though played as a scene in a play. During the rehearsals for *Lovers' Vows*, first Mary and then Edmund separately seek out Fanny to hear their lines in the crucial proposal scene between Amelia and Anhalt. Fanny plays her role reluctantly enough:

> To prompt them must be enough for her; and it was sometimes *more* than enough; for she could not always pay attention to the book. . . . And agitated by the increasing spirit of Edmund's manner, had once closed the page and turned away exactly as he wanted help. It was imputed to very reasonable weariness, and she was thanked and pitied; but she deserved their pity, more than she hoped they would ever surmise. (170)

Fanny has been disliked by many because she has so much the air of a martyr; but her martyrdom is very real, for she is made to witness, and even to prompt, exchanges where the private signification is perfectly understandable and deeply painful to her.

Readers of *Mansfield Park* have more often objected to what they take to be Jane Austen's summary treatment of the important matter of how Edmund, once he has lost Mary, comes to transfer his affections to Fanny:

> Scarcely had he done regretting Mary Crawford, and observing to Fanny how impossible it was that he should ever meet with such another woman, before it began to strike him whether a very different kind of woman might not do just as well – or a great deal better. . . . I purposely abstain from dates on this occasion. (470)

But such readers have I think missed one of the major subsurface movements of the novel: Edmund's unconscious courtship of Fanny, which is concurrent with his deliberate courtship of Mary. The reader is constantly informed of how his love for Mary and his love for Fanny grow *together*. The three are always "in a cluster together" (86), they seem "naturally to unite" (90). The more Edmund's ardour kindles for Mary, the more fervent become his feelings for Fanny. He speaks of them as "the two dearest objects I have on earth" (264). When he confesses his love for Mary to Fanny, he calls *her* "Dearest Fanny!" and presses "her hand to his lips, with almost as much warmth as if it had been Miss Crawford's" (269). And when he writes to Fanny of his beloved, he tells her, "There is something soothing in the idea, that we have the same friend, and that whatever unhappy differences of opinion may exist between us, we are united in our love of you" (420). He had indeed needed Fanny's "prompting," even in his courtship of the other woman.

Of course the psychological probability of the confidante's becoming a principal in the love affair is frequently demonstrated in literature as in life. Ritualized comic versions of the situation appear several times in Shakespeare alone (not to mention *Lovers' Vows* itself), and Fanny in her role as prompter for Edmund might well say with Viola, "A barful strife! / Whoe'er I woo, myself would be his wife!" A more serious psychological study appears in *Henry Esmond*, where the hero woos Beatrix for a decade, making a confidante of her mother, and finally marries the mother instead. And George Eliot exploited the same situation for irony and pathos in the relation of Farebrother, Mary Garth and Fred Vincy, in *Middlemarch*.

Mary Crawford and Fanny, for Edmund, are a package deal; and at the end he simply discovers that he has mistaken the wrapping for the gift. So, in the scene at Sotherton I have been discussing, Edmund's decorous place between the two young ladies, courteously lending an arm to each, is an objective correlative for the passionate tensions of the eternal triangle.

The next scene I would like to mine is from *Persuasion*. It occurs during the walk to Winthrop, when Louisa Musgrove has just urged her sister Henrietta to visit her cousin and admirer Charles Hayter, in spite of the disapproval of the status-seeking Mary Musgrove, who feels Henrietta should connect herself better. Louisa boasts to Captain Wentworth of her part in the affair, while Anne accidentally overhears:

"And so, I made her go. I could not bear that she should be frightened from the visit by such nonsense. What! – would I be turned back from doing a thing that I had determined to do, and that I knew to be right, by the airs and interference of such a person? – or, of any person I may say. No, – I have no idea of being so easily persuaded. When I have made up my mind, I have made it. And Henrietta seemed entirely to have made up hers to call at Winthrop to-day – and yet, she was as near giving it up, out of nonsensical complaisance!"
"She would have turned back then, but for you?"
"She would indeed. I am almost ashamed to say it."
"Happy for her, to have such a mind as yours at hand!" (87)

Anyone with sense and discrimination can see that Louisa is expressing herself with more force than intelligence: the sister who urges a persuadable mind in one direction may be as blameworthy as the sister-in-law who urges it in the other. But, with the kind of deafness to nuance and delicacy that characterizes the Mrs. Eltons of the world, she insists on her own irreproachable rectitude. Louisa's strengths and deficiencies, however, are not so interesting to us as Wentworth's misjudgements of them. For him all discussions on the influence of one person over another relate to himself, and his broken engagement to Anne, and Lady Russell's persuasion that caused the breach. When he says, "Happy for her, to have such a mind as yours at hand!" he has mentally recast all the people in question, so that Henrietta has become Anne, himself Charles Hayter, Mary Lady Russell, and Louisa the advocate he wishes he himself had had eight years ago. The rights and wrongs of the case he has not yet come to terms with. All he feels now is, "*I* have suffered because Anne yielded to persuasion; therefore the others must have been wrong." This is the premise on which he bases his moral philosophy.

"Your sister is an amiable creature; but *yours* is the character of decision and firmness, I see. If you value her conduct or happiness, infuse as much of your own spirit into her, as you can. But this, no doubt, you have been always doing. It is the worst evil of too yielding and indecisive a character, that no influence over it can be depended on. – You are never sure of a good impression being durable. Every body may sway it." (88)

Here, of course, there is an irony for the reader. Wentworth is supposing that because Anne gave him up she is inconstant in her heart, whereas we know, as we listen with her, that *her* feelings have scarcely altered through eight years, and we will soon find out that the "firm" Louisa will transfer her affections in a few weeks.

"Let those who would be happy be firm [he continues]. – Here is a nut," said he, catching one down from an upper bough. "To exemplify, – a beautiful glossy nut, which, blessed with original strength, has outlived all the storms of autumn. Not a puncture, not a weak spot any where. – This nut," he continued, with playful solemnity, – "while so many of its brethren have fallen and been trodden under foot, is still in possession of all the happiness that a hazel-nut can be supposed capable of." Then, returning to his former earnest tone: "My first wish for all, whom I am interested in, is that they should be firm. If Louisa Musgrove would be beautiful and happy in her November of life, she will cherish all her present powers of mind." (88)

His solemnity is not really playful, though he is conducting an entertaining conversation – speaking aphoristically, and illustrating his maxims by apt analogy with elements of the autumn landscape. If we did not know the circumstances, we would be forced to suppose that this man has a bee in his bonnet about firmness: he is almost obsessive. "My first wish for all, whom I am interested in, is that they should be firm" – a curious priority! And then, "If Louisa Musgrove would be beautiful and happy in her November of life, she will cherish all her present powers of mind." He is thinking of the contrast with Anne. Anne, as he resentfully thinks of her now, is not beautiful and happy, but faded and miserable, and so she deserves to be in this and every other November of her life. That is the feeling that underlies his analogy. And in his little parable of the nut he is wiser than he knows. Louisa, in comparison with Anne, does have a limited range of sensibility, and can perhaps hope to achieve not very much more than "all the happiness that a hazel-nut can be supposed capable of." We need hardly pause over the quality of his advice – thus encouraged by him, Louisa does "cherish all her present powers of mind," and, through her stubborn persistence on the Cobb at Lyme, nearly knocks out her brains altogether.

Captain Wentworth speaks with a weight of implication of which he is not, as Edmund is in the other scene, in control. His speech has been essentially an expression of his resentment against the persuadability of Anne Elliot, but the form it has taken is earnest praise of Louisa Musgrove.

He had done, – and was unanswered. It would have surprised Anne, if Louisa could have readily answered such a speech – words of such interest, spoken with such serious warmth! – she could imagine what Louisa was feeling. For herself – [//] she feared to move, lest she should be seen. (88)

Captain Wentworth has essentially been saying: "Anne made me miserable by listening to someone else's advice"; Louisa has heard "What an admirable woman you are! I would like to make you happy." Anne has heard some combination of both. And from this time, particularly as Henrietta is now out of the picture, Captain Wentworth is considered by Anne and others to be virtually engaged to Louisa. He has committed himself to one woman because of her unlikeness to the one he is really thinking of.

From his commitment he is happily released by Louisa's fortunate facility in falling in love with Captain Benwick. He must then inform Anne that he had never been in love with Louisa. They are at a public assembly in Bath, and he must again make his declaration by indirection: "I regard Louisa Musgrove as a very amiable, sweet-tempered girl, and not deficient in understanding; but Benwick is something more" (182). *Now* he is in control of his language of implication, and Anne is perfectly able to translate it: "His opinion of Louisa Musgrove's inferiority, an opinion which he had seemed solicitous to give, his wonder at Captain Benwick . . . – all, all declared that he had a heart returning to her" (185). The full declaration – and it is fuller in this novel than in any of the six – is to come in a scene that exactly parallels the scene with the hazel-nut. Anne, in the fullness of her experience of eight years of fidelity to her love, speaks to Harville on the subject of constancy in men and women, while this time Wentworth is the eavesdropper. There is the same oblique communication between the two, and Wentworth like Anne has been put through the agony of jealousy. The spurious virtue of firmness has been re-categorized as obstinacy, and the real virtue of constancy is given due credit. As he listens, Wentworth is able to write, without indirection, words that are for Anne's eyes alone: "I am half agony, half hope. . . . I offer myself to you again with a heart even more your own, than when you almost broke it eight years and a half ago" (237). Anne had a smaller proportion of hope to agony in the previous scene, but she had the same feelings, though they were never voiced, there and through most of the novel.

Captain Wentworth is closer to being a Mr. Rochester than any other of Jane Austen's heroes. When Mr. Rochester finds himself tied to a woman he doesn't love, he "unlocked a trunk which contained a brace of loaded pistols" (*Jane Eyre*, ch. 27), and when he is deserted by the one he does, "He grew savage – quite savage on his disappointment. . . . he got dangerous after he lost her. He would be alone, too" (ch. 36). Now, perhaps Wentworth is not quite the stuff that Mr. Rochester is made of, and Jane Austen gives us no expanded account of his behaviour in his darkest hours after Anne rejected him. But we do have, in the course of conversation in the drawing-room at Uppercross, sufficient indication that he too has passed through the valley of the shadow. The Musgrove girls look for his first command, the *Asp*, in the navy list.

> "You will not find her there. [he tells them] – Quite worn out and broken up. I was the last man who commanded her. – Hardly fit for service then. – Reported fit for home service for a year or two, – and so I was sent off to the West Indies."
> The girls looked all amazement.
> "The admiralty," he continued, "entertain themselves now and then, with sending a few hundred men to sea, in a ship not fit to be employed." (64–5)

And when his brother-in-law tells him he was lucky to get even such a command as the *Asp*, he admits, "I was as well satisfied with my appointment as you can desire. It was a great object with me, at that time, to be at sea, – a very great object. I wanted to be doing something" (65). The reference to his state of mind on being dismissed by Anne is clear. We have seen "no tear-floods, nor sigh-tempests," no pistols removed from the trunk, no alienation from all society – just a light-toned conversation with new acquaintance about the course of his profession. But Anne and the reader can understand that his mood was as close to being suicidal as Mr. Rochester's was, that he went to sea in a leaky ship, and would as soon have gone to the bottom as not. He has been Jane Austen's restrained version of Childe Harold, a "gloomy wanderer o'er the wave."

As we have seen, in *Emma* the characters' skill in delivering secret messages to each other in social gatherings is highly developed – so much so that Jane Fairfax and Frank Churchill can carry on a lovers' quarrel in general company at Box Hill, and even break off their engagement, without any of the surrounding characters' being aware of what is happening. The scene is a vivid testimony of Jane Austen's power to advance the private and the public – the individual love affair and the surface of the lives of genteel English people – simultaneously. This kind of double communication is quite accessible to the awakened personnel of her novels. As Frank Churchill says after the quarrel scene, "She spoke her resentment in a form of words perfectly intelligible to me" (441).

That form of words is not, I suspect, perfectly intelligible to Charlotte Brontë and her allies. She accused Jane Austen of being deaf to the rhythms of the human heart, but she herself had no ear for the still small voice. She was attuned to what Scott called "The Big Bow-wow strain."[16]

In general terms I have been talking about the power of form to liberate rather than to limit. In art the restrictions of form and discipline do not confine, but rather define. "As well a well wrought urne becomes / The greatest ashes, as halfe-acre tombes" – the sentiment was shared and practised by Jane Austen, even if the metaphor would be hardly characteristic. Her novels are well wrought urns, where Charlotte Brontë's preference was more in the line of half-acre tombs. I have had occasion to quote Donne once before in this chapter; and, strange bedfellows as they seem at first sight, Donne and Jane Austen have much in common. They both have the conviction that it is not the quantity of experience that counts, but the quality; and they both have the concomitant power to make "one little roome, an every where." They find the world's room in a bed, in a relationship, or in Highbury, or in those "3 or 4 Families in a Country Village" that Jane Austen delighted in writing about (*Letters*, 401).

We all know that Jane Austen was an ironist. Studies of her irony have formed the mainstay of much twentieth-century criticism of her novels. But we usually associate irony with the intellect: we think of it as a polemical tool, or as a means of creating comedy through its illumination of incongruity; we assume that the ironist maintains a cerebral detachment, like Mr. Bennet's in *Pride and Prejudice*. Marvin Mudrick even heads one of the chapters of his book on Jane Austen's irony "Irony and Convention *versus* Feeling."[17] But irony and feeling are not necessarily opposed: there is an irony used to express emotion as well as an irony used to make fun of it. Arthur Sidgwick pointed this out in an early and illuminating article on the term: "It often comes about," he said, "that while the lower stages of feeling can be expressed, the higher stages must be suggested. In the ascent the full truth will do; but the climax can only be reached by irony."[18] I do not claim quite this much for Jane Austen – she does not deal in the tragic experience of an Oedipus or an Othello; but her power of understatement, and ability to express feelings by indirection, inform her novels with emotional intensity. She offers us far more than the *surface* of the lives of genteel English people.

Notes

1. A version of this paper was originally published in *Ariel*, 5:2 (April, 1974), pp. 5–24. Since then, further discussions of Jane Austen's handling of love and the passions have emerged. I refer the interested reader particularly to Barbara Hardy, "The Feelings and the Passions," the second chapter of her *A Reading of Jane Austen* (London: Owen, 1975), pp. 37–65; Mark Kinkead-Weekes, "This Old Maid: Jane Austen Replies to Charlotte Brontë and D.H. Lawrence," *Nineteenth-Century Fiction*, 30:3 (December, 1975), pp. 399–419; and A. O. J. Cockshut, *Man and Woman: A Study of Love and the Novel, 1740–1940* (London: Collins, 1977). It would be anachronistic to update further for this 1978 essay.

2. Letter to W.S. Williams, April 12, 1850. *The Shakespeare Head Brontë* (Oxford, 1931), xiv, p. 99. Reprinted in *Jane Austen: The Critical Heritage*, ed. B.C. Southam (London: Routledge & Kegan Paul, 1928), p. 128.

3. Letter to W.D. Howells, January 18, 1909. *Mark Twain's Letters*, ed. A.B. Paine (New York: Harper, 1917).

4. Unpublished manuscript entitled "Jane Austen." I quote from Ian Watt's introduction to *Jane Austen: a Collection of Critical Essays* (Englewood Cliffs: Prentice-Hall, 1963), p. 7.

5. "The Lady Novelists," *Westminster Review*, 58 (July, 1852), p. 134. See *Critical Heritage*, p. 140.

6. Letter to Ruskin, 5 November 1855. *Letters of Elizabeth Barrett Browning*, ed. F.G. Kenyon (London, 1897), ii, p. 217. See *Jane Austen: The Critical Heritage*, ed. B.C. Southam (London: Routledge & Kegan Paul, 1968), p. 25.

7. *Jane Austen: a Collection of Critical Essays*, p. 4.

8. Howard Babb has pointed out how "most of Jane Austen's critics are obsessed by a sense of her limitations." *Jane Austen's Novels: the Fabric of Dialogue* (Ohio: Ohio State University Press, 1962), p. 3.

9. "Biographical Notice" in her introduction to *Wuthering Heights*.

10. The earlier novels have the most of this kind of traditional satire: General Tilney, Lucy Steele, and Caroline Bingley are deceitful; but Elizabeth, Mary Crawford, Emma and Captain Wentworth are self-deluded.

11. Howard Babb has provided excellent analyses of these and other passages in *Jane Austen: the Fabric of Dialogue*. My emphasis differs from his, however.

12. Lionel Trilling points out how Mary Crawford "cultivates the *style* of sensitivity, virtue, and intelligence." *The Opposing Self* (New York: Viking Press, 1955), p. 220.

13. Marvin Mudrick comments perversely on this passage, "Mary has suddenly become Satan," and calls this final view of her "a grotesque makeshift." *Jane Austen: Irony as Defense and Discovery* (Princeton:

Princeton University Press, 1952), p. 165. But the imagery throughout has prepared us for such a view of Mary.

14. In "Apropos of *Lady Chatterley's Lover*" (1930). See Mark Kinkead-Weekes, cited above.

15. *John Thomas and Lady Jane* (New York: Viking Press, 1972), p. 114.

16. Scott was opposing this to what he called Jane Austen's "exquisite touch," and her "talent for describing the involvement and feelings and characters of ordinary life." See *Critical Heritage*, p. 106.

17. *Jane Austen: Irony as Defense and Discovery*, p. 60.

18. "On Some Forms of Irony in Literature," *Cornhill*, 58 (April, 1907), p. 499.

10

Love and Pedagogy[1]

"Your lessons found the weakest part," Vanessa complained to her tutor Cadenus, "Aim'd at the head, and reach'd the heart." Swift and Vanessa weren't the first couple, not yet the last, to discover that the master–pupil relationship can be a highly aphrodisiac one.[2] From Heloise and Abelard to Eliza Doolittle and Henry Higgins, history and literature produce recurrent examples of relations that evolve from the academic to the erotic. And Jane Austen's novels afford in themselves a range of possibilities in the operations of teaching and learning as an emotional bond. As Lionel Trilling points out, Jane Austen "was committed to the ideal of 'intelligent love,' according to which the deepest and truest relationship that can exist between human beings is pedagogic. This relationship consists in the giving and receiving of knowledge about right conduct, in the formation of one person's character by another, the acceptance of another's guidance in one's own growth."[3]

Jane Austen, in exploring this subject so thoroughly, perhaps sets a standard for the nineteenth-century novel, which continued, partly because of its strongly didactic intention, to present love stories in which the heroine falls in love with a man who is her tutor, or her mentor, or her superior in age, experience or authority. No doubt there is an Oedipal element in the relationship: the daughter is sexually attracted to the embodiment of her father's loving role.[4] But society generally condones and even encourages this attitude, where it usually looks with disapproval or disgust on the young man who marries the older woman, however wise she may be.

Charlotte Brontë, in spite of her scorn of Jane Austen for knowing nothing of the Passions, nonetheless fastened on the same central relationship for her most passionate attachments. Mr. Rochester is "the master," and Jane, equal soul though she is, looks up to him from the stance of servant, daughter, pupil:[5] "I love Thornfield," she acknowledges; "I love it, because I have lived in it a full and delightful life . . . I have talked, face to face, with what I reverence; with what I delight in, – with an original, a vigorous, an expanded mind. I have known

150

you, Mr. Rochester" (*Jane Eyre*, ch. 23). Lucy Snowe's relation to Monsieur Paul is literally pedagogic, since he becomes her tutor: "His mind was indeed my library, and whenever it was opened to me, I entered bliss" (*Villette*, ch. 33). Charlotte Brontë, pupil of Monsieur Héger, knew what it was like to be in love with the master, and in her novels she charges the pedagogic relationships with a passion which, though she apparently did not notice it in Jane Austen's novels, she might well have found there in a refined but still intense form.

George Eliot too examined how "potent in us is the infused action of another soul, before which we bow in complete love" (*Daniel Deronda*, ch. 65); but her treatment of the pedagogic relationship differs from Charlotte Brontë's in that it introduces an element of grim irony. Perhaps she remembered with some qualms of embarrassment her adolescent susceptibility to handsome language teachers and elderly pedants,[6] and sought to exorcise the memories. Maggie Tulliver begs Philip Wakem, "Teach me everything, wouldn't you? Greek and everything" (*The Mill on the Floss*, II, ch. 6), and he does undertake to develop her and direct her reading, falling deeply in love with her in the process; but her love for him is a thin cerebral quantity that cannot match the force of her strong sexual attraction to Stephen Guest. Dorothea Brooke looks joyfully forward to a marriage in which "she would be allowed to live continually in the light of a mind that she could reverence," but finds that Mr. Casaubon's mind is only a series of dark "vaults where he walked taper in hand" (*Middlemarch*, I, chs. 5, 10). And Gwendolen Harleth, eager to receive Deronda's instruction and render her self in return, discovers that though he is ready enough with instruction, he doesn't want *her*.

Henry James goes further still in exploring the sinister implications in the pedagogic relationship. That it fascinated him is testified by his first novel, *Watch and Ward*, which is about a man who brings up his ward, educates her, and marries her at last. But he leads us through a series of disturbing speculations about the right of one mind to govern another, in presenting Maisie, who is used for dubious purposes in the sexual relations of her parents and parent surrogates; Miles and Flora, who apparently either pervert or are perverted by their governess; and Isabel Archer, who negates herself by trying to conform to the aesthetic standards of the manipulators who surround her. The culmination is the horrible premise of the narrator of *The Sacred Fount*, that what one gives – of youth, of wisdom, of joy – is by definition no longer one's own: that the donor becomes, in the process of giving, correspondingly depleted. You can't eat your cake and have it too.

When he hears of how much grace and intelligence a certain lady has imparted to a man, he asks incredulously, "She keeps her wit then, . . . in spite of all she pumps into others?" (ch. 1). And he gradually persuades his interlocutor,

> "Whoever she is, she gives all she has. She keeps nothing back – nothing for herself."
> "I see – because *he* takes everything. He just cleans her out."
> (ch. 3)

Similar metaphors are multiplied, until the one who gives is seen as a "victim," the one who receives as "the author of the sacrifice," and we are presented with a complete theory of human relations as a system of parasitism, of society as composed of vampires and victims. The narrator of *The Sacred Fount* may be a crazy hypothesizer, but James gives his theory a certain authority when he returns to the giving and taking relationships again in *The Ambassadors*, where it is hard to resist the conclusion that Chad Newsome has grown fat and sleek while Madame de Vionnet has dwindled to a diaphanous wraith.

Such a progression suggests why Lionel Trilling notes that "the idea of a love based in pedagogy may seem quaint to some modern readers and repellent to others." But he goes on – "unquestionably it plays a decisive part in the power and charm of Jane Austen's art."[7] What to James is suspect and potentially horrible, for Jane Austen is a source of power and charm. For her the pedagogic relationship is not parasitic but symbiotic, a relationship that is mutual and joyful: it blesseth him that gives, and him that takes. The happy resolutions of her novels celebrate the achieved integration of head and heart that is represented by the pupil and teacher coming to loving accord. Novelists of more tragic vision are unable to visualize so complete a reconcilement. A recurring pattern in the novels of the Brontës, George Eliot, Hardy, Lawrence and others shows a split between the intellectual and the passionate, the Apollonian and the Dionysian, the spiritual and the physical; and the task of the central character is to choose *between* alternatives – between Edgar Linton and Heathcliff, St. John Rivers and Mr. Rochester, Philip Wakem and Stephen Guest, Angel Clare and Alec d'Urberville, Hermione Roddice and Ursula Brangwen. The final choice may be too difficult, and Cathy, Maggie and Tess are destroyed in the process of making it; but even where the choice is made and a fortunate resolution achieved, some loss is implied in the rejected alternative.

The alternative men for the Austen heroine – Wickham, Crawford, Churchill *et al.* – are far from presenting the same agonizing choice of alternatives. Her feelings for them – if aroused at all, which is doubtful – are transitory and swiftly recognized as a delusion. She generally recognizes joyfully that "We needs must love the highest when we see it, / Not Lancelot, nor another" – and without having to go through the extent of Guinevere's pain and error in the process. The union of Fanny Price with Edmund, say, can be entire and satisfying (at least to those readers they don't exasperate) – because Edmund has not only "formed her mind" but also "gained her affections" (*MP*, 64), and at the same time, while Fanny has not only made his knowledge and principles her own, but graduated and exceeded her teacher in discrimination and judgement.

Richard Simpson, in his fine early study of Jane Austen, pointed out her commitment to "the Platonic idea that the giving and receiving of knowledge . . . is the truest and strongest foundation of love." But he goes on to suggest that this love between her heroes and heroines doesn't amount to much: "Friendship, to judge from her novels, was enough for her; she did not want to exaggerate it into passionate love."[8] Strongly as he is convinced of her merits, he seems to agree with Charlotte Brontë that the stormy sisterhood of the passions has no place in her work, and that she opts for esteem rather than passion as the basis of a successful marriage. But Jane Austen will not accept that division – for her the full and mutual engagement of head and heart is what *is* passionate; and any substitute, like Marianne's love for Willoughby, is not only founded on a delusion, but a delusion in itself.

The pattern, however, is of course far more varied than this simplification suggests. Ian Watt comments, "As has often been observed, [Jane Austen's] young heroines finally marry older men – comprehensive epitomes of the Augustan norms such as Mr. Darcy and Mr. Knightley. Her novels in fact dramatize the process whereby feminine and adolescent values are painfully educated in the norms of the mature, rational and educated male world."[9] One doesn't need to be a woman to react to so dangerous a generalization. Elizabeth teaches Darcy as much as he teaches her; Anne and Fanny, in the main course of their novels' action, remain morally static while Wentworth and Edmund get the painful education; and Marianne, though she certainly has plenty to learn, learns from her sister. That leaves Catherine and Emma, who do get educated in the norms of their men; but even they have a certain power whereby their Pygmalions find that Galatea has turned the tables on them.

Characteristically enough, Jane Austen starts out by being ironic, even satiric, on the theme that she continues to develop through the whole body of her novels. In walking with the Tilneys, Catherine Morland discovers her ignorance on the subject of landscape and the picturesque:

> She was heartily ashamed of her ignorance. A misplaced shame. Where people wish to attach, they should always be ignorant. To come with a well-informed mind, is to come with an inability of administering to the vanity of others, which a sensible person would always wish to avoid. A woman especially, if she have the misfortune of knowing any thing, should conceal it as well as she can. (*NA*, 110–11)

And the narrator proceeds with an aphoristic discussion of how, though some men will be content with mere ignorance in a woman, most will be satisfied with nothing less than imbecility. Such satire leaves Catherine comparatively unscathed; it is Tilney who needs his vanity administering to.

The satire on the pedagogic relation notwithstanding, Jane Austen goes on to study its operation in realistic terms, and sympathetically:

> In the present instance, she confessed and lamented her want of knowledge; . . . and a lecture on the picturesque immediately followed, in which his instructions were so clear that she soon began to see beauty in every thing admired by him, and her attention was so earnest, that he became perfectly satisfied of her having a great deal of natural taste. (111)

He sounds like Emma concluding of Harriet that she is "so pleasantly grateful for being admitted to Hartfield, and so artlessly impressed by the appearance of every thing in so superior a style to what she had been used to, that she must have good sense and deserve encouragement" (*E*, 23). Jane Austen was perfectly aware of the element of self-love in the pedagogic relationship, as was Swift:

> What he had planted, now was grown;
> His Virtues she might call her own . . .
> Self-love, in Nature rooted fast,
> Attends us first, and leaves us last:
> Why she likes him, admire not at her,
> She loves her self, and that's the matter. ("Cadenus and Vanessa")

Tilney is a kind of god to Catherine – "It was no effort to Catherine to believe that Henry Tilney could never be wrong" (114): but the creature has a concomitant power over the creator, as we find in numbers of such incidents as his dance with her, during which she "enjoyed her usual happiness with Henry Tilney, listening with sparkling eyes to every thing he said; and, in finding him irresistible, becoming so herself" (131). Tilney may well find that "a teachableness of disposition in a young lady is a great blessing" (174). He needs her as much as she needs him.

He does have much to teach her, and she duly benefits from his instruction. His insistence on precision with language, as Stuart Tave suggests,[10] teaches her not only to have the right word by which to express herself, but also to define and refine the sentiment that is to be expressed. Like Henry Higgins, to some extent he creates a new identity for her by giving her a new language. And if novel readers are disposed to be disappointed, as Jane Austen predicted, "that his affection originated in nothing better than gratitude" (243), that he loves her only because she has made it so plain that she loves him, it is compensation to reflect that the woman for once is the initiator of this courtship. Catherine doesn't lecture him or consciously re-form him; but she does recognize that "he indulged himself a little too much with the foibles of others" (29) – an indulgence we later see more dangerously practised by Mr. Bennet. And in fact Tilney is not much to be admired in drawing out the absurdities of Mrs. Allen. However just his ridicule of affectation, however minute his discriminations, he is occasionally on the verge of becoming a rather glib satirist, what Isabella Thorpe would call a "quiz." He is captivated by Catherine's fresh responses and quickly engaged feelings – so that when, like Miranda looking on the brave new world, she exclaims, "Oh! who can ever be tired of Bath?" he answers with genuine appreciation, "Not those who bring such fresh feelings of every sort to it, as you do" (79). Charmingly disenchanted as he is, he needs those fresh feelings, and responds to them.

Nevertheless, we are not again to find in Jane Austen's novels so apt and so docile a pupil as Catherine Morland. To move from *Northanger Abbey* to *Pride and Prejudice* is like turning from *The Taming of the Shrew* to *Much Ado*. Henry Tilney and Petruchio have things stacked in their favour, and learn comparatively little from their two Catherines; but between Elizabeth and Darcy, as between Beatrice and Benedick, matters are even more evenly balanced. They are both student-teachers; not that either deliberately sets out to instruct or learn from the other – but they do very resoundingly teach each other a lesson. And, again as with Beatrice and Benedick, the state that exists between them is war: "They never meet but there's a skirmish of wit between them" (*Much Ado About Nothing*, I, i).

The similarity between these two gayest of their authors' works has tempted me to speculate whether Jane Austen was consciously following Shakespeare's play.[11] Beatrice, "born in a merry hour" (II, i) is surely kin to Elizabeth, who "dearly love[s] a laugh" (*PP*, 57), and her comment, "I was born to speak all mirth and no matter" (II, i), seems echoed in Jane Austen's famous admission that her novel was "rather too light, and bright, and sparkling; . . . it wants to be stretched out here and there with a long chapter of sense, if it could be had" (*Letters*, 299).

The analogy is pertinent not only for suggesting the exuberant quality of both works, but for illuminating the sexual piquancy of the love–war relation, that gives such delightful force and suggestiveness to works like *The Rape of the Lock*, *Pamela*, *Jane Eyre*, and the Wife of Bath's prologue and tale. I find it hard to credit that anyone who has read *Pride and Prejudice* could subscribe to the view of Miss Austen as an old maid who wrote sexless novels – this novel to my ear fairly rings with the jubilant fertility of spring.[12] Elizabeth's physical vitality, expressing itself in her running, her "jumping over stiles and springing over puddles" (32), and so on, is a sexual vitality too; and Darcy's strongly sexual response to her, as he gradually and unwillingly succumbs to her "fine eyes," is quite sufficiently dramatized. We see in Elizabeth as in Beatrice the subsumed attraction that is behind their antagonism – although they always fight with their men, they are always thinking of them. Beatrice, separated as she thinks from Benedick in the masked dance, says almost wistfully, "I would he had boarded me"; and Elizabeth can't see Miss de Bourgh without reflecting, "She looks sickly and cross. – Yes, she will do for him very well" – the "him" in her consciousness being Darcy (158). But relations between her and Darcy proceed stormily: she refuses to dance with him, and he is the more attracted. When she does dance with him, she quarrels with him about Wickham. They spar in the dance, skirmish at the piano, fence in conversation. Beatrice's sallies on "Signior Mountanto" are echoed in Elizabeth's witticisms at Darcy's expense: "I am perfectly convinced . . . that Mr. Darcy has no defect. He owns it himself without disguise" (57). Such is their "merry war" – very provocative, very delightful.

But the battles are not love play only – they have their serious issues, in which, without usually intending it, the antagonists set up their standards for the other to conform to or reject. Elizabeth is initially closest to being the pedagogue. Bingley recognizes her as "a studier of character" (42); and in admitting, "Follies and nonsense, whims and inconsistencies *do* divert me, I own, and I laugh at them whenever I can" (57), she achieves the status of a kind of licensed satirist during her brief stay at Netherfield. She makes full use of that licence in her critical analyses of character. In a playful context, she is a teacher catechizing a potential student in order to place him:

"Follies and nonsense, . . . I suppose, are precisely what you are without."

"Perhaps that is not possible for any one [replies Darcy]. But it has been the study of my life to avoid those weaknesses which often expose a strong understanding to ridicule."

"Such as vanity and pride."

"Yes, vanity is a weakness indeed. But pride – where there is a real superiority of mind, pride will be always under good regulation."

Elizabeth turned away to hide a smile.

"Your examination of Mr. Darcy is over, I presume," said Miss Bingley; – "and pray what is the result?" (57)

"The study of my life," "real superiority of mind," "good regulation," "examination" – this is classroom terminology. And though Darcy goes through this play catechism with the smiling detachment of an adult who has already done with exams, he is to recall and eventually be changed by Elizabeth's standards as implied in these dialogues.

There are three main subjects on which Elizabeth "examines" him in the course of the novel, and in which he acquits himself with varying degrees of credit, at various attempts.

The first issue is his right of influence over Bingley, canvassed at length, in a Netherfield discussion complete with a hypothetical case, as in an exam question (48-51). Ironically Elizabeth, who is far from being an infallible teacher, takes the opposite side in this argument from that she is to take in practice afterwards – here she defends Bingley's "merit" in his readiness "to yield readily – easily – to the *persuasion* of a friend" (50), whereas later she is to be indignant that Darcy makes him do just that.

The second aspect of Darcy's character that Elizabeth probes at Netherfield is what she calls, when he admits, "my good opinion once lost is lost for ever," his "implacable resentment" (58). Here the practical test Elizabeth administers is Wickham, against whom she believes that that resentment has been unjustly vented. Unjustifiable influence over his friend, and brutal persecution of his enemy: these are the two offences she accuses Darcy of in the first proposal scene. She has examined him as a candidate for her hand, and she fails him resoundingly. Having failed the *viva*, Darcy voluntarily sits a written exam – his letter – not to qualify himself for the same position, but to justify himself as a man of right conduct. This paper is enough to teach the teacher how wrong she has been, how "blind, partial, prejudiced, absurd."

> "How despicably have I acted!" she cried. – "I, who have prided myself on my discernment! – I, who have valued myself on my abilities! . . . I have courted prepossession and ignorance, and driven reason away, where either were concerned. Till this moment, I never knew myself." (208).

It is a salutary lesson for one who has been more fond of detecting short-comings in others than in herself.

Darcy is to be further exonerated from the charge of implacable resentment by his remarkably forbearing behaviour to Elizabeth herself, who certainly gives provocation for resentment: after she quarrels with him in the dance, his feelings for her "soon procured her pardon" (94); and though his letter after her insulting refusal begins in bitterness, "the adieu is charity itself" (368). He has been tested by having had a lot to put up with; and he has been admirably tolerant and forgiving.

However, on the third issue Darcy has more to learn, and does not acquit himself creditably until the last part of the novel. It is not a question of conduct or principle, but of manners. Again the matter is playfully canvassed between them in conversation – as usual, with an audience at hand – this time at the piano at Rosings. Elizabeth threatens to tell Colonel Fitzwilliam of Darcy's misdemeanours in Hertfordshire:

> "You shall hear then – but prepare yourself for something very dreadful. The first time of my ever seeing him in Hertfordshire, you must know, was at a ball – and at this ball, what do you think he did? He danced only four dances! I am sorry to pain you – but so it was. He danced only four dances, though gentlemen were scarce; and, to my certain knowledge, more than one young lady was sitting down in want of a partner. Mr. Darcy, you cannot deny the fact." . . .

"I certainly have not the talent which some people possess," said Darcy, "of conversing easily with those I have never seen before. I cannot catch their tone of conversation, or appear interested in their concerns, as I often see done."

"My fingers," said Elizabeth, "do not move over this instrument in the masterly manner which I see so many women's do. They have not the same force or rapidity, and do not produce the same expression. But then I have always supposed it to be my own fault – because I would not take the trouble of practising. It is not that I do not believe *my* fingers as capable as any other woman's of superior execution." (175)

Elizabeth's shortcomings as a pedagogue are still apparent in the continuing operation of that initial incident at the Meryton assembly that wounded her vanity, but here in essence she is right. Her analogy is apt – she lets Darcy know that gracious manners are not acquired simply as a ready-made gift from heaven, but that they are a skill, to be developed like other skills by exertion and practice. But Darcy, though he accepts her analogy, misapplies it and so doesn't profit from her instruction: "You are perfectly right," he acknowledges, ". . . No one admitted to the privilege of hearing you, can think any thing wanting. We neither of us perform to strangers" (176). But piano-playing is an accomplishment that anyone may choose or not choose to develop; gracious manners are a duty that everyone must practise, and most particularly those with Darcy's prominent position in the world. Again, it takes a practical issue to make the point. Darcy's churlish first proposal brings a fierce rebuke which this time sinks in, so that he can even quote it months afterwards: "Your reproof, so well applied, I shall never forget: 'had you behaved in a more gentleman-like manner.' Those were your words" (367). In the interval, like a good pupil, he has made a conscious effort "to correct my temper," and he displays his newly acquired skill when they meet at Pemberley:

"My object *then*," replied Darcy, "was to shew you, by every civility in my power, that I was not so mean as to resent the past; and I hoped to obtain your forgiveness, to lessen your ill opinion, by letting you see that your reproofs had been attended to." (370)

In this matter he has acknowledged his shortcomings and studied to correct them; and he has been an apt scholar: "You taught me a lesson," he acknowledges fervently (369). Like Benedick, he has resolved,

"I must not seem proud: happy are they that hear their detractions and can put them to mending" (II, iii).

Elizabeth has had plenty to learn too, but Darcy, though he is the occasion of her increased self-knowledge, is not so clearly the agent. The theoretical discussions at Netherfield and Rosings, which are subsequently so neatly put to the test, are about Darcy's behaviour, not Elizabeth's. Hers have been the faults of the examiner who has overestimated her qualifications and totally misjudged her examinees. They are faults not of conduct but of judgement; so that in the process whereby her failing candidate proves himself eminently qualified, and her favoured student does the reverse, she has come to know her shortcomings and herself.

On the question of Wickham's wrongs and Darcy's supposedly implacable resentment, she was entirely misguided, and Darcy had no fault to correct; and on the first issue canvassed between them, his influence on Bingley, she has learned that it is wrong only if exerted in the wrong direction; she ceases to be fanatical in her views here, but it is an issue that will arise again for playful debate between them. Darcy does still unblushingly keep Bingley under strict if friendly surveillance, and Bingley dares propose to Jane only with Darcy's permission:

> Elizabeth longed to observe that Mr. Bingley had been a most delightful friend; so easily guided that his worth was invaluable; but she checked herself. She remembered that he had yet to learn to be laught at, and it was rather too early to begin. (371)

That is a charming little preview of their marriage, confirming Elizabeth's conviction that "It was an union that must have been to the advantage of both" (312). Elizabeth, by the time they are engaged, has learned some tact and forbearance in the exercise of her wit; and Darcy, having learned manners, must go on learning – he must learn to be laughed at.

In *Pride and Prejudice* we see the pedagogic relationship stormily in process; in *Mansfield Park* it is virtually a *fait accompli* by the time the main action of the novel begins. By the end of the second chapter we get a summary of Edmund's central role in Fanny's education, and her response:

> His attentions were . . . of the highest importance in assisting the improvement of her mind, and extending its pleasures. He knew her to be clever, to have a quick apprehension as well as good sense.

... He recommended the books which charmed her leisure hours, he encouraged her taste, and corrected her judgment. . . . In return for such services she loved him better than any body in the world except William; her heart was divided between the two. (22)

By his early pedagogic role he has "formed her mind and gained her affections" (64). That state of affairs is memorably dramatized in the stargazing scene, where Fanny seeks to hold Edmund's attention by rhapsodizing over the natural beauty he has taught her to admire. "Here's harmony!" she exclaims, "Here's repose . . ."

"I like to hear your enthusiasm, Fanny. It is a lovely night, and they are much to be pitied who have not been taught to feel in some degree as you do – who have not at least been given a taste for nature in early life. They lose a great deal."
"*You* taught me to think and feel on the subject, cousin."
"I had a very apt scholar." (113)

At this point, however, Edmund is disposed to turn from his faithful creature to metal more attractive. Fanny's story is to begin when, as the now qualified star pupil, she watches her honoured master stray into error and pain, – led there by her rival the wayward pupil. What she has learned is put to its severest test when she must detach the learning from the tutor, and subject him to the tests of the very principles he has taught her.

It is noteworthy that "the first actual pain" that Mary Crawford occasions Fanny is caused when Edmund adopts the pedagogic stance with her – he teaches her to ride. His instructions to Fanny have always had a strongly moral cast: "You are sorry to leave Mamma, my dear little Fanny," he once comforted her, "which shows you to be a very good girl" (15) – and to maintain that role of the good girl in Edmund's estimation becomes her constant practice. But to Mary Crawford, whose attractions are more overtly physical, he initially teaches a physical activity. When Fanny, neglected and sorry for herself, watches from afar, she has cause to feel a pang at the physical intimacy that his instruction promotes:

After a few minutes, they stopt entirely, Edmund was close to her, he was speaking to her, he was evidently directing her management of the bridle, he had hold of her hand; she saw it, or the imagination supplied what the eye could not reach. (67)

Fanny as a child had her own feelings warmed by such attentions from Edmund, when he ruled her lines for her letters, and stood by "to assist her with his penknife or his orthography, as either were wanted" (16). Now she is naturally quick to discover Edmund's attraction to his new pupil; and he is soon making her his confidante in his discussion of the shortcomings and charms of her rival.

"I am glad you saw it all as I did" [he tells her after one such discussion].

Having formed her mind and gained her affections, he had a good chance of her thinking like him; though at this period, and on this subject, there began now to be some danger of dissimilarity, for he was in a line of admiration of Miss Crawford, which might lead him where Fanny could not follow. (64)

It is in this direction that Fanny's story is to develop. She has been and is a good pupil, and the love that grew out of the pedagogic relation is to remain constant; but Fanny is to graduate from the status of pupil to adult in the process of separating her judgement from Edmund's, and detecting him in error. Fanny as pupil "regarded her cousin as an example of every thing good and great. . . . Her sentiments towards him were compounded of all that was respectful, grateful, confiding, and tender" (37). Fanny as adolescent wonders, "Could it be possible? Edmund so inconsistent. . . . Was he not wrong?" (156). Fanny as adult discovers, "He is blinded, and nothing will open his eyes" (424). But the pupil is morally debarred from opening her master's eyes, even though he recognizes her sound judgement and even reverses their roles by applying to her for advice: she cannot in honour denigrate her rival; hence her story must be a "trial," like Pamela's; and like Jane Austen's other actively passive heroines, Elinor and Anne, she must achieve through endurance rather than through action.

Mary Crawford, though she outclasses Fanny as a horsewoman, proves to be morally a totally intractable pupil. Edmund's most sustained effort in instructing her, as we have seen, is the conversation in the wood at Sotherton, where he carefully justifies his decision to enter the ministry, and persuasively explains the importance of a clergyman's duties. His lecture elicits an earnest "Certainly" from Fanny, but Mary Crawford asserts, "I am just as much surprised now as I was at first that you should intend to take orders" (93). She is simply determined not to listen: her mind is closed. And her very recalcitrance has its attractions for the teacher, who begins to succumb to that danger, not unknown to many of us, of paying most attention to the worst students: "He still reasoned with her, but in vain. She would not calculate, she would not compare. She would only smile and assert. The greatest degree of rational consistency could not have been more engaging, and they talked with mutual satisfaction" (96). And – again a familiar fault in pedagogues – he excuses her shortcomings as a moral student by blaming her previous educators: "Yes, that uncle and aunt! They have injured the finest mind!" (269)

Though Mary closes her mind to Edmund's influence, she is ambitious to influence *him*. And in her case it is not that her chief end is his moral welfare, but that she enjoys power. When she urges him to go into law she could conceivably have his good, as well as her own, in view; but in the matter of the play her tactics in persuading him to take the part of Anhalt are directed not only to getting him to play opposite her, but also to conquering him, because she relishes the triumph of making him act against his principles. Her fondest memory is of this victory: "His sturdy spirit to bend as it did! Oh, it was sweet beyond expression" (358). This sinister bit of gloating is another of the touches that remind us of Mary as temptress, seductress – as even Satanic.

Lovers' Vows provides a paradigm for the novel in that Edmund's role is Anhalt, who is literally the tutor of the heroine, Amelia. There are some crude statements there of themes Jane Austen enlarges on more subtly in the novel. Amelia tells her tutor, for instance, "My father has more than once told me that he who forms my mind I should always consider as my greatest benefactor. [*looking down*] And my heart tells me the same" (503–4).[13] And when Anhalt admits that "love" is the subject of their discourse, Amelia pursues, "[*going up to him*]. Come, then, teach it me – teach it me as you taught me geography, languages, and other important things" (506). Such might well be Fanny's sentiments, though of course it will be long before she can voice them. But it is Mary who plays Amelia's part: Mary has Amelia's brass, and Amelia's sense that her tutor is her social inferior – a sense that ultimately makes her unable to accept Edmund. But Fanny has been the docile and loving pupil – until she perceives Edmund's clouded judgement. Amelia's role of the enamoured pupil combines Edmund's two women.

Emma, like Mary Crawford, is a bad pupil. They both have the talents to be good students, but the temperament to resist instruction. But though that is the whole of Mary's story, it is only a part of Emma's.

The novel opens on the evening of Miss Taylor's withdrawal from Hartfield, and Mr. Knightley's consequent friendly visit. Miss Taylor, we hear at the outset, has long been Emma's friend rather than her governess, and Emma, though "highly esteeming Miss Taylor's judgment," has been "directed chiefly by her own" (*E*, 5). Mr. Knightley is to tell Miss Taylor affectionately that she is "very fit for a wife, but not at all for a governess" (38). Still, she has been there, and now she has gone. That scene introduces not only the marriage theme of the novel, and "the question of dependence or independence" (10),[14] but also the theme of Emma's education. Exit governess, enter governor: "Mr. Knightley, in fact, was one of the few people who could see faults in Emma Woodhouse, and the only one who ever told her of them: . . . this was not particularly agreeable to Emma herself" (11). That is the initial situation, which we see dramatised at length in subsequent scenes. Emma doesn't like to be told she has anything to learn, and she argues.

On nearly all the questions at issue between them – and the working out of these constitutes the novel's structure – Mr. Knightley is right and Emma is wrong. Mr. Knightley condemns her matchmaking propensity: "Your time has been properly and delicately spent," he says with sarcasm, "if you have been endeavouring for the last four years to bring about this marriage" (12). But Emma insists, "Only one more [match] . . .; only for Mr. Elton" (13). And at the end she realizes how "with unpardonable arrogance [she had] proposed to arrange everybody's destiny" (413). Mr. Knightley objects to Emma's intimacy with Harriet, whom he calls "the very worst sort of companion that Emma could possibly have" (38). Emma maintains the intimacy notwithstanding, but is to exclaim at last, "Oh God! that I had never seen her!" (411). Mr. Knightley wants her to recognize Jane Fairfax's better claims to attention, but Emma persists in neglecting her, until she is made aware of her "past injustice towards Miss Fairfax" (421). Mr. Knightley tells her she is not sufficiently considerate towards Miss Bates, but his hints are not "equal to counteract the persuasion of its being very disagreeable" (155); until she eventually reproaches herself bitterly, "How could she have been so brutal, so cruel to Miss Bates!" (376). The only matter on which Mr. Knightley's judgement is not fully to be trusted is the merits, or lack of them, of Frank Churchill, and here Emma is shrewd:

"You seem determined to think ill of him."
"Me! – not at all," replied Mr. Knightley, rather displeased. (149)

His forgivable jealousy is the only passion that will lead his otherwise sound judgement astray.

So, as in *Pride and Prejudice*, there is the beautifully symmetrical pattern of the precept laid down and discussed in theory, the practical test, and the access of knowledge with experience. Emma is the wayward pupil; she does not simply close her mind like Mary Crawford, but she refuses to acknowledge she has anything to learn for as long as she can. And there is a focus of emotional intensity in their arguments – in Mr. Knightley's pleasure when Emma seems to have taken his advice, his disappointment when she turns out to be unreformed; in Emma's fluctuations of rebelliousness and fear of him in his "tall indignation" (60), and her schemes for placating him without actually taking his advice. In the scene where he exclaims, "Nonsense, errant nonsense, as ever was talked!" to her argument that Robert Martin is not fit for Harriet,

> Emma made no answer, and tried to look cheerfully unconcerned, but was really feeling uncomfortable and wanting him very much to be gone. She did not repent what she had done; she still thought herself a better judge of such a point of female right and refinement than he could be; but yet she had a sort of habitual respect for his judgement in general, which made her dislike having it so loudly against her; and to have him sitting just opposite to her in angry state, was very disagreeable. (65)

She cares about his disapproval, "she was sorry, but could not repent" (69). Like other wayward pupils who would rather resort to wiles than learn the lesson, she contrives a reconciliation with him while they are in physical contact, dandling their niece. "It did assist; for though he began with grave looks and short questions, he was soon led on to . . . take the child out of her arms with all the unceremoniousness of perfect amity" (98).

On another occasion she plays with his eagerness for her properly appreciating Jane Fairfax. He warmly praises her attentions as hostess; "I am happy you approved," she says, smiling; but deliberately adds her old objection, "Miss Fairfax is reserved" (170–1).

> "My dear Emma," said he, moving from his chair into one close by her, "you are not going to tell me, I hope, that you had not a pleasant evening."
>
> "Oh! no; I was pleased with my own perseverance in asking questions, and amused to think how little information I obtained."

"I am disappointed," was his only answer. . . .

Emma saw his anxiety, and wishing to appease it, at least for the present, said, and with a sincerity which no one could question –

"She is a sort of elegant creature that one cannot keep one's eyes from. I am always watching her to admire; and I do pity her from my heart."

Mr. Knightley looked as if he were more gratified than he cared to express. (171)

Here we trace the emotions of the pedagogue, eager for his student's progress: his warm physical approach, his distress in her backsliding, his gratification in the appeasement. We read also the pupil's conscious withholding of complete conformity with the instructor's demands, so that her response is chosen acquiescence rather than obedience or subjection.

Emma as rebellious student often tries to bring Mr. Knightley round to her way of thinking, and occasionally has the pedagogue's pleasure in success. When he acknowledges Harriet's claims by dancing with her after Mr. Elton's slight, Emma is jubilant. "Never had she been more surprised, seldom more delighted, than at that instant. She was all pleasure and gratitude, . . . and longed to be thanking him; and though too distant for speech, her countenance said much, as soon as she could catch his eye again" (328). Even here, where Emma is delighting in his attention to her own star pupil, we are reminded of her subconscious love by a hint of jealousy: "Harriet would have seemed almost too lucky, if it had not been for the cruel state of things before" (328).

The culmination of all these arguments, the pedagogic battles and the latent love, is of course the Miss Bates incident. It is the emotional climax of the novel. Mr. Knightley believes Emma will very soon marry his rival, but claims his privilege for the last time – "once more" – of remonstrating when he sees her acting wrongly. "Emma recollected, blushed, was sorry, but tried to laugh it off" (374) – the usual pattern. He persists in his reproach, however, and this time deeply disturbs her – "she felt it at her heart" (376). But there is no time for placation or reconciliation, and after the hurried parting, Emma is utterly desolate. All her confidence in her own judgement, her perseverance in her own courses, her determination not to give in, are done away with. She mends her ways and calls on Miss Bates, rather hoping Mr. Knightley will find her so creditably occupied: "She had no objection. She would not be ashamed of the appearance of the penitence, so justly and truly hers" (377-8). For this occasion, she is a new Emma. And when Mr. Knightley does understand she is conciliating and not resentful, it is a moment of full and loving accord, and physically expressed:

> He looked at her with a glow of regard. . . . He took her hand; – whether she had not herself made the first motion, she could not say – she might, perhaps, have rather offered it – but he took her hand, pressed it, and certainly was on the point of carrying it to his lips. (385–6)

Emma and Mr. Knightley have both more to learn about each other's feelings before that kiss can happen; but the spontaneous and simultaneous clasp of the hands, in the moment of harmony between master and pupil, is a memorable image for the mutually passionate and joyful commitment implied in the pedagogic relationship in Jane Austen's novels.

Emma's and Mr. Knightley's love has grown and been manifested in their relations as master and pupil. When Emma discovers her love for him, it is in terms of his teaching role: "He had loved her, and watched over her from a girl, with an endeavour to improve her, and an anxiety for her doing right, which no other creature had at all shared" (415); and when he avows his love for her, it is in the same terms; "You hear nothing but truth from me. – I have blamed you, and lectured you, and you have borne it as no other woman in England would have borne it" (430). Mind and heart have been fully and simultaneously involved, so that the love has found its existence and expression through the teaching and the learning. In Mr. Knightley's case, by his own avowal, it is the love that has taken precedence of the education: "My interference was quite as likely to do harm as good. . . . The good was all to myself, by making you an object of the tenderest affection to me" (462).

In *Persuasion* it is the hero who must learn, while the heroine remains morally static. But we do not have a full reversal of the Emma–Mr. Knightley situation, in that Anne teaches Wentworth not by precept but by example, so that she doesn't really qualify for the pedagogue's role in that relation. As in *Pride and Prejudice*, the principals of this novel are in a sense antagonists – Wentworth is determined to stay angry with Anne as Elizabeth is determined to dislike Darcy – but here we have no merry war. The "perpetual estrangement" (64) is a cause not of merriment but of pain, and gives the novel its emotional poignancy. Anne is isolated from the man she loves, and can neither influence him nor be influenced by him for much of the novel. This estrangement is emphasized by the fact that hero and heroine – briefly and abortively – set up pedagogic relations elsewhere.

As we have seen, Wentworth takes on the role of pedagogue for his other woman: and being offended by Anne's persuadability, lectures Louisa on the virtues of firmness: "My first wish for all, whom I am interested in, is that they should be firm" (88). The misguided teacher finds an enthusiastic pupil, and Louisa, "being now armed with the idea of merit in maintaining her own way" (94), insists on going to Lyme, insists on being jumped from stiles, insists on leaping from the Cobb. "I am determined I will," she declares (109) – and so she comes a cropper.

In the interval Anne has become instructress for another man too, the bereaved Captain Benwick, who like her is grieving over a lost love. She gives him a bracing lecture on fortitude, and, "feeling in herself the right of seniority of mind," directs him to read "such works of our best moralists . . . as occurred to her at the moment as calculated to rouse and fortify the mind by the highest precepts" (101). She is not without a wry sense of the irony of her role as instructress:

> Anne could not but be amused at the idea of her coming to Lyme, to preach patience and resignation to a young man whom she had never seen before; nor could she help fearing, on more serious reflection, that, like many other great moralists and preachers, she had been eloquent on a point in which her own conduct would ill bear examination. (101)

For all this, Benwick responds as warmly to her instructions as Louisa does to Wentworth's, and seems so ready and eager to be consoled that he is in a fair way to forgetting his lost fiancée in falling in love with Anne.

However, by that symmetrical recoupling caused by the accident on the Cobb, the two facile pupils are thrown together and very plausibly united, so clearing away at least some of the obstacles between their instructors.

> [Anne] saw no reason against their being happy. . . . They would soon grow more alike. He would gain cheerfulness, and she would learn to be an enthusiast for Scott and Lord Byron; nay, that was

probably learnt already; of course they had fallen in love over poetry. (167)

There is a little history in miniature of a pedagogic relationship,
stripped of the perils and pitfalls encountered by more complex souls
like Elizabeth, Darcy and Emma.

Anne has not been Wentworth's instructress, except indirectly in
the scene where he overhears her fervent speech on constancy; but
she has been the occasion of his learning. He tells her how at Lyme
he had "received lessons of more than one sort. . . . There, he had
learnt to distinguish between the steadiness of principle and the obstinacy of self-will" (242). Anne is more fortunate than many a teacher
in being able to claim, "I must believe that I was right, much as I suffered from it" (246). But Wentworth, like Darcy who must learn to be
laughed at, is to continue his education: "I must learn to brook being
happier than I deserve" (247). It is a propitious ending.

Jane Austen has greater faith than most writers in the love fully com-
bined with knowledge of self and esteem for the partner that is implied
in her version of the pedagogic relationship. That mutual contribu-
tion to the formation of character, that mingling of minds as well as
hearts and bodies, is joyful and totally fulfilling. But in Jane Austen
there is always a qualification. I have been talking about the pedagogic relationship in its successful operation, as it occurs between
hero and heroine, with its emotional and sexual implications. But it
is not always successful. And Jane Austen examines with a critical
eye both the right of one mind to influence another, and the com-
plicity of the mind that allows itself to be influenced. She is fully aware
of the possible arrogance of the pedagogic enterprise between falli-
ble human beings: we need only remember Emma and Harriet. She
occasionally endorses Elizabeth's touch of cynicism (it is before
Elizabeth learns that she has indeed taught Darcy a lesson): "We all
love to instruct, though we can teach only what is not worth knowing" (*PP*, 343). And she gives full attention to the mischief done by
misguided mentors, however well-intentioned, like Sir Thomas
Bertram and Mrs. Norris, and finally says of the original Persuader,
"There was nothing less for Lady Russell to do, than to admit that she
had been pretty completely wrong, and to take up a new set of opinions and of hopes" (*P*, 249).

"Persuasion" is an issue not only in the last novel. Darcy's control
of Bingley, Emma's of Harriet, Mary's of Edmund, are critically exam-

ined and the characters are judged – as arrogant, as pliable, as silly, in their different degrees. Ultimately Jane Austen insists that a pupil, however richly receiving or disastrously misled, is responsible. He (if it's a man) cannot be a mere passive receptacle of wisdom, or a mere victim of bad advice. The pupil makes choices – she (if it's a woman) may choose or not choose to be instructed; she may elect her instructor; she may select which of the instructions to attend to. In all these choices pupils define themselves, and have themselves to accuse if they are wrong. There can be no shrugging off the blame. Emma is blameworthy in her influence on Harriet, and is certainly fortunate that Robert Martin is so bravely persistent as to get Harriet in the end anyway; but then Harriet had no business allowing Emma to run her life for her in the first place; and, had he lost her, Martin's loss would have been so much the less. This issue of responsibility is fully explored in *Mansfield Park*, where Edmund tries to excuse Mary's behaviour by putting the blame on her education, and at last extorts Fanny's impatient outburst, "Her friends leading her astray for years! She is quite as likely to have led *them* astray" (*MP*, 424). Jane Fairfax carefully avoids Edmund's kind of injustice in her apology to Mrs. Weston: "Do not imagine, madam, . . . that I was taught wrong. Do not let any reflection fall on the principles or the care of the friends who brought me up. The error has been all my own" (*E*, 419). It is a noble declaration: a brave and full acceptance of responsibility.

Embedded in all Jane Austen's novels is a pedagogic story, a story not just of learning – most novels are that – but of teaching too. We see courses of instruction proceeding through initiation, lectures, examination, graduation, qualification. We hear of pupils apt, and too eager, and recalcitrant; of teachers discerning, misguided, perverse. All of this bears much of the moral import of the novels, as the reader learns along with the lecturers and the students. But it also carries the emotional interest, as hero and heroine respond to each other, fully and consciously, come to share their experience, their feelings, and themselves, and are thus wholly united. T.S. Eliot[15] would perhaps have disclaimed the analogy, but it seems to me that the "felt thought" that he finds as the characteristic of metaphysical poetry has some kinship with the "intelligent love" that Lionel Trilling finds as Jane Austen's ideal. She too presents an intense and simultaneous commitment of feeling and intelligence, and her novels dramatize the achievement of that commitment. She shows us what is for her the most passionate love, a love that is fully aware. Emma comes to realize that her first endeavour must be "to understand, thoroughly understand her own heart" (*E*, 412). There is no need to apologize for the spinster Jane, even though she may never show us her lovers in bed. In the fullest sense, she *understood* love, and made sure her best men and women come to do so too.

Notes

1. This was first published in *Jane Austen Today*, ed. Joel Weinsheimer (Athens, Ga.: University of Georgia Press, 1975).
2. The phrase is Pamela Hansford Johnson's. "The Sexual Life in Dickens's Novels," *Dickens 1970*, ed. Michael Slater (London: Chapman & Hall, 1970), p. 179.
3. *Sincerity and Authenticity* (Cambridge: Harvard University Press, 1972), p. 82. Professor Trilling elsewhere sardonically commented, "I know that pedagogy is a depressing subject to all persons of sensibility." "On the Teaching of Modern Literature," *Beyond Culture* (New York: Viking Press, 1965), p. 3.
4. Geoffrey Gorer explored this aspect in the novels in "The Myth in Jane Austen," *American Imago*, 2:3 (1941), pp. 197–204.
5. See David Smith, "Incest Patterns in two Victorian Novels," *Literature and Psychology*, 15:3 (Summer, 1965), pp. 135–62.
6. See Gordon S. Haight, *George Eliot: A Biography* (Oxford: Clarendon Press, 1968), pp. 27, 49–50.
7. *Sincerity and Authenticity*, p. 82. Since I wrote this essay, a great deal has been written on the mentor–pupil relationship in the eighteenth- and nineteenth-century novel. It would be anachronistic to attempt an updating, but one treatment of the subject that stands out and needs mention is Susan Morgan's "Why There's No Sex in Jane Austen's Fiction," *Sisters in Time: Imagining Genders in Nineteenth-Century British Fiction* (New York and Oxford: Oxford University Press, 1989), 23-55.
8. Unsigned review of James Austen-Leigh's *Memoir of Jane Austen* in the *North British Review* (April, 1870). Reprinted in *Jane Austen: The Critical Heritage*, ed. B.C. Southam (London: Routledge & Kegan Paul, 1968), pp. 244 and 246.
9. "Serious Reflections on *The Rise of the Novel*," *Novel: a Forum on Fiction*, 1 (1968), p. 218. Sylvia Myers challenged Professor Watt for this characteristic bit of swashbuckling in her article in the same journal, "Womanhood in Jane Austen's Novels," 3 (1970), pp. 225–32, and much more has followed since then.
10. See *Some Words of Jane Austen* (Chicago: University of Chicago Press, 1973), chapters 1 and 2.
11. The similarity between *Pride and Prejudice* and *Much Ado About Nothing* extends not only to the main plot, where hero and heroine come to accord only after having pointedly singled each other out for abuse, but also to the subplots – the making and breaking of the Hero/Claudio and Jane/Bingley matches being a point at fierce issue between the main characters. "God help the noble Claudio! If he have caught the

Benedick, it will cost him a thousand pounds ere 'a be cured" (I, i), says Beatrice, and so might Elizabeth say of Bingley and Darcy. Hero's description of Beatrice, who "turns . . . every man the wrong side out" (III, i), sounds like the unreformed Elizabeth:

> Disdain and scorn ride sparkling in her eyes,
> Misprising what they look on, and her wit
> Values itself so highly that to her
> All matter else seems weak. She cannot love . . .
> She is so self-endeared.

And when Beatrice brings herself to love Benedick, she might be Elizabeth soliloquizing after talking to the housekeeper at Pemberley: "For others say thou dost deserve, and I / Believe it better than reportingly" (III, i). Darcy is obviously not so like Benedick. But he too is confident – as well he might be with Miss Bingley and Miss de Bourgh visibly eager to snap him up – that "It is certain I am loved of all ladies, only you excepted" (I, i). Benedick's determination that "till all graces be in one woman, one woman shall not come in my grace" (II, iii) is echoed in Darcy's exacting notions of what constitutes accomplishment in a woman. And when it comes to the point, Benedick, like Darcy, finds it difficult to express himself warmly and captivatingly: "No, I was not born under a rhyming planet, nor I cannot woo in festival terms" (V, ii). Amen to that, Elizabeth at Hunsford might well have agreed!

12. Cf. Lloyd W. Brown: "The myth of the asexual Jane Austen novel is more revealing of our surfeited twentieth-century 'senses' than it is of Jane Austen's work." "Jane Austen and the Feminist Tradition," *Nineteenth-Century Fiction*, 28:3 (1973), p. 333.

13. I use Chapman's edition of the play, included with his edition of *Mansfield Park*.

14. See Arnold Kettle's section on *Emma* in *An Introduction to the English Novel* (London: Hutchinson's Universal Library, 1951).

15. I refer to his essay of 1921, "The Metaphysical Poets," reprinted in *Selected Essays* (London: Faber & Faber, 1932).

11

Women in Love

In Jane Austen's wicked little burlesque "Jack & Alice," written when she was fourteen or so, she tells the story of the love of Lucy, a tailor's daughter, for the irresistible country gentleman Charles Adams, who is so dazzlingly beautiful that "none but Eagles could look him in the Face" (13). Lucy is so smitten with his charms that, as she says,

> I was determined to make a bold push & therefore wrote him a very kind letter, offering him with great tenderness my hand & heart. To this I received an angry & peremptory refusal, but thinking it might be rather the effect of his modesty than any thing else, I pressed him again on the subject. But he never answered any more of my Letters & very soon afterwards left the Country. (*MW*, 21)

Nothing daunted, she writes to him at his other estate, suggesting she should come to visit him there; and again receives no answer. Choosing to take "Silence for Consent," she immediately sets out in pursuit of him. He has taken his precautions, however, and while she is penetrating the woods surrounding his estate, she is caught by the leg in one of the steel person-traps "so common in gentlemen's grounds" (22). "O, cruel Charles," exclaims another female victim of his charms, in perfect iambics, when she hears the story, "to wound the hearts & legs of all the fair" (22).

As an outrageous teenager, Jane Austen was cheerfully reversing all the stereotypes. The beautiful Charles Adams is like the usual heroine, irresistibly lovely and remote, and like Pope's Belinda in being the rival of the sun's beams. He is in fact a sex-object hotly contended for by a number of rapacious and predatory women. His No does not mean no, and his coy withdrawals make him all the more desirable. As for the women, they are shown as warmly desiring and shamelessly pursuing this male in a moated grange. They disguise their passion neither from its object nor from each other, and they make their moves in the courtship hunt with unabashed directness.

The young Jane Austen was rousingly participating in the ongoing debate on women, their capacity – or lack of it – to feel sexual desire, and the degrees to which they were allowed to be conscious of it, to show it, to speak it, and to act on it. The genteel culture of the eighteenth century, enunciated and dramatized by Richardson, and reinforced by the conduct books and even the medical experts, taught that woman's sexuality was not an independent free-standing entity, but only reflective of man's. Two popular and authoritative documents in this debate that Jane Austen knew well were Richardson's *Rambler* essay of 1751, and the letter on courtship that Frances Burney attributed to the heroine's father, the Reverend Tyrold, in *Camilla*, of 1796. Both were considered sufficiently striking and important to be reprinted and issued separately, out of context and in large numbers; and they became part of the larger literature on the important conduct-book topic of female delicacy.

Richardson's famous dictum in the *Rambler* was a central statement of the doctrine:

> That a young lady should be in love, and the love of the gentleman undeclared, is an heterodoxy which prudence, and even policy, must not allow.[1]

Woman is not allowed to be the subject of her own desire; she may only be the object of the man's, of which she is then permitted to produce the shadow. So, in *Pamela*, we are presented with the basic situation of the male as the ravening sexual beast, while the virtuous female Pamela spends much of the book resisting his sexual advances and invoking her "Virtue." There are carefully planted signs that she has some subliminal response to his attractions. But it is only when he makes an honourable proposal of marriage that – bingo! – she recognizes that this unknown quantity in her heart was Love, no less, and it waited only for the litmus test of his proposal of marriage to become recognizable.[2]

The powerful stereotype of unawakened female desire, a variant on the Sleeping Beauty myth, was followed through dozens of eighteenth-century novels by R.P. Utter and G.B. Needham, in their erudite and amusing book of 1936, *Pamela's Daughters*.[3]

Like many literary conventions, this convention of non-existent or unawakened female desire gathered power and influenced life, as we all know. The Proper Lady, "guardian and nemesis of the female self," as Mary Poovey has characterized the sexually unawakened woman,[4] was a powerful role model for women in novels, particularly those in novels *by* women. To deviate from this model was to risk very damaging moral opprobrium.

Frances Burney, the novelist Austen most admired, and identified as her model in the famous passage about novels in chapter 5 of *Northanger Abbey*, was clearly agonized by the whole issue of propriety and woman's sexuality. She did not buy in to the convention of a woman's sexuality as reflective only: her heroines do fall in love before the hero proposes, and suffer accordingly. But each successive heroine, from Evelina to Juliet in *The Wanderer*, is put to more painful trials in the mandatory concealment of her love. *Camilla*, the Burney novel Austen knew best,[5] is simply obsessive about the issue of female desire and the necessity to conceal it. And it was from *Camilla* that a full statement of the principle derived, and one that became as influential as Richardson's dictum in the *Rambler*.

Camilla deeply loves Edgar Mandlebert, and becomes aware of her love. This should make for a swift and fortunate conclusion, because Edgar loves her and longs to know that she loves him too. But, as Jane Austen noted, the course of this true love is made to occupy five volumes (*Letters*, 13), and largely because of the elaborate conventions surrounding woman's desire and its necessary concealment.[6] For however the hero Edgar longs for Camilla to manifest her love, her father is ready to snatch her out of the relationship forever rather than let Edgar discover that Camilla loves him. This father is a parson, and he delivers a written sermon to his daughter on this occasion, a careful statement and justification of the principle that woman in love must *never*, by word or sign, let the man she loves, or anyone else, deduce the state of her heart. Mr. Tyrold's sermon, which like Richardson's *Rambler* essay achieved large separate publication, occupies a whole chapter at the very heart and centre of the novel.

Mr. Tyrold, like his author, can admit the possibility of "prepossession," even of "passions," and even in a virtuous girl like his daughter. But so strong in him is the paradigm of the unawakened maiden that he imposes a terrible penance on the girl whose own desire has outstripped that of the man. She must, he tells her, "struggle ... against yourself as you would struggle against an enemy" (358). As her "prepossession" (the word carries within it the assumption that a woman may only be passively possessed, may never actively possess another) must be "what you would rather perish than utter," so she must "shut up every avenue by which a secret which should die untold can further escape you" (360). Not speaking her love is not enough. She must control her body language, her gestures, the very trembling, blushing and pallor that are the involuntary and recognizable signs of emotion. She must neither seek nor avoid meetings with the man who prompts her emotion. She must appear to "behave with the same open esteem as in your days of unconsciousness" (360). While struggling against herself as against an enemy, and "in a state of utter constraint" (361), she must nevertheless act as normal. But she must not be hypocritical (361). The whole set of instructions seems designed to induce terrible stress, self-alienation and dementia. And in fact ultimately Camilla in this agonizing situation does go mad.

Why is this terrible penance for a woman's virtuous love necessary? One large answer is that "delicacy" demands the concealment of the unsolicited passion. But a more pragmatic reason Tyrold also urges is that the man who perceives it will lose his "respect" for her (360). It is a familiar story. In the case of Camilla, though – and who knows in how many other cases besides? – it happens not to be true. Edgar is simply longing for some sign that Camilla loves him, and doesn't proceed in his own courtship until he perceives it. The whole huge novel hangs on this delicate matter of the need for the lovers to learn each others' feelings, and the principle of delicacy would seem to be not the solution but the problem.

The problem and its solution similarly occupy Jane Austen in her novels. But she is able to move confidently towards solution by a relative abandonment of delicacy.

Given the extraordinary prevalence of this set of moral, social, sexual and psychological restraints, generations of women have internalized the convention, and believed themselves to be exempt from sexual longing. They have taken their sexual satisfaction, such as it is, from a state not of desiring and possessing, but of *being* desired, *being* possessed. They have been trained to say no, whether they mean it or not; for a hearty Yes is open to charges of indelicacy; and the negative voice is the only power left to them. It is not surprising that this subject of woman's sexuality, or lack of it, became an issue as crucial to women of the eighteenth and nineteenth centuries as issues of the franchise or abortion have been to the women's movements of our own century. Deprived of desire and the right to express it, woman is doomed to a passive role in courtship, and thus by implication deprived of effective control in her life as daughter, wife, and mother.

Fanny Burney shows her women intensely feeling desire, but forced to conceal and repress it. Today's feminists insist on woman's independent sexuality and her right to pursue its gratification. I want to explore Jane Austen's stand on this crucial women's issue of her day. Where does she stand on the issue of the woman as *subject* of desire, rather than object? What initiatives does she allow to her women in love and in courtship, especially to the women we are meant to approve of? Are the loves of her heroines direct and independent, or only secondary, and reflexive of the males' love? To what extent are they allowed consciousness of their own love? To what extent do they dare voice it, and like Lucy in "Jack and Alice" boldly pursue the man? Does Jane Austen endorse a healthy sexuality in her heroines, and champion their right to its expression? Or did she indeed create "proper," unawakened heroines, who have no erotic desire of their own, and merely tolerate or reflect their men's?

Before I get to a consideration of individual heroines in Austen's novels, it's worth noting that the most socially advanced heroines are those who are most psychologically retarded in the matter of recognizing their own desire. Elizabeth Bennet, for all her social aplomb, doesn't feel or recognize her own developing love for Darcy until well after his declaration of love for her; and she admits to the influence of the compliment of his love. Emma Woodhouse, believing herself above romantic entanglements, can confidently assert that she will never marry; and she does not recognize her own growing love for Mr. Knightley until very late in the day, when she is threatened with his loss.

By contrast, the socially mousy or inexperienced heroines, Fanny and Catherine, are much more revolutionary in taking the initiative in loving, and in having access to their own emotions. Anne Elliot is perhaps the most revolutionary of all, in that she not only loves on when she believes Wentworth has ceased to love her, but brings herself to take active steps towards winning him back.

Catherine Morland falls in love in the third chapter of *Northanger Abbey*, on her first encounter with Henry Tilney; and in spite of all the vicissitudes in the relationship, and in spite of Jane Austen's sardonic stance elsewhere on the matter of first impressions and love at first sight, this first love is prosperous, and leads to a happy marriage. Right at the outset of her career as novelist, Austen mocks and exposes the Richardsonian stereotype. Her note reference to Richardson's *Rambler* paper (the only note reference in her novels, so far as I can recall) not only testifies to the wide currency of his doctrine, but also constitutes her own challenge to the "celebrated writer." She decorously but unequivocally throws down the gauntlet. The narrator speculates with mock solemnity:

> Whether she thought of [Mr. Tilney] so much, while she drank her warm wine and water, and prepared herself for bed, as to dream of him when there, cannot be ascertained; but I hope it was no more than a slight slumber, or a morning doze at most; for if it be true, as a celebrated writer has maintained, that no young lady can be justified in falling in love before the gentleman's love is declared,* [here Austen supplies her reference to Richardson's *Rambler* paper] it must be very improper that a young lady should dream of a gentleman before the gentleman is first known to have dreamt of her. (*NA*, 29–30)

The joke, elaborated through all the careful political distinctions between degrees of impropriety in dreams of deep sleep, or slight slumber, or early morning dozes, is the whole assumption that considerations of propriety must pertain even where control is impossible, as in dreams. Thought Police are bad enough. Dream Police would be even worse. The implication of the passage about Catherine's improper dreaming is not only that she can't be expected to control her dreams, but that she can't be expected to control her love. There are some forces of nature and of the mind that are beyond the rules of propriety.

Among the rags and tags of poetry that the young Catherine was expected to commit to memory is the passage from *Twelfth Night* about "Patience on a Monument" (16). The approved model is the young woman who never told her love, but let concealment like a worm in the bud feed on her damask cheek – an image well calculated to reinforce Parson Tyrold's message about "what you would rather perish than utter" (*Camilla*, 360).

Catherine is an uncomplicated soul, and she is not apt to agonize over the Richardsonian maxims any more in her falling in love than in her dreaming. But even she knows that she should not tell her love. In her case, though, telling is superfluous: after a short conversation with Miss Tilney about her brother Henry, they part " – on Miss Tilney's side with some knowledge of her new acquaintance's feelings, and on Catherine's, without the smallest consciousness of having explained them" (*NA*, 73). That naive transparency of Catherine's is one of her charms; and Henry Tilney is certainly not immune from it.

Tilney can discover Catherine's feelings for him as easily as his sister can. According to Tyrold's sermon, the man who finds himself beloved feels "tenderness without respect. . . . A certainty of success in many destroys, in all weakens, its charm" (*Camilla*, 360). But Jane Austen abandons this othodoxy in favour of a pattern she considers more true to life, if less morally elevated. The passage, for all its playful tone, is a frank rejection of the Pamela's Daughter stereotype, and a brave assertion of woman's sexuality as a free-standing entity rather than as merely reflective, and of Catherine's in particular as healthy and fortunate:

> Though Henry was now sincerely attached to her, . . . I must confess that his affection originated in nothing better than gratitude, or, in other words, that a persuasion of her partiality for him had been the only cause of his giving her a serious thought. It is a new circumstance in romance, I acknowledge, and dreadfully derogatory of an heroine's dignity; but if it be as new in common life, the credit of a wild imagination will at least be all my own. (*NA*, 243)

Catherine loved first, and loved effectively. It is Henry's love that is merely reflexive. In the context of its time, the apparently joking ending is a fairly tough political statement.

Sense and Sensibility, in the issue of women in love as in many others, presents what seems to be a conservative position, but then proceeds to modulate and complicate it. In Marianne's case, we are initially presented with a romantic tableau that is almost hackneyed: beautiful young girl disports herself on hillside, falls, and sprains her ankle; whereupon handsome young stranger sweeps her off her feet, literally and metaphorically, and carries her home, while she and surrounding characters admire the "manly beauty and more than common gracefulness" of her "preserver" (*SS*, 43, 46). The romance blossoms at breakneck speed (to mix my clichés), and Marianne makes no effort to conceal her growing love for Willoughby. They talk to each other in whispers, go on secret excursions together, and she allows him the rape of her lock. Marianne, if anything, takes more initiatives in advancing the relation than Willoughby does himself. When she gets to London, for instance, it is she who begins a correspondence. We hear that his "ardour of mind . . . was now roused and increased by the example of her own" (48). (Not only "increased," we notice, but actually "roused.") Of course we know that such behaviour is imprudent, even improper: Elinor laments that Marianne sets "propriety at naught" (56); and in the pertaining social system she is made to suffer cruelly for her clear and unconcealed love. Since she has so plainly manifested her feelings before the man has ever declared his own love, or proposed marriage, she is open to the accusation of having "chased" him; and Willoughby in his outrageous letter can deeply humiliate her by referring to "the lock of hair, which you so obligingly bestowed on me" (183). To talk of the lock for which he had earnestly begged (60) as having been "obligingly bestowed" is to imply a campaign of the woman to capture and subdue the man. Meanwhile, because he had carefully *not* made an explicit declaration or proposal, Willoughby gets out. The woman pays, the man gets off scot-free.

Well, not quite. Had the story ended there, it would have been a cautionary tale that Mr. Tyrold would love to cite, about how girls, if they have the misfortune to fall in love while the gentleman's love is yet undeclared, should repress any sign, and so avoid painful humiliation. That is indeed the prudent course. But prudence is a virtue of a not very exalted kind.

It's certainly the case that Marianne loved not wisely but too well. Society is apt to condemn her for her imprudence and her impropriety. But Marianne's eager and undisguised participation in the relationship is a direct expression of her self, and her integrity is unblemished. Willoughby, on the other hand, because of his cautious circumspection, essentially abdicates his subjectivity. To examine the account of their swift progress to intimacy is to discover not the fortunate "general conformity of judgement" that Marianne believes in and enjoys, but a duplication more mechanical.

> Encouraged . . . to a further examination of his opinions, she proceeded to question him on the subject of books; her favourite authors were brought forward and dwelt upon with so rapturous a delight, that any young man of five and twenty must have been insensible indeed, not to have become an immediate convert to the excellence of such works, however disregarded before. Their taste was strikingly alike. The same books, the same passages, were idolized by each – or if any difference arose, it lasted no longer than till the force of her arguments and the brightness of her eyes could be displayed. He acquiesced in all her decisions, caught all her enthusiasm. (47)

"Strikingly alike" is a phrase in Marianne's consciousness. But the narrator provides enough further information to suggest that in fact the likeness is "striking" only if one finds the likeness of a mirror image to its original so. Willoughby simply adopts and reiterates Marianne's views, and more automatically than ever Catherine took instruction on the picturesque from Tilney. His taste is only reflective, as a woman's desire is meant to be. Austen has reversed the stereotype again.

Willoughby, in fact, has no stable centre of self. To a surprising degree, he takes on the colouring of others. He becomes Marianne's echo and duplicate. "Her taste, her opinions – I believe they are better known to me than my own," he admits ingenuously in his last scene (325). And when Marianne's influence is not in the ascendant, it is perfectly in character that he should sign himself over to his fiancée, Miss Grey, and allow her to dictate his letter to Marianne. He shrugs off responsibility for this gross piece of charlatanism – "what did it signify . . . in what language my answer was couched?" he says irresponsibly (328). This propensity to neutralize himself and take his language, taste and responses from others becomes a key to his character. Even his casual and callous affair with Eliza seems to have followed the same pattern: Eliza's "tenderness . . . had the power of creating [a] return" (322). With luxurious passivity, he lets himself be taken over in a relationship, and so renounces responsibility for it; but he retains all along his male's privilege of collecting himself again and walking out of it, leaving the woman with the burden of guilt for having created her own humiliation.

Willoughby is not a victim of other people's influence, but an exploiter of it, since he can always renounce the influence and resume his own personality (what there is of it) when it suits him. He mimics others, makes himself over, because of an emptiness in his own soul; and so gains power over them. Even at the end, we see him winning over Elinor by mirroring her anger against himself.

He loves to be loved; in a society that frowns upon males who boast about their conquests, he nevertheless harps on how the ladies love him. "Her affection for me deserved better treatment," he admits of Eliza, when he recalls "the tenderness which . . . had the power of creating any return" (322). "I had reason to believe myself secure of my present wife, if I chose to address her," he ingenuously acknowledges (323). And of Marianne: "to have resisted such attractions, to have withstood such tenderness! – Is there a man on earth who could have done it?" (321). His appetite for adoration knows no bounds. He can't resist trying to soften Elinor towards him, too. "You do think something better of me than you did?" he pleads (331). He has certainly worked hard to win her over; he even partially succeeds.

In creating a *male* who habitually plays the passive role in the courtship, and who to this extent allows his impulses and his behaviour simply to reflect those of the partner of the moment, Jane Austen throws the spotlight on the absurd and unequal allotment of active and passive roles in courtship. We have seen how she makes something positive of Catherine's initiative in *her* courtship: the fact that Henry's love is reflective of Catherine's is a compensating factor in a relationship in which he is otherwise dominant (a good deal *too* dominant, as some read him). But in Willoughby's case the passivity, the lotos-eating numbness, is the keynote; and the abrogation of responsibility that goes with it makes Willoughby thoroughly contemptible, for all Elinor's propensity to forgive him. Austen's best people are those who, in Henry James's phrase, are "richly responsible." She carefully negotiates the initiatives and accommodations in a relationship to achieve a balance; no one side can elect passivity and resign responsibility. As with the giving and receiving of knowledge in the pedagogic relationship, so in the matter of desire and its fulfilment, the principals in a relationship must find, between them, some equity of impulse and reaction, initiative and reflection; in the best matchings we are assured of a precious achieved mutuality.

Lucy Steele provides a useful contrast to Willoughby, as well as to Elinor. (Her character is so sharp and hard-edged that she recurrently assists in definition, whether of character or theme.) She is the predatory woman who, in a world that is tough for portionless unmarried girls, learns how to look after herself and capture the most eligible man available. But all the time she is taking her calculated steps to make sure of this husband or that, she is busy maintaining the pose of the passive and altruistic maiden who only acquiesces in the importunate love of her fiancé. She cultivates the "amiably bashful" look (129). She claims to have been "very unwilling" to enter the engagement with Edward (130), and to have begged him "earnestly" to withdraw from it when it is discovered (277). But by her sister's testimony we know that she won't let Edward off the hook until the better-heeled Robert is safely *on*. What is interesting is not so much Lucy's pirating tactics in her search for matrimonial prizes, as her sense that it behoves her to seem coy and retiring in the process. She has a keen sense of what society expects of a girl, and she works energetically at seeming passive and retiring.

The patriarchal doctrine of women as sexually unawakened and hence necessarily passive and even resistant in the courtship situation has never taken such a beating as in *Pride and Prejudice*; and the beating is all the more effective for being oblique. Jane Austen finds the sure-fire way to pour scorn on the proposition that a woman's No doesn't *mean* No: she puts it in the mouth of Mr. Collins:[7]

"I am not now to learn," replied Mr. Collins, with a formal wave of the hand, "that it is usual with young ladies to reject the addresses of the man whom they secretly mean to accept, when he first applies for the favour; and that sometimes the refusal is repeated a second or even a third time." (107)

We have grown so used to laughing at Mr. Collins, and he is made so absurd in all his sayings and doings, that it is easy to miss the pointedness of this satire. There still *was* strong social pressure on girls to act in the way he describes – Mr. Collins himself will no doubt urge his daughters to do so. Jane Austen was the shrewder psychologist, and a sharper social critic, for sending up the pattern of the conduct books.

In spite of Collins's theoretic devotion to "the true delicacy of the female character" (108), he himself is swiftly snapped up by a lady who has no intention of refusing even a first proposal. From the moment that Charlotte Lucas "instantly set out to meet him accidentally in the lane" (121), Mr. Collins's options are reduced to one. Charlotte knows how to make her moves, and also how to make Mr. Collins believe that the moves have been all his own. Charlotte's principles are the very opposite of his; and they prove to be far more effective. When Elizabeth takes satisfaction in Jane's undemonstrativeness in her promising relation with Bingley, Charlotte produces her less delicate but much more practical strategy: "In nine cases out of ten, a woman had better show *more* affection than she feels," she tells Lizzie (22). If Jane likes Bingley, according to Charlotte, she should show him so, and in no uncertain terms: love needs encouragement. "Bingley likes your sister undoubtedly; but he may never do more than like her, if she does not help him on" (22). Elizabeth laughs at Charlotte's doctrine, thinking she's joking; but Charlotte, who certainly profits by following this practice in her own amours, turns out to be right. Because Bingley has no confidence that Jane loves him – he too "has great natural modesty," the usual attribute of the girl (199) – Darcy is able to detach him from her.

In this thorny matter of the extent to which a woman may manifest her love, the love story of Jane and Bingley, although they are not the principal characters, becomes, as we have seen, a case study for the surrounding characters, and for the readers of the novel as well.

Charlotte, Elizabeth and Darcy, as well as Miss Bingley, Mrs. Bennet and the rest of Highbury, make the couple their study, examine the signs, and take their steps according to their deductions and their own preferences. Jane and Bingley both suffer from this degree of publicity.

Given the dispute over the manifestation of love that centres on the couple, I like to see the delicacy with which the Bingley–Jane affair is settled. Bingley has had Darcy's permission to come back to Longbourn; Mrs. Bennet's hopes are burgeoning, and she has secured him for dinner. In the dining room all eyes are upon him to see where he will choose to sit.

> On entering the room, he seemed to hesitate; but Jane happened to look round, and happened to smile: it was decided. He placed himself by her. (340)

Instantly Elizabeth, Darcy, Bingley, and Mrs. Bennet are all aware that all is settled. It's a happy conclusion. The debate on whether Jane should show her feeling, or conceal it, is lightly side-stepped: she only "happened" to deliver the inviting look that brings Bingley to her side once and for all. But the arch repetition of that "happened" can signal, to those who choose so to understand it, that Jane has learned to exceed the stereotype, and to take her own active role in the courtship, a role which yet falls short of Charlotte's contrived and predatory tactics; and also that no opprobrium attaches to her charming and spontaneous initiative. Here is the achieved mutuality between the lovers in the courtship situation.

Elizabeth's strong attachment to her father goes along with a certain proud aloofness in sexual relations – just as Lydia's attachment to her mother comprehends a high degree of susceptibility to masculine charms. At the outset of the novel Elizabeth is the kind of daughter that Mr. Tyrold would be proud of, for she would be unlikely to fall in love easily, or to show it if she did. As we have seen, she takes particular satisfaction in the fact that though Jane is in love, no one would guess it (21). Her pride would never allow her to descend either to Charlotte's strategy of vigorous encouragement or Miss Bingley's tactics of constant flattery and persevering assaults on Darcy's attention. She has in fact gone some way towards internalizing the Richardson model of the unawakened girl who must await the male's declaration before she discovers any sexual desire of her own. The first declaration she receives, however, emphatically doesn't do the trick. For Elizabeth, like the model girls imagined by Richardson in the *Rambler* paper, is not fully in touch with her own sexuality, or aware of her own desire. With a mind so powerful, and an observation so acute about so much in the world around her, she is nevertheless rather ignorant about her own psychological operations. The reader can deduce her increasingly intense response to Darcy long before she recognizes it herself.

And in fact her sexual aloofness does much to engage Darcy's attention – his confidence in himself and his position being strong enough that he doesn't need "encouragement," as the more humble Bingley does. Near the end, Elizabeth accounts for his love – playfully, but also fairly accurately.

> "The fact is . . . you were disgusted with the women who were always speaking and looking, and thinking for *your* approbation alone. I roused, and interested you, because I was so unlike *them*. . . . In your heart, you thoroughly despised the persons who so assiduously courted you." (380)

To this extent, her story is a rather conservative one, in the sense that it reinforces the principle that men don't like to be courted, that courtship is an exclusively masculine province. But, with her usual subtlety, Austen complicates the issue. After Elizabeth's severe rebuff of Darcy, he is no longer the confident wooer, and Elizabeth cannot leave all the initiatives to him. "You were grave and silent, and gave me no encouragement," he recalls later (381). Their relation is at a standstill. On that memorable walk, when Jane and Bingley linger behind, Elizabeth has only to get rid of Kitty to be alone with Darcy. She shows as much resourcefulness and determination on her own behalf as her mother ever did on her daughters'.

> When Kitty left them, she went boldly on with him alone. Now was the moment for her resolution to be executed, and, while her courage was high, she immediately said,
> "Mr. Darcy, I am a very selfish creature; and, for the sake of giving relief to my own feelings, care not how much I may be wounding your's. I can no longer help thanking you for your unexampled kindness . . ." (365).

There! The ice is broken; and her wording even carries an echo of his first importunate declaration ("In vain have I struggled. It will not do.

My feelings will not be repressed ..." [189]). In any case, she has taken active steps to provide him with his opportunity to renew his proposal, and he takes advantage of it promptly. In fact we are reminded at the same time of that precious mutuality in courtship initiatives; for the narrator has just told us, "Elizabeth was secretly forming a desperate resolution; and perhaps he might be doing the same" (365). Elizabeth is amused later to recall the extent to which she took the proposal into her own hands. "I wonder how long you *would* have gone on [that is, being distant and embarrassed], if you had been left to yourself. I wonder when you *would* have spoken, if I had not asked you!" (381). Darcy staunchly asserts that he "was not in a humour to wait for any opening of your's." And they end the matter amicably by giving the credit of their engagement to Lady Catherine's intervention.

Both sisters' matches show, however, that a woman in search of happiness, no less (or not *much* less) than a woman in search of an establishment, should take an active role in courtship; to be delicate, passive, unawakened, negative, like the Richardson model, is to be only half alive, like Anne de Bourgh, or like the "pictures of perfection" in novels which we know made Jane Austen "sick and wicked" (*Letters*, 487).

The heroine of *Mansfield Park* delivers a No to an unwanted suitor, and would like very much to deliver a Yes to the one she does want. But Fanny too is up against a strong set of masculine and patriarchal assumptions, and she has to fight hard even for the woman's poor right to a negative.

> "No, no, no," she cried [three times!], hiding her face. "This is all nonsense. Do not distress me. I can hear no more of this. . . . I do not want, I cannot bear, I must not listen to such – No, no [two more times], don't think of me." (*MP*, 301–2)

One would have thought the message would be clear enough. But Henry Crawford, though a far more sensible and sensitive man than Mr. Collins, won't hear the reiterated and emphatic negatives: "her modesty alone seemed to his sanguine and pre-assured mind to stand in the way of the happiness he sought" (302). From Henry's report of the interview, Sir Thomas concludes that he "received as much encouragement to proceed as a well-judging young woman could permit herself to give" (315). If that is "encouragement," what would Sir

Thomas think of Elizabeth's initiatives! Crawford's and Sir Thomas's assumptions, which are not hilariously sent up as are Mr. Collins's, remind us how current that Richardson stereotype still was. Moreover, the stereotype is to be reinforced, especially by the patriarch. Sir Thomas congratulates Fanny on what he supposes to be mere modest hesitancy: "I was very much pleased with what I collected to have been your behaviour on the occasion; it shewed a discretion highly to be commended" (315). Fanny does not have the self-assurance of an Elizabeth Bennet, who can tell Mr. Collins, "You must give me leave to judge for myself, and pay me the compliment of believing what I say" (*PP*, 107). Fanny of course is just as capable of judging for herself; but because of her disadvantaged social position, she would never dare to assert her *right* to judge for herself.

Sir Thomas, Henry Crawford, his sisters, and even Edmund, essentially assume that Fanny, courted by a Henry, must at once respond by loving him, almost as by physical necessity. That is the way women work, they tacitly assume: their love automatically reflects the man's. It would have been improper for her to love him *before* his declaration; but the moment he declares his love for *her*, bingo! she is expected to be just as much in love with *him*. When she mildly tells her uncle, "I – I cannot like him, Sir, well enough to marry him," he responds in displeasure, "This is very strange!" – "strange" in Austen's language being a very strong word, suggesting, if not quite an alien from outer space, at least something outside the expected course of nature (315). Edmund reports his discussion with Mary Crawford and Mrs. Grant: "That you could refuse such a man as Henry Crawford, seems more than they can understand. I said what I could for you; but in good truth, as they stated the case – you must prove yourself to be in your senses as soon as you can, by a different conduct" (352-3). This is strong language: and it shows how deeply ingrained was the notion, even with women, that a woman's love must automatically be awakened by the man's. Edmund's speech gives Fanny a cue to deliver a little lecture on a matter that seems close to her author's heart.

"I *should* have thought," said Fanny after a pause of recollection and exertion, "that every woman must have felt the possibility of a man's not being approved, not being loved by some one of her sex, at least, let him be ever so generally agreeable." (353)

There is her reproof to the women who buy in to the patriarchal stereotype. She enlarges also on the issue of reflective love:

"Even . . . allowing Mr. Crawford to have all the claims which his sisters think he has, how was I to be prepared to meet him with any feeling answerable to his own? He took me wholly by surprise . . . . How then was I to be – to be in love with him the very moment he said he was with me. How was I to have an attachment at his service, as soon as it was asked for?" (353)

These are searching questions. For those who accept the stereotype, the answer is easy: since the woman's love mirrors the man's, it appears automatically as soon as the man's is manifested. Fanny, however, insists on the woman's right to *choose*: her love is not determined by any irresistible qualities of the man who woos her; and moreover, it must be *hers*, developed over time within herself, and not merely triggered by the man, or reflective of *his* love. All of this, of course, seems sufficiently obvious to us in the twentieth century. But for Austen these were still hard-won rights; and one reason she chose a mousy and socially disadvantaged heroine like Fanny was to show how grievous could be the pressure on woman to renounce her own sexuality, and subsist merely on the second-hand article of the male.

Fanny is of course well qualified, in experience though not in social confidence, to develop these views; being secretly and unrequitedly in love with her cousin, she knows that a woman's love doesn't always wait on the man's. But her *declaration* of it must: Fanny is not sufficiently advanced to do her own proposing. In fact, she conforms closely to that other stereotype, of patience on a monument: she does a good deal of never telling her love, and pining in thought.

So far as Sir Thomas is concerned, there can be only one reasonable explanation of Fanny's rejection of Henry Crawford: prepossession.

"This requires explanation. Young as you are, and having scarcely seen any one, it is hardly possible that your affections – "

He paused and eyed her fixedly. He saw her lips formed into a *no*, though the sound was inarticulate, but her face was like scarlet. That, however, in so modest a girl might be very compatible with innocence; and choosing at least to appear satisfied, he quickly added, "No, no, I know *that* is quite out of the question – quite impossible." (316)

It is a charged moment. Fanny is on the brink of having her precious secret discovered; and as she knows very well, an unrequited love in a woman is not compatible with "innocence." Even in this emergency she cannot speak a lie; she mouths one – but her body declares her in other ways, at least to us. His conviction of her modesty, however, saves her from exposure. He is convinced she must be modest because she delivered the unintended negative to Crawford; and of course if she's modest she can't be in love. "*That* is quite out of the question – quite impossible."

We get the full story of Fanny's negative, and her difficulty in delivering it effectively. Sadly, though, Jane Austen skimped on her positive; and for me that is the most unsatisfactory thing about *Mansfield Park*. With all the other love stories except that of Marianne and Brandon we have some dramatic proposal scene that brings the lovers together and allows them behaviour, and a voice. In several there is also the debriefing scene, where they discuss the vicissitudes of the relationship in tranquillity. But Fanny and Edmund are deprived of both kinds of scene. The pen that won't "dwell on guilt and misery" (461) dwells even less on merit and happiness: we hear only that "exactly at the time when it was quite natural that it should be so, and not a week earlier," Edmund ceases to care about Mary and becomes anxious to marry Fanny (470). There is no room in such a telescoped account to discover whether or how Fanny finds a way to make Edmund see her with new and loving eyes, or to what extent she takes initiatives herself. We do hear, though, that when he does learn "the whole delightful and astonishing truth" about her long love, a love that predated his own, "it must have been a delightful happiness!" (471). There is no word of the "tenderness without respect" that the Reverend Tyrold says is the portion of the woman who loves before the man does.

Emma, as we have seen, is a fully socialized young woman of her time, and one a father – even such a one as Mr. Tyrold – could be proud of. She plans not to marry; and though she does believe herself susceptible to Frank Churchill's charms, even at the height of what she thinks is her susceptibility, she plans to refuse him. Her love for Mr. Knightley – or rather, her *consciousness* of it, does predate his declaration; but only by a very short time. Until her awakening, she is perhaps the least passionate of the heroines, and the one who has least access to her own heart. However, Austen is still in the business of putting down the stereotype of the delicate, sexless maiden who is all morality and no desire. When, after believing he loves Harriet, she receives Mr. Knightley's welcome proposal, the narrator pointedly informs us that Emma doesn't aspire to "that heroism of sentiment which might have prompted her to entreat him to transfer his affection from herself to Harriet" (43). Though this irony on "heroism of sentiment" is undoubtedly aimed at the literary convention of the perfectly delicate heroine, Austen has sufficiently shown the prevalence of her culture's expectation of women as sexually unconscious to make this passage too a politically pointed one. Emma has been, up to now, a conventionally unawakened heroine. But once she has discovered her desire, she is not going to annihilate it.

As an example of the perfectly mutual love, I must quote again the passage in which Mr. Knightley *almost* kisses Emma's hand, in a moment of reconciliation:

> He looked at her with a glow of regard. She was warmly gratified – and in another moment still more so, by a little movement of more than common friendliness on his part. – He took her hand; – whether she had not herself made the first motion, she could not say – she might, perhaps, have rather offered it – but he took her hand, pressed it, and . . . (385–6)

As we know, the meditated kiss of her hand doesn't happen this time. But the incident remains as an emblem of the best and happiest kind of courtship in the novels. Did he take her hand, or did she offer it? Because we can't tell, because Emma herself can't tell, we know that this is that preciously mutual relationship in which the woman's desire is engaged equally with the man's, and equally manifested.

In *Persuasion* the relation of the heroine's parents neatly reverses that in *Pride and Prejudice*.[8] Mr. Bennet, otherwise a man of sense, had been "captivated by youth and beauty" (*PP*, 236), had married a foolish woman, and had lived to regret it. Anne Elliot's mother, a "sensible and amiable" woman, likewise succumbed to a "youthful infatuation" for the "good looks and rank" of a foolish man (*P*, 4). The man too can be a sex object, even among parents. It is an early signal that this novel, more even than those that precede it, is to focus on woman's desire.

Anne's particular agony is that, having early fallen "rapidly and deeply in love" (*P*, 26), she has had her sexual awakening, both in fact and by convention. But, that love not having prospered, she must close down all channels, and school herself into being once more the pure, passive, unawakened maid – in Keats's phrase, "As though a rose should shut, and be a bud again." Her society, and her own pride, will not allow any open acknowledgement of the fact of this passion. Like Tyrold's daughter, she must cover up every sign of her intense love. This severe repression results in the almost masochistic self-denial that we find Anne practising in the first few chapters. It is not only Sir Walter and Elizabeth who consider her as "nobody" (5); she cancels herself, preferring the torpor of numbness to the pain of full self-consciousness. She insists on staying home with little Charles, rather than going to dinner with the Musgroves to meet Captain Wentworth again; she plays the piano while he dances with other people, her eyes filling with tears. She is in fact fulfilling to the letter Mr. Tyrold's instructions on concealing unrequited love. She schools herself to desire "nothing . . . but to be unobserved" (71). She connives at her own annihilation.

Anne's emotionally conflicted state, as passionate woman constrained to appear passive and unawakened, is rendered in a series of contrarieties and oxymorons. Typically, as she renews her relationship with Wentworth she feels "a something between delight and misery" (175).[9]

Although these painful contrarities sustain our sympathy for Anne, they also often have the effect of prolonging her paralysis and inhibiting her action. Like a wounded animal she has sought darkness and obscurity; and she is necessarily the passive recipient of Wentworth's active rescues. With her emotional reawakening the contrary impulses keep her inactive. For full recovery and achieved happiness, however, Anne must play an active role in recalling Wentworth.

A turning-point is their first meeting in Bath, at Mollands, in the rain. Anne sees him in the street, and "For a few minutes she saw nothing before her. It was all confusion" (175). The scene that follows, delivered as Anne's stream of consciousness, presents a psychomachia, almost an allegory of her conflicting impulses, and a battle between her learned propriety and her irrepressible love.

She now felt a great inclination to go to the outer door; she wanted to see if it rained. Why was she to suspect herself of another motive? Captain Wentworth must be out of sight. She left her seat, she would go, one half of her should not be always so much wiser than the other half, or always suspecting the other half of being worse than it was. She would see if it rained. She was sent back, however, in a moment by the entrance of Captain Wentworth himself. (175)

Jane Austen makes fine creative use of the conflict between Anne's socialized consciousness of proper feminine behaviour, and her strong passionate impulse of love. Her "inclination to go to the door," her natural desire to look after him, go after him, must be disguised even from herself, as only a rational curiosity to see if it is still raining. She is conscious of her own self-division, and constructs one half of herself "wiser" and the other "worse": presumably it would be "wise" *not* to look after Wentworth, to stay quiet, passive, unmoved. It would be "worse" to give in to her impulse of love. But then it is also wise to be fully aware of her own real motivation, and to stop disguising it from herself. On this impulse she rises to go to the door; but as soon as her object appears, she retires again in confusion. It is a wonderful dramatization of the fluctuating battle of social constraint with sexual desire.

As Wentworth hesitatingly renews his approaches (one cannot yet call it courtship) they must equally find ways to deliver the message each knows the other needs to hear. Wentworth must let Anne know that he does not care for Louisa, and never did. He achieves that at the concert, by telling her he is surprised that "a clever man, a reading man" like Benwick (182), who had once been in love with such "a very superior creature" as Fanny Harville, should attach himself to Louisa, who is not his equal in these respects. As we have seen, Anne clearly understands the subsurface message: "all, all declared that he had a heart returning to her" (185). And she is eager to find further opportunities of carrying on the promising conversation. She is even allowed "a little scheming of her own" in her manoeuvres to save a seat by herself and lure him to it (189). But now comes the other impediment. Louisa being out of Anne's way, William Walter Elliot plays the same separating role for Wentworth. The concert chapter ends with his depressed withdrawal, and Anne's realization that Elliot's attentions to her have driven Wentworth away. As the well-trained passive woman, Anne faces the likelihood of Wentworth's total withdrawal. "How," she hopelessly asks herself, "in all the peculiar disadvantages of their respective situations, would he ever learn her real sentiments?" (191)

The answer is that the passive woman must become active. She can't, in our modern way, say "Look, Frederick, I want you to know that William Walter means absolutely nothing to me; and while we're on the subject, I might as well tell you that I really regret breaking off our engagement the last time, and I suggest we get back together. What do you say?" How destructive such modern openness would be to so much that we find fascinating in Austen's novels! *But* Austen requires Anne to take, within the limits of the formal bounds set on behaviour in the ritual of courtship, some firm steps in the *direction* of our modern outspokenness. She is not allowed to be a picture of perfection who never felt or owned to an impulse of desire. She is not allowed even to be her old masochistic self, avoiding his company and seeking solitude like a wounded deer. She must get busy and *tell* him, as he told her, that her affections are not engaged elsewhere. She must find a way, and she does. In the debate on whether the Musgroves should break their prior engagement to go to the evening party where Mr. Elliot is an honoured guest, or go to the theatre instead, Anne finds the "opportunity" to say, in front of Wentworth, "I have no pleasure in the sort of meeting, and should be too happy to change it for a play" (224–5). The words sound ordinary enough, but we are alerted as to how bold a move this is by Anne's internal tremor: "She had spoken it; but she trembled when it was done, conscious that her words were listened to, and daring not even to try to observe their effect" (225). She has told Wentworth, though by an indirection difficult to track, that she cares nothing for an evening with Mr. Elliot. The effect is immediate. After her "declaration" of an unengaged heart, Wentworth approaches her warmly, and for the first time since the renewal of their acquaintance, makes an open reference to their past engagement. "It is a period indeed! Eight years and a half is a period!" (225)

In this breathless process of their gradual coming together after their agonizing years of estrangement, Austen keeps the two principals apart by some deliberate delaying tactics. Each promising conversation is interrupted, and a new impediment is introduced. Each delay requires Anne to take a new active step towards recapturing happiness, to assert herself equally with Wentworth, to overcome her earlier numb paralysis and convention's embargo on the woman's initiatives in courtship.

Wentworth and Anne have now each successfully delivered the message (he first) that their hearts are unengaged elsewhere. But, in the fine incremental advances in this renewed courtship, there still remains the question, of huge import to both, of whether they love each other. I suggest that in this part of the communication Anne takes the lead; though the scene is so written that those who would disapprove of such an initiative need not believe in it. As we saw, in the crucial moment in *Pride and Prejudice* when "Jane happened to look round, and happened to smile" the question of the deliberateness of the inviting look is left open. So it is with Anne, and on a more extended scale. She speaks her love, but under camouflage. In fact her declaration is doubly camouflaged, in that she refers to the particular in the guise of the general, and in that she speaks, apparently, not to Wentworth but to Harville.

"We certainly do not forget you, so soon as you forget us," she says. "Our [feelings] are the most tender." "All the privilege I claim . . . is that of loving longest, when existence or when hope is gone" (232, 233, 235). For "we" and "my sex" read "I". For "you" read not Captain Harville, nor men in general, but "Wentworth." Such adjustments, in the complex communication that characters undertake in Austen's novels, are simple enough. The message is clear. She has loved long and tenderly.

But she doesn't know Wentworth can hear her (I hear you argue). Well, *doesn't* she? In the middle of her conversation with Harville, "Anne was startled at finding him nearer than she had supposed, and half inclined to suspect that the pen had only fallen, because he had been occupied by them, striving to catch sounds, which yet she did not think he could have caught" (233–4). She continues her conversation with Harville, however, and the unburdening of her heart. Is she disingenuous, scheming, proceeding by cunning tricks? We can't be sure. We know only that she *happened* to keep talking of her love, and he *happened* to overhear. It is enough. We can pick the level of consciousness to suit ourselves.

Wentworth himself, however, wants more certainty. Her indirect declaration prompts his direct one. He writes of his own attachment, his own constancy. His language is the more fervent for its direct engagement with hers: her claim of constant love, if it doesn't quite create his love, at least intensifies it, and prompts his expression. But still he wants to be *sure* of her love, to extort a declaration that is less camouflaged. He sends his letter: "I must go, uncertain of my fate; but I shall return hither, or follow your party, as soon as possible. A word, a look will be enough to decide whether I enter your father's house this evening, or never" (237–8). Or *never*? He is certainly pinning a great deal on the "word" or the "look"; particularly considering the received orthodoxy of the day on woman's proper behaviour in courtship. To return to Richardson's *Rambler* essay: we hear there of the appropriate eye motions of the properly modest girl:

Women are always most observed, when they seem themselves least to observe, or to lay out for observation. The eye of the respectful lover loves rather to receive confidence from the withdrawn eye of the fair-one, than to find itself obliged to retreat.[10]

The orthodox view is that the woman is to *receive* the gaze, not perpetrate it herself. In this context, Wentworth's requirement of a-look-or-else becomes more weighted. Like Darcy, he has been rebuffed in the past, and so needs, all the more, clear signals from the woman that he won't be rebuffed again. But the standard imperatives of modesty in a woman, including the downcast or "withdrawn eye of the fair-one," make Wentworth's requirements difficult to comply with. Her society has trained Anne to be absolutely undemonstrative in courtship; and moreover for many years she has schooled herself to cover up her love, to stifle every sign. Now her happiness is made to hinge on her willingness to reverse that ingrained behaviour and deliver a clear and unequivocal signal – to participate fully in the final phase of courtship.

What happens?

> They [Anne and Charles Musgrove, her reluctant attendant] were in Union-street, when a quicker step behind, a something of familiar sound, gave her two moments' preparation for the sight of Captain Wentworth. He joined them; but, as if irresolute whether to join or pass on, said nothing – only looked. Anne could command herself enough to receive that look, and not repulsively. The cheeks which had been pale now glowed, and the movements which had hesitated were decided. He walked by her side. (239–40)

Only if we are acquainted with the ritual and convention which surrounded courtship in her day can we fully appreciate the force that informs that mild and apparently cautious double negative, "to receive that look, and not repulsively." Therein lies a revolution, and a victory. It declares, once and for all, that women are, and should be, agents and active participants in the courtship process, and not mere objects. Their power is not to be limited to the negative vote; they have a positive choice, and they can and do take steps towards its advancement and accomplishment. Moreover, we learn, the men rejoice in the women's participation. They don't want to do all the loving and courting by themselves; their love is a complex and mutually responsive process. In Donne's phrase, it "interinanimates two souls."

After Anne has delivered her crucial welcoming look, we hear, "The cheeks which had been pale now glowed . . ." It is not immediately clear *whose* cheeks are being referred to (though as we read on we gather that the cheeks are Wentworth's). This momentary doubt is perfectly appropriate. *All* the cheeks that matter are a-glow, we can infer. Similarly, when Charles bows out of the scene to visit his gun-smith, the grammar insists on mutuality. "There could not be an objection. There could be only a most proper alacrity, a most obliging compliance for public view; and smiles reined in and spirits dancing in private rapture" (240). Whose smiles? whose spirits dancing? whose rapture? – His *and* hers, surely. The paragraph continues, "Soon words enough had passed between them to decide their direction ..." (Not "Soon he had said enough"); "There they exchanged again those feelings and those promises ..." (Not "There he told her again and promised again...") "They," not "he" or "she," is the subject of every main clause that follows, until the last sentence of the paragraph.

When "he" and "she" are next discriminated, by their separate feelings and responses as they re-examine their relationship in the past days, it emerges that Anne's strong initiatives, which would be censured as "forward" by any moral authority of the time, are what have saved the day. His jealousy of Mr. Elliot had been a force to separate them, Wentworth acknowledges. But that jealousy

> had been gradually yielding to the better hopes which her looks, or words, or actions occasionally encouraged; it had been vanquished at last by those sentiments and those tones which had reached him while she talked with Captain Harville; and under the irresistible governance of which he had seized a sheet of paper, and poured out his feelings. (241)

The vocabulary suggests a dominant woman, a receptive man. His resistance "yields" and is "vanquished"; her sentiments and tones provide "irresistible governance," just as earlier he wrote that she had "penetrated" his feelings (237). The question of who proposed to whom becomes a genuinely debatable matter.

Claudia Johnson, in her impressive feminist study, sees Austen as not particularly advanced in the matter of women's initiatives in courtship. "In Austen's novels," she says, "... as in most others, women simply do not have 'the advantage of choice' (*NA*, 77) ... They can only wait for proposals .... Of course waiting is practically all that Fanny Price and Anne Elliot ever do."[11] One knows what she means, and from a long view this may be true. But a close scrutiny of *Persuasion*, particularly, shows that after Anne has emerged from her passive torpor, and has some hope, she can and *must* do plenty to ensure that she won't lose Wentworth a second time. Her author requires it of her; and Wentworth does too. The same attentive examination of all the novels reveals the women's initiatives, and Austen's pointed and brave insistence on woman's active engagement in the courtship process, and her rejection of the stereotype of passive femininity.

I realize that for those who have imbibed Jane Austen with their mother's milk, I have probably said nothing surprising. *Of course* her heroines participate in the courtship process, as they and all women should. We have accepted the behaviour she describes as natural and proper; and the fact that we read it in Jane Austen may have quite a lot to do with our thinking it so. What I have tried to suggest is that for her time, and in the context of the exacting codes of proper female behaviour, she was brave, and politically advanced. From the gleefully imagined predatory behaviour of Lucy in "Jack & Alice," who takes upon herself the active pursuit of a desirable male, and adopts male tactics, to the highly self-conscious and hesitant advances of the gentle Anne Elliot, who knows she must choose between strict propriety and happiness, Jane Austen continues to explore the possibilities for a woman's honest recognition of her own desire, and her active initiatives for achieving it.

Notes

1. Samuel Richardson, paper contributed to *The Rambler*, no. 97 (19 February 1751), p. 156 in *The Rambler*, vol. 4 of the Yale edition of the *Works of Samuel Johnson*, ed. W.J. Bate and Albrecht B. Strauss, 153–9. The editors note that this issue of the *Rambler* "had a large sale because it was widely bought by Richardson's admirers" (153n). The large separate sale is analogous to that of the Tyrold sermon in Burney's *Camilla*, discussed below, and suggests the popularity of the topic of women's delicacy.

2. "Heroines are inherently defined as reactive," as Susan Morgan characterizes pre-Austen fiction. *Sisters in Time: Imagining Gender in 19th-Century British Fiction* (New York: Oxford University Press, 1989), p. 31. I should say that in representing Richardson as something of a patriarchal villain in the following pages, I refer to Richardson the essayist, particularly of this widely promulgated *Rambler* essay. Richardson the novelist was far less intransigent, and indeed in his Harriet Byron, beloved of Jane Austen, he permitted emotional and sexual responses that as essayist he would reprove.

3. Robert Palfrey Utter and Gwendolyn Bridges Needham, *Pamela's Daughters* (New York: Macmillan, 1936).

4. Mary Poovey, *The Proper Lady and the Woman Writer: Ideology as Style in the Works of Mary Wollstonecraft, Mary Shelley, and Jane Austen* (Chicago: University of Chicago Press, 1984), p. 47.

5. Fanny Burney, *Camilla: or, A Picture of Youth* (1796), ed. Edward A. Bloom and Lillian D. Bloom (Oxford and New York: Oxford University Press, 1983). References for quotations from *Camilla* are supplied in the text. In the first edition of *Camilla*, "Miss J. Austen, Steventon," appears in the subscription list. Having devoted some of her scarce income to *Camilla*, Austen was faithful to it, and mentioned it several times in her letters, besides giving it the best of recommendations, the abuse of John Thorpe in *Northanger Abbey* (49).

6. See my essay: "The Silent Angel: Impediments to Female Expression in Frances Burney's Novels," *Studies in the Novel*, 21:3 (Fall, 1989), 235–52.

7. See Ruth Bernard Yeazell, *Fictions of Modesty: Women and Courtship in the English Novel* (Chicago: Chicago University Press, 1991): "In ... [Mr. Collins'] routine equation of 'natural delicacy' with secrecy and dissembling, Austen gleefully sends up the familiar double-talk of the conduct books, even as she devastatingly identifies such rhetoric with the demands of masculine vanity and the complacent assumption of power" (144).

8. Isobel Grundy notes this as well as other interesting role reversals in "*Persuasion*: The Triumph of Cheerfulness," *Jane Austen's Business*, ed. Juliet McMaster and Bruce Stovel (London: Macmillan [in press]).

9. I can't resist reference to Paula Schwartz's lyric in *An Accident at Lyme*, her musical version of *Persuasion*: Anne and Wentworth share a number called "Between despair and delight."

10. Richardson's essay in the *Rambler* (cited above), p. 155.

11. Claudia L. Johnson, *Jane Austen: Women, Politics and the Novel* (Chicago and London: Chicago University Press, 1988), p. 59.

Index

Separate entries are provided for Jane Austen's works, by title, and for those of her characters who receive more than passing mention. References to works or characters by other authors are indexed under the author's name. A sustained treatment of a subject is indicated by page numbers in italics.